The Eridanos Library

Felisberto Hernández

PIANO STORIES

Translated from the Spanish by
LUIS HARSS

The Eridanos Library
MARSILIO PUBLISHERS

CONTENTS

INTRODUCTION

Italo Calvino

The adventures of a penniless pianist, in which humor transforms the bitterness of a life riddled with defeats, are the initial premise from which the tales of the Uruguayan Felisberto Hernández (1902–1964) take their cue. No sooner does he set about recounting the petty woes of a life lived between the orchestras of the cafés of Montevideo and concert tours through small provincial towns of the Rio de la Plata region, than the page begins to fill with gags, hallucinations and metaphors in which objects take on as much life as people. But this is just the beginning. What really unleashes the imagination of Felisberto Hernández are the unexpected invitations that admit the shy pianist behind the doors of mysterious houses, lonely *quintas* inhabited by rich, eccentric characters, women full of secrets and neuroses.

A secluded mansion, the inevitable piano, a daintily maniacal and perverse gentleman, a visionary or sleepwalking maiden, a matron who obsessively celebrates her misfortunes in love: one would say we have here all the ingredients of a romantic tale à la Hoffmann. And there's even the doll that seems in every way a young woman. In fact, the story *The Daisy Dolls* involves a whole series of dolls (cousins to "Gogol's Wife" according to Landolfi) who rival real women: created by a devilish manufacturer to stoke the fantasies of an eccentric collector, they end up unleashing marital jealousies and stirring up murky dramas. Yet any possible reminiscence of a Germanic imagination is immediately dispelled by the atmosphere of these afternoons spent sitting in a patio slowly sipping *mate* or at a café watching a *ñandú* ostrich walk between the tables.

Hernández's most typical stories are those that are centered on a rather complicated *mise en scène*, a spectacular ritual that unfolds within the depths of an elegant house: a flooded patio in which lighted candles float; a little theatre of dolls large as real women striking enigmatic poses; a dark gallery in which one is supposed to recognize by touch objects that elicit associations of images and thoughts. If the point of the game is to guess the story represented by the scene of the dolls, or to recognize what is placed on the table in the dark gallery, what matters most to the emotions of the participants are not so much these innocent riddles as the chance occurrences, the overlapping noises, the premonitions that invade one's consciousness.

The association of ideas is not only the favorite game of Hernández's characters, it is the dominant and avowed passion of the author himself. It is also the procedure through which these tales build themselves up, connecting one motif with another as in a musical composition. And it seems as if the most ordinary everyday experiences set in motion the most unpredictable mental sarabands, while fancies and manias requiring complex premeditation and elaborate choreography aim at nothing more than to evoke forgotten sensations of the most elementary sort. Hernández is forever pursuing an analogy that for a split second has peeped into the remotest corner of his brain circuits, an image foreshadowing another corresponding image several pages ahead, an incongruous juxtaposition that helps him to capture a very precise feeling; and to reach it he must venture onto foot-bridges cast over the void. Out of the tension between a very precise imagination that always knows what it wants and the word that gropes along behind it, is born a charm not unlike that of the paintings of a naif artist.

By this, however, we certainly do not mean to give credence to the classification of Hernandez as a "Sunday writer," an autodidact "out of touch," which is probably untrue. A surrealism of his own, a Proustianism of his own, a psychoanalysis of his own must, after all, have been reference points in his long search for means of expression. (He too, like all respectable literati of the Rio de la Plata, had put in his obligatory time in Paris.) His way of making room for a play within a play, of setting up games within the story, the rules of which he lays down each time anew, is the solution he has found for giving a traditional narrative structure to the quasi oneiric automatism of his imagination.

What is most astonishing in his writing is the rendering of the physicality of objects and people. An unmade bed, for example: "its nickel-plated bars made me think of a young whore giving herself to the first passerby." Or a girl's hair: "Now she was showing me her full head of hair. Between two waves I could see a bit of scalp and it reminded me of the skin of a hen when the wind ruffles her feathers." Or another girl about to recite a poem: "Her attitude made me think of something between infinity and a sneeze."

Sensations provoke visual echoes that continue to reverberate in the mind. "The theater where I was giving my concerts was also half empty and invaded by silence: I could see it growing on the big black lid of the piano. The silence liked to listen to the music, slowly taking it in and thinking it over before venturing an opinion. But once it felt at home it took part in the music. Then it was like a cat with a long black tail slipping in between the notes, leaving them full of intentions." In this instance, the mysterious correlation established between cat and piano is only metaphorical, but in another story it materializes into a Chaplinesque gag of a cat walking across the stage.

Felisberto Hernández is a writer like no other: like no European, nor any Latin American. He is an "irregular" who eludes all classification and labeling, yet is unmistakable on any page to which one might randomly open one of his books.

Translated from the Italian by Stephen Sartarelli.

Translator's Note

Felisberto Hernández (1902–1964) never wrote anything he called a "piano story." But his stories are told from the piano, one might say. He was a professional pianist who started out at the age of fifteen accompanying silent movies. Often he seems to project the story onto an imaginary screen, from the keyboard. At other times he seems to play the story on the piano itself, as if drawing music from one of the mysterious notebooks he kept in a secret shorthand. Most are told in the first person, in the conversational tone in which he enjoyed reading them to his friends, and evoke childhood scenes or the quirky small-town characters and misadventures he met with on his lonely tours of the provinces, where he earned a meager living as a café pianist, staying in seedy hotels while trying to finance his concerts. Many are deceptively simple anecdotes built around a piano incident or memory. Gradually they become more involved, until in some the piano vanishes entirely, although its presence may still make itself felt in strange ways, as it does, for instance, in the groping hands of "Except Julia" or the seeing eyes of "The Usher." The stories are brooding, humorous, dreamlike fantasies, sometimes with animal faces. The best are small masterpieces of erotic poetry.

Hernández's life was unspectacular. He was born and he died in Uruguay. Once he spent some shadowy months on a grant in France (an experience reflected in the chase along the river bank with bookstalls in "The Usher" and the student hotel-brothel of "The Daisy Dolls"). He married four times; was a great eater and raconteur at literary soirées; had a passion for fat women; loved to improvise on the piano in the styles of various classical composers; once toured Argentina with his own trio, other times with a flamboyant bearded impresario called Venus González. He preferred to write in shuttered rooms or basements; suffered a life-long emotional dependence on his mother; was haunted by morbid vanity and a sense of failure; became ill-humored and reactionary in middle age; and died of leukemia, his body so bloated it had to be removed through the window of the funeral home in a box as large as a piano.

Most of the stories in this sampling are from his only commercially published collection, *No One Had Lit a Lamp* (1947). "The Daisy Dolls," in which he achieved something like total piano vision, came out as a booklet with whimsical illustrations in 1949. "The Flooded House," with its watery world moved by rowing hands, was his last finished work, published in 1960. *The Stray Horse* (1943) is a short novel with self-commentary in his earlier rambling style. "How Not to Explain My Stories" (1955) is his charming *ars poetica*. "Just Before Falling Asleep," a revealing fragment dealing with peephole memory, was composed around 1946.

L.H.

PIANO STORIES

How Not to Explain My Stories

Anything I may feel obliged to reveal—or betray—about how I write my stories will be external to them. They are not completely natural, in the sense of having been free from all conscious interference—I would find that distressing. Nor are they ruled by some theory of consciousness—I would find that even more distressing. I would rather say the conscious mind acts mysteriously in them. My stories have no logical structures. Even the consciousness undeviatingly watching over them is unknown to me. At a given moment I think a plant is about to be born in some corner of me. Aware of something strange going on, I begin to watch for it, sensing that it may have artistic promise. I would be happy if the idea weren't a complete loss. But I can only watch and wait, indefinitely: I don't know how to nurture the plant or make it bloom. All I have is the feeling or hope that it will grow leaves of poetry or of something that could become poetry when seen by certain eyes. I must take care that it does not occupy too much space or try to be beautiful or intense, helping it to become only what it was meant to be. At the same time, it will be on guard against the mind contemplating it when that mind suggests too many grand meanings or intentions. If the plant is true to itself, it will give out a natural poetry it is unaware of. It must be like a person who does not know how long he will live but has his own needs and modest pride, carried a bit awkwardly so as to seem improvised. The plant will not know its own laws, although it may have them, deep down, out of reach of consciousness. It will not know to what degree or in what way consciousness is interfering, but will prevail over it in the end, teaching it to be a disinterested onlooker.

My only certainty is that I can't say how I write my stories, because each of them has a strange life of its own. But I am also aware of their constant battle against the strangers consciousness keeps urging on them.

JUST BEFORE FALLING ASLEEP

Many times, just before falling asleep, I've remembered my family, as if putting an eye to a small hole and blinking to light them up in the back yard of my house. It was noon and I was returning from a town in the provinces and they had not yet seen me. They were gathered around the lunch table, under the trees, and I knew spots of light and shade fell like large coins on the tablecloth, combining each time the leaves stirred in the breeze. Engrossed in their small feast and their bit of happiness, they seemed to have forgotten me. One night the memory kept recurring, like a self-repeating mechanism: again and again they sat down at the table and seemed to have forgotten me. But suddenly the mechanism stopped and it dawned on me that those heads bent over their plates had a living image of me in their minds and carried this image around with them in a way that was probably very different from the way you carry around the image of a dead person. In any case, I had learned how my absence felt to them and what they were like when they remembered me. But I had also learned something else: that even as I opened the door soundlessly that day and watched them from behind some reeds, I was already seeing them as if I were remembering them, and I already knew the memory would follow me. And I decided that if some day I had to survive them, that was how I would remember them, some distance away and in silence. At times, when the memory has followed me and caught up with me at night, the colors of the day were like those of an ordinary postcard, but their smiles were unchanged.

THE STRAY HORSE

I

First you saw only white: the large slipcovers on the piano and the sofa and the smaller ones on the chairs and armchairs. And underneath was the furniture, which you knew was black because of the legs sticking out from under the white skirts.

Once when I was alone in the room, I raised a chair's skirt and found that although the wood was black the seat was a silky green.

As it often happened that neither my mother nor my grandmother accompanied me to my afternoon lesson, and as Celina—my piano teacher when I was ten years old—almost always kept me waiting, I had plenty of time to get into close touch with everything in the room. Of course, when Celina came in the furniture and I behaved as if nothing had happened.

To reach Celina's house I had to take a last turn up a rather quiet street. There I looked forward to crossing toward some huge trees. Usually I broke off that thought to watch for traffic. Then I looked up at the trees, knowing, even before I was in their shade, what their trunks were like, rising from their big squares of earth between timidly encroaching tiles. The trunks were very thick where they began, as if they had foreseen the height they would reach and the weight they would have to bear, loaded as they were with dark leaves and big white blossoms that spread their strong scent all around because they were magnolias.

Entering Celina's house, my eyes were full of the shapes they had gathered in the street. When they were suddenly invaded by the white and black shapes in the room, it seemed the others would fade. But as I sat down to rest—not yet daring to disturb the furniture for fear of the unexpected in a strange house—the shapes of the street lit up in me again, and it was a while before they settled down to sleep.

What never quite went to sleep was the specter of the magnolias. Although I had left behind the trees where they lived, they were with me, hidden in the back of my eyes, and suddenly I felt their presence, light as a breath somehow blown into the air by thought, scattered around the room, and blending into the furniture. Which was why, later on—in spite of the miseries I went through in that room—I never stopped seeing the faint glow of magnolias on the furniture and among the white and black shapes.

The shapes of the street had not yet fallen asleep when I began to roam—on tiptoes so Celina wouldn't hear me—and to poke into the secrets of the room.

First I went toward a marble woman and ran my fingers over her throat. The bust was on a little table with spindly legs that rocked the first times I touched it. I held the woman by the hair with one hand while I stroked her with the other. Needless to say, the hair was not hair but marble. But the first time I steadied her that way I suddenly felt troubled and confused. For a moment she seemed so much like a real woman that I could not help thinking of the respectful behavior I owed her as a woman. That was when I suddenly felt troubled. But then I began to enjoy the sense I had of giving in to a forbidden pleasure. To me she was a mixture of the known—her suggestion of flesh and blood, the fact that she was of marble, and other minor considerations—and the unknown: the ways in which she differed from other women, her personal history (I vaguely supposed she had been brought from Europe and even more vaguely supposed what Europe might be, where she might have been bought, who might have touched her, etc.) and above all her connection with Celina. But there were a lot of other things mixed in with the pleasure of stroking her neck. I was disappointed in her eyes: the holes meant to suggest irises or pupils made them look like fish eyes. It was annoying that they hadn't bothered to put streaks in her hair: it was a solid block of marble that made your hands cold. Where the breast began the bust ended in a cube that supported the whole figure. Also, just where the breast began, there was a flower with such sharp edges that if you moved too fast you could cut your fingers on it (and I couldn't see why anyone would have wanted to reproduce a flower that grew wild on every fence along the road).

After looking at the woman and touching her for a while I was left only with a kind of sad memory of pieces of marble that, once explored, were no longer much like the pieces of a real woman. Yet the moment we were alone, I couldn't keep my fingers from her throat. At times, when there were other people around—Mother and Celina engaged in some boring conversation—I even felt a certain complicity with her. Seen at a glance from across the room, her pieces formed a whole again and suddenly I was as confused as before.

In a portrait frame were two ovals with the pictures of a couple related to Celina. The woman's head was tilted in a kindly way, but her bulging throat reminded me of a frog. Looking at her once, I don't know why but I felt her husband's eyes on me. No matter how I slanted my glance, he went on staring me straight in the eye. Even as I moved about the room, until I tripped over a chair, he kept his gaze fastened on me, and I was inevitably the one who had to look down. The wife expressed her kindliness not only in the tilt of her head but in all her features, even the raised hairdo and the bulging throat. Everything about her suggested a goodness and sweetness that made you think of a great big tasty dessert, no matter what part of it you tried first. And there was something about the goodness that didn't just exist but was directed at me: I could see it in her eyes. When I worried about not being able to get my fill of her because of her watchful husband, she had a way of looking into my eyes that seemed to say, "Don't pay any attention to him, sweetheart, I understand you." And that set me to worrying again. I had always thought the good people who loved me best had never understood me, had never realized I betrayed them with evil thoughts. If that good woman had still been young, if she had been under the spell of that sleeping sickness in which people are alive but don't realize when they are being touched, and if she had been alone in the room with me, I probably would have done something to embarrass us.

When I inadvertently caught the husband's eye and quickly looked down, I felt frustrated and upset. And since this happened a number of times, the memory of the anguish and humiliation lingered on my eyelids, so that the moment I met his eyes I knew what to expect. Sometimes I held his look just long enough to figure out some way to remove mine without feeling humiliated: I tried slipping it out sideways, suddenly focusing on the frame, as if interested in its shape. But shifting my eyes, with my attention still on him, made his overbearing presence even more humiliating; I also felt I was cheating. Yet I did once manage to forget his look or my humiliation a little. I had quickly withdrawn my eyes from his and fixed them on his mustache. The thick black tuft over his lip narrowed in either direction into pointed whiskers that stretched for some considerable distance. I thought of my grandmother's round, pudgy fingers—once she had pricked a finger and the blood had squirted to the ceiling—and imagined the whiskers had been twisted by her. (She would spend ages twisting a black thread with perspiring fingers to pass it through a needle. Because of her poor eyesight she held the thread and needle too far away, cocking her head to see better, so the job never got done.) It seemed the man in the picture must have spent just as long twisting his mustache. And while he twisted and stared, who knew what was on his mind.

Although the secrets of grownups could be glimpsed in their actions and conversations, I had my favorite way of uncovering them—when the people were absent and I could find their traces in something they had left behind. It might be a forgotten object or simply one left temporarily in place—or, better yet, hurriedly, out of place—while they were gone. Whatever it was, it had to have been in use for some time before I noticed it. It might have entered a person's life by chance or secret choice or for whatever other unknown reason: what mattered was that it had started to fulfill some purpose or to mean something to the person who used it, so that the moment it was left unattended I could begin to trace that person's secrets in it.

In Celina's parlor there were many things that made me want to look for secrets. Just being in an unfamiliar place was one of them. Knowing, besides, that everything there belonged to Celina and that she was so stern and likely to keep such a tight hold on her secrets quickened the strange desire I felt to break into those secrets.

At first I had glanced at things casually. Then I had wondered about the secrets they had in themselves. And suddenly it had occurred to me that they—or other things that I wasn't seeing at that moment—might be intermediaries in the world of grownups and have hidden meanings or be involved in mysterious actions. Then it seemed to me that I had caught one making a secret sign at another and a third pretending not to notice when the second returned the sign to the first and so on, making fun of me, until they wore me down playing their game back and forth, always leaving me out. It must have been at one of those moments that my attention was caught, without my quite realizing it, by the suggestive curves and undulations of women and I must have felt carried along in the ripples, only to be snatched back by the watchful eyes of the husband in the picture. But by the time I had intercepted several calls from the various characters in different parts of the room playing their game at my expense, I realized that at first I had been drawn toward a secret that interested me more and then my attention had been interrupted and sidetracked by a lesser secret, and that I had probably been more on track when I was raising the skirts of the chairs.

Once when my hands were reaching out for the skirt of a chair they were stopped short by the loud noise of the hallway door as Celina hurried in from the street. I barely had time to pull the hands back when she came up in her usual way and kissed me. (The habit was ruthlessly suppressed as we parted one afternoon and she told my mother something in the order of, "This young gentlemen is growing up and from now on we'll have to shake hands.") She was in black, her tall, slim figure bound tight in her heavy wool dress, as if she had run her hands many times down the curves formed by the corset to smooth out every wrinkle and then up to choke her neck in the high collar that reached to her ears. Topping it all was her very white face with very black eyes, a very white forehead and very black hair done up in a bun like that of a queen I had seen on some coins: it reminded me of a burned pudding.

I was just beginning to digest the surprise of Celina's noisy entrance and her kiss when she reappeared in the room. But now, over the stern black dress, she wore white: a starched smock of lightweight material that had short flared sleeves with ruffles. From each ruffle emerged an arm still bound—down to the wrist—in the long black sleeve of the street dress. That was in winter: in summer the arm emerging from the ruffle was completely naked. Something about the bare arm in its starched ruffle reminded me of the artificial flowers made by a lady who lived just around the corner from my house. (Once my mother had stopped to chat with this lady. She was enormously fat and cheerful; seen from the sidewalk when she stood on her doorstep, she seemed immense. My mother told her she was taking me to my piano lesson, and for some reason the lady got worked up and said: "I also used to study the piano. I studied and studied and nothing happened, I never had anything to show for it. But since I've been making my wax fruit and flowers . . . At least I can see them, touch them . . .

and that's something, anyway." The fruit in question was big yellow bananas and big red apples. She was a coalman's daughter: very white, blonde, with naturally ruddy cheeks, and the wax fruit could have been her children.)

One winter day my grandmother had taken me to my lesson. Seeing my ten-year-old child's hands turn blue from the cold on the white and black keys, she was moved to warm them in hers. (On lesson days she scented her hands with a mixture of cologne and plain water: a milky blend that looked like orgeat. She used the same stuff as a mouthwash to rinse out the smell of the cigars my father brought her in packages of twenty-five and over which she went into such a rage when he couldn't find her exact brand, size and flavor.)

Since it was winter, night came early. But the windows had not seen it come in: they had gone on absently gazing at the clear sky until the last bit of light faded. The night floated up around our legs from under the furniture, where the black souls of the chairs grew and spread. Soon the white slip covers were quietly suspended in the air, like small harmless ghosts. Suddenly Celina would rise, light a small lamp on a coil and attach it to the candleholder on the piano. When my grandmother and I lit up in the light it was like being in a blaze of bright hay. Then Celina would put the shade on the lamp and her heavily powdered face was no longer so ghostly white. Her eyes also seemed less raw, her hair less starkly black.

When Celina was seated next to me I never dared to look at her: I sat stiff-backed as if I were in a cart, braking a horse. (If it was a slow horse it would be lashed on, if a spirited horse it might bolt and be punished even more severely.)

Only when Celina spoke to my grandmother, leaning her forearm on one of the boards of the piano, did I sneak a look at her hand. At the same time my eyes took in the long black sleeve running down to her wrist.

The three of us had bent forward toward the light and sound (or, rather, to wait for the sound, because my notes came spaced painfully far apart and we kept listening for more but were almost never rewarded for our effort, our three heads slowly working together, as in a dream, eyes glued to my poor fingers). My grandmother had remained in part darkness because she hadn't drawn her armchair up close enough and she seemed to hang in midair. She was so fat that her bulk—stuffed into an unchanging gray house-coat with a little black velvet collar—blotted out the chair, leaving only a bit of backrest clear on either side of her head. The half shadow she was in disguised her wrinkles. The ones on her cheeks were round and spread out, like ripples on a pond when a stone has dropped in, the ones on her forehead straight and piled up on each other, like still water ruffled by a soft wind. Her full, kindly face seemed to portray the word "grandmother": she made me feel how round that word was. (Whenever a friend's grandmother had a thin face, I thought the word "grandmother" didn't fit her and she would probably not be as kindhearted as mine.)

For long moments during the lesson my grandmother settled in her shadow beyond the edge of the light, gathered into herself. She was closer to me than Celina, but at such moments she withdrew into the darkness of things so familiar that their presence is forgotten. At other times she was spontaneously moved to express thoughts I could never predict but always recognized immediately as hers. Some of those thoughts were abstruse, and—especially if they had to do with music—she used ridiculous words for them. They were always the same words and after a while I ignored them, like objects left lying around a room until you no longer notice them. But then suddenly they managed to stand out again, irritating me with what I thought was their devious attempt to seem new when they were old. I also hated the insistence with which she kept bringing them up, forcing me to take another look at them, as if to convince me of their value and make me regret the injustice I had committed in not recognizing them to begin with. Of course it's possible that her thoughts were different each time and she just couldn't find new words for them, no matter how hard she tried, so they ended up all sounding alike, as if she had changed the contents of a jar but when she showed it to me all I could see was the same old jar. Sometimes, after dragging out the same old words, she seemed to realize she was not only not saying what she meant but repeating herself endlessly. Then she was the one who got annoyed and, trying to be sarcastic but beginning to splutter, she said, "How about listening to your teacher? Or doesn't she know more than you do?"

In Celina's house—even when Celina wasn't there—my grandmother's rages were not dangerous. Something in that parlor cooled her off in time. It had to do with our feeling that we both had to be on our best behavior there. She was naturally kindhearted and many of my attitudes amused her. Although generally those attitudes were similar in style, she found them new if they occurred differently in different situations: she enjoyed recognizing things in me that were at once familiar and unpredictable. I can still see her laughing, her stomach bouncing under her apron and a sticky green paper bouncing up and down between her fingers as she wound it around a wire stalk when she was making artificial flowers: the stalks were always too thick, grotesquely misshapen where the gobs of paste made bulges in the paper, and out of proportion to the flowers. Her kerchief also bounced up and down, and so did the stub of the cigar she kept in her mouth. But she was also easy to anger, and then she became all fiery cheeks, curses, and grimaces and headed, in ponderous haste, for the spot where she hung a fancy riding crop with silver bands that had belonged to her husband.

In Celina's house she hardly let out the hint of a threat, let alone a slap: I could sit next to her without worrying. Moreover, when Celina was too strict or forgot I hadn't been able to study for some reason beyond my control, I tried to catch her eye or, if I dared not look her way, I summoned her with my will, concentrating my attention on her and hardening my silence. It took her a while to react, but finally I would hear her lumbering toward me like a great big heavy contraption on a rough road, blowing steam and making all sorts of strange noises. At those moments, when Celina's cool surface took on jagged edges, when I was braking my cart and my grandmother was bearing down on us like an old steamroller, it seemed we had been invited to a small nightmare.

Across the piano keys, like a rail over sleepers, lay a long red pencil. I never lost sight of it because I wanted one just like it. When Celina picked it up to number the notes of the score for my fingering, the pencil was anxious to be allowed to write. Since Celina would not let it loose, it moved eagerly between the fingers that held it, its single pointed eye wavering as if in doubt and swinging back and forth.

When it was allowed to approach the page, the tip of the pencil was like a snout sniffing out something only a pencil's instinct could recognize, searching between the legs of the notes for a white spot it could bite into. Finally Celina would let it loose and, like a piglet suckling in quick, short bursts, it would cling hungrily to the white of the page, leaving little sharp footprints with its short black hoof and merrily wagging its long red tail.

Celina would make me spread my hands on the keys and, with her fingers, she bent mine back, as if she were teaching a spider to move its legs. She was more closely in touch with my hands than I was myself. When she made them crawl like slow crabs over white and black pebbles, suddenly the hands came upon sounds that cast a spell on everything in the circle of lamplight, giving each object a new charm.

Once Celina kept drumming something into me that I understood with my head but not with my hands. We reached a point where she was angry. Her anger grew faster than usual and took me by surprise, as if I had forgotten a pot on the fire until suddenly it boiled over. In her impatience she had already picked up the pretty red pencil, and I heard its sharp rap on my knuckles even before I had time to realize it was striking me. I had to divide my attention between many things coming at me from all sides, but gradually the pain took over until it stood out over everything else. An irresistible desire to cry was bloating up in me. I held it back with all my strength while a nightmarish silence fell about my ears and from my head and face down my whole body. Everything around me— the piano, the lamp, Celina still holding the pencil— radiated a strange heat. At that moment the objects were more alive than we were. Celina and my grandmother sat very still, smothered in the silence that seemed to flow from the watchful furniture in the dark corners of the room. In my first moment of surprise I had felt an emptiness in me which soon began to fill up with anguish. Then I had made a great effort to come out of the emptiness and let it fill up without me. Now I had taken a sort of jump back to the beginning of the silence, imagining Celina and my grandmother must also be filling it up with something. I thought I had felt them exchange a look that grazed my back, and that the look meant, "We had to punish him for his fault, but it wasn't all that serious—and he's suffering so much." But this unhappy supposition was the sign for the river to burst its dam, and that was when my silence poured in. Rushing toward me in the current I had glimpsed—but not recognized—a belated thought that made a furtive appearance, lurking nearby, and then exploded: How could Celina be hitting and dominating me when I had secretly promised myself to dominate her? For a long time I had been hoping she would fall in love with me—if it hadn't happened already—and my unhappy supposition of a minute before—that she felt sorry for me—was what had attracted and quickened its opposite: my private intention to dominate her.

I removed my hands from the keyboard and clenched my fists on my lap. No doubt to keep me from crying—I clearly remember I didn't cry—she ordered me to go on with my lesson. I sat there for a long while refusing to raise my head or my hands, until she blew up again and said, "If he won't take his lesson he may leave." She went on talking to my grandmother and I stood up. We parted curtly at the front door and my grandmother and I headed into the night. As soon as we had passed under some big trees—the darkened magnolias—my grandmother threatened me with the beating that awaited me when we got home, not only for incurring Celina's wrath but for refusing to go on with the lesson. I didn't care what happened any more: I was thinking it was all over between me and Celina. Our story had ended sadly, and not just because she was older—by some thirty years—than I was.

Our affair had begun, as so often happens, because of an old family relationship. (Celina had studied the piano with my mother sitting on her lap. My mother was then about four years old.) This relationship had been interrupted before I was born. When the two families met again and exchanged news of recent events, I was one of them. And Celina had made me want to be an interesting event for her. In spite of her unsmiling sternness, the way she looked at me and fussed over me tempted me to search for signs of the affection I knew she must be feeling for me. When she spoke to my mother, you could see she was fond of her. During one of our first lessons she told me I looked like my mother. After that, whenever she compared our features, it seemed as though her black eyes transferred some of the warmth inspired by my mother's features to mine. But once in a while she lingered over mine a bit longer, probably when she was discovering what was new and different about me, and that must have been when I began wanting to hold on to her attention, to make her realize I differed from my mother not only in some of my features but in my way of being. I had a way of standing by a chair, with an arm on the backrest and one leg crossed behind the other, that my mother didn't have.

Since it was always hard for me to deceive grownups, or at least to sustain my deceit for any length of time, I didn't think my poses had fooled Celina until once, much later, when I heard her remark to my mother on my natural ability to maintain a good posture. I believed her because just before that they had been discussing the postures people adopted when they slept, and it was true: an affectionate truth, I could almost say, in which she had lovingly enclosed my lie. Celina's unexpected words surprised and moved me. She had no idea what feelings she had stirred in me. A moment earlier I had been like a glass of still water on a table. Then she had come by and inadvertently jolted the table and the water's calm had been disturbed.

I couldn't believe I had managed to fool Celina. I stole a look at her, wondering if she was making fun of me, and then began to ask myself whether I might not really be striking poses without meaning to. Finally I remembered that when she had made me want to make her like me, when I had begun to enjoy imagining what she could be thinking of me because I had started to believe I might be the least bit interesting to her, I had decided to watch my posture and try to find constant new ways in which to seem original to her. Remembering this slowly calmed me, as if the water in the glass unconsciously disturbed by Celina had settled again. Now that I had managed to fool her—as grown-ups fooled others, especially when they were visiting—I felt more in possession of myself, and I would probably even find a way to have her fall in love with me. Of course, it would be very difficult, and I was too shy to dare ask anyone how it was done. I would have to go on just being interesting and original and wait for her to make the first move. Meantime I would be watching for signs of affection and hiding in the bushes that I assumed would line the road leading to her. Besides, if she had the feelings I thought she had, she would see into my silence and guess my wish. I couldn't help trying to imagine what such a stern person would be like when she softened and yielded to someone she loved. Perhaps her gnarled hand, the one with the scar on it, would be capable of a gentle caress, in spite of the thick black sleeve stretching down to her wrist. Perhaps the whole scene would take on the beauty and charm of the objects around us when struck by the sounds rising from the piano. Perhaps caressing me she would bend forward, as she did to light the lamp, and meantime the piano, like an old man half asleep, wouldn't mind holding the lamp on its back.

Now Celina had torn up all the roads between us, she had torn up secrets before knowing what they contained. Of course, grownups were full of secrets: the words they spoke out loud were always surrounded by others you couldn't hear. Sometimes they pretended to agree on something even though they were saying different things, and it was as surprising as if they thought they were face to face while turning their backs on each other or in the same room while wandering far apart. Being a child, I was free to roam among the chairs where the grownups sat—and also among the words they used. But now I was no longer in a mood for uncovering secrets. After what had happened with the pencil, Celina and I would have to tread lightly in our relations, as if picking our way through broken glass. From then on, I realized sadly, things between us would be clear but desolate. My illusions had been as violently shattered as if the light had come on in the middle of a dramatic scene in a movie: to her I was just a child, as my mother had been when Celina held her on her lap.

I got through that night—in spite of my grandmother's threats in the street—without a beating. The road home was dark. My grandmother helped me make out the shapes we passed. Some were shapes that stayed in place: columns, stones, tree trunks. Others were persons coming in the opposite direction. There was even a stray horse. While we were busy with these things, my grandmother's anger died down and her threats were blotted out, like more vanishing shapes, or were carried off on the back of the stray horse.

At home they noticed I was sad and attributed it to the unaccustomed punishment Celina had inflicted on me. But they never suspected what had been going on between us.

It was on one of those sad nights, in bed, as my thoughts edged toward sleep, that I began to feel the presences in the house around me, like furniture that kept changing position. From then on I often had that thought at night: they were furniture that could hold still or move, at will. The ones that held still were easy to love because they made no demands on you, while the ones that moved demanded not only love and kisses but harsher things, and were also likely to spring suddenly open and spill out on you. But they did not always surprise you in violent or unpleasant ways: some provided slow, silent surprises, as if they had a bottom drawer that gradually slid open to reveal unfamiliar objects. (Celina kept her drawers locked.) I even knew some persons with closed drawers who were nevertheless so pleasant that if you listened quietly you heard music in them: they were like instruments playing to themselves. Those persons had an aunt who was like a wardrobe in a corner, facing the door: there was nothing she didn't catch in her mirrors and you couldn't even dress without consulting her. The piano was a nice person. When I sat close to him, pressing a lot of his white or black fingers with a few of mine, he let out drops of sound, and combining the sounds with our fingers we both felt sad.

One night I had a strange dream. I was in Celina's dining room. There was a family of blond furniture: the sideboard and a table with its chairs around it. Then Celina was running around the table. She looked a bit different and skipped along, like a little girl, and I chased her, holding a stick with the tip wrapped in a piece of paper.

II

Something unexpected has happened and I've had to interrupt my story. For days now I've been at a standstill. Not only am I unable to write, but it's a great effort for me to live in the present, to live forward. Without meaning to, I had started to live backward, and there came a moment when I couldn't even live many of the events of that past time but could only concentrate on a very few, perhaps a single one, and I preferred to spend night and day just sitting or lying here. In the end I had lost even my desire to write. And, as it happens, this desire was my last tie to the present. But before this tie came loose, the following occurred: I was quietly enjoying one of those nights of the past. Although I had been stepping slowly, like a sleepwalker, suddenly I tripped over the wisp of an idea and fell into a moment full of events. The place into which I'd fallen was like an irresistible center of attraction, where a number of muffled secrets lying in wait for me seized and tied down my thoughts, and it has been a struggle ever since. My first impulse, after recovering from my surprise, was to give the secrets away. Then I started to feel more relaxed and to find a certain cozy pleasure in dwelling on those secrets, watching them silently at work, and I let myself sink into the pleasure without bothering to free my thoughts. That was when my last ties to the present gradually came undone. But at the same time something else happened: among the thoughts tied down by the muffled secrets there was one that broke loose on its own after a few days. What I was thinking just then was, "If I spend much longer in the past I'll never get out again and I'll go mad: I'll be like one of those unhappy souls trapped by a secret in his past for the rest of his life. I've got to row with all my might back to the present."

"Up until a few days ago I was in the present because I was writing. Now I'll do the same, even if the only land in sight is the island with Celina's house and I have to keep returning to it. I'll look through it again in case I missed something."

Then, preparing to go back over those same memories, I came on a lot of strange events. Most of them had occurred not back in the days of Celina but quite recently, while I was remembering and writing and perceiving the obscure or only dimly understood links between those events of the past and the ones that occurred later, during all the years I went on living. I couldn't quite recognize myself or make out what moods or impulses those distant events and the more recent ones had in common, or if they were equivalent in some way, or whether they might not all disguise the same mystery.

So now I'll try to tell what was happening to me a short time ago, while I remembered those days in the past.

One summer night I was walking home to my room, tired and depressed. I had let myself sink under the dead weight that thoughts take on when you feel the perverse need to pile them up for no particular reason other than to make yourself even more miserable and to convince yourself that life has lost its charm. Perhaps my disenchantment showed in my willingness to play with danger and risk having things become as bad as I thought they were, or maybe I was preparing for the next day's imaginings, and the feeling of spent hope was in itself a charm. Perhaps while I foundered in despair I was clutching the last few coins in the bottom of my pocket.

When I got home you could still see the white shirts of the neighbors who had come out to sit in the cool evening air under the crooked old trees, which hadn't been pruned yet. Later, in bed, with the light out, it felt good to complain and be a pessimist, stretching your legs out in sheets that were whiter than the neighbor's shirts.

It was on such a night, when I was running past times through my mind, carelessly, the way you let coins slip through your fingers, that the memory of Celina visited me. I was no more surprised than I would have been by the visit of an old friend who was in the habit of dropping in every once in a long while. No matter how tired I felt, I could always manage a smile for such a visitor. The memory of Celina returned the next day and for several days after that. By then I was accustomed to having the visitor around and I could leave him there, attend to other matters, and come back to him later. But while I was gone he was up to things I didn't know about. I can't say what small changes he made in my room or whether he was in touch with other people now living nearby. Once, when he came in and greeted me, I even thought he was looking past me, as if addressing someone in the back of the room. But he and other memories weren't the only ones who looked beyond me:

certain thoughts also went through me and beyond, after accompanying me for a few minutes in my sadness.

And then one night I woke up in anguish when I became aware of another presence in the room. It must be a friend—or perhaps not exactly a friend: a partner. It was distressing suddenly to realize that you had been sharing your work with someone else and that the one in charge was the other person. I didn't have to look far for proofs: they were plainly visible behind my suspicions, like shapes behind a veil. As they burst into the present and took it over, I was thinking the "someone" in the back of the room communicating over my shoulder with my memories must have been this partner of mine, who was speculating with those memories as if they belonged to him: he was the one who had written my story. No wonder I distrusted the precision the story took on whenever Celina appeared in it: it was nothing like what I myself was really going through. So then I tried to be myself alone, to find out how I myself remembered things—and I waited for the events and memories to recur.

On the last night of my theater of memories there is a moment when Celina comes in and I don't know I am remembering her. She simply comes in—all my senses are aware of her. The fleeting moment is long enough for me to realize I have felt a shiver of pleasure because she has come. My soul settles down comfortably to remember, the way my body does in a seat at the movies. I can't tell whether the image before my eyes is clear, whether I am seated too far back, who my neighbors are, or if anyone is watching me. I don't know whether I am working the projector myself or even whether I came on my own or

someone prepared the memory for me and brought me to
it. I would not be surprised if it had been Celina herself: all
these years, ever since I left her side, I may have been on
threads stretching into the future but still controlled by her.

Celina does not always come to mind the way she came in
the door of her parlor: sometimes she comes already seated
next to the piano or in the act of lighting the lamp. I don't
remember her myself, with the eyes I have now: I remember the eyes that saw her then. The images that come to me
now are transmitted by those other eyes, and so is the
feeling that moves them. It is the original feeling I had for
Celina. The eyes of the child in me stare in amazement but
unsteadily. Celina may be caught in motion or just after she
has moved, but her movements displace no air in space:
they are the movements of remembering eyes.
   My mother or my grandmother has asked her to play and
she sits down at the piano. My grandmother must be
thinking, "The teacher is going to play"; my mother,
"Celina is going to play"; and I, "*She* is going to play." It
must be summer because her arms are bare. In the lamplight
they and their flared sleeves look translucent. The arms
move in waves that end in hands, keys and sounds. Summer
is when I can taste the night best with its plant-shaped
shadows and hints of the unexpected, its waiting for
something to happen, its false alarms, reveries, nightmares,
and good food. I can also taste Celina most, and not just in
my mouth: all her movements taste of her, so do her clothes
and the shapes of her body. Her voice must also have tasted
of her in those days, but I have no direct memory of
anything related to hearing—of her voice, of the piano, of
the street noises—only of what was going on while the
sounds were in the air. My memories are a silent movie: I

can put my old eyes on to see them, but my ears are deaf to them.

Now, for a few moments, my imagination has flown out the window like a night bug, drawn to the tastes of summer over distances unknown, even to night and to the deep. Nor does the imagination know who the night is or who in its dark landscape chooses the spots where a digger turns over the soil of memory and seeds it again. At the same time, someone dumps chunks of the past at the feet of the imagination, who hastily sorts through them in the swaying light of a small lantern it holds over them, mixing earth and shadows. Suddenly it drops the lantern on the soil of memory and the light goes out. Then once more the imagination is an insect flying over forgotten distances to land again on the edge of the present. Now the present into which it has fallen is again Celina's parlor, and at the moment she is not playing the piano. The insect flying in memory has gone back one more wingbeat in time and arrived just before Celina will sit down to play. My grandmother and my mother ask her once more to play, though in a different tone of voice than before. This time Celina says she is not sure she remembers the piece. She is nervous, and on her way to the piano she trips over a chair, which must make a noise—but we are not supposed to notice. She has gathered enough speed that the impulse carries her past the chair and the accident is immediately forgotten. She sits down at the piano: we are hoping nothing unpleasant happens to her. Before she begins, we have just enough time to imagine she will play something impressive which will make us recommend her to our acquaintances. She is so nervous, and so aware of being the teacher, that my grandmother and my mother both try to advance her a bit of success, willing their favorable expectations on her and anxiously awaiting the performance that will allow them to match their expectations with reality.

The things I have to imagine are very lazy and slow in composing themselves to come. It's like when I'm waiting for sleep, and I soon grow accustomed to certain sounds and can go on imagining or fall asleep as if they weren't there. But the sounds and small happenings with which those three women filled the room keep me tossing my head right and left.

When Celina performed for us that time I took in everything that reached my eyes and ears. Before that, I had been letting things become too familiar, until they had almost stopped surprising me and I no longer really appreciated what she did.

My mother and grandmother seemed to be halfway into a sigh from which they hung suspended, as if afraid that at the supreme moment, just when their effort to understand was supposed to take off, their wings would carry them about as far as useless hens' wings.

I was probably very bored, after a while.

Here I've stopped again. I'm very tired. I've had to keep watch all around myself to make sure that he—my partner—doesn't sneak in with my memories. As I said before, I want to be myself alone. But, to keep him out, I'm forced to think of him constantly. With a part of myself I've made a sentry who stands guard over my memories and thoughts, but that means I also have to watch the sentry so he won't start listening to the story of the memories and get so caught up in it that he falls asleep. On top of everything, I've got to lend him my eyes—the ones I have now.

My eyes, now, are cruel, insistent: they demand a great effort from the eyes of the child, who must be old and tired by now. Besides, he has to see everything in reverse: he is not allowed to remember the past but obliged to perform the miracle of remembering toward the future. But how is it that, while still being myself, I suddenly see everything differently? Can my partner have put on my eyes? Can we be sharing the same pair of eyes? Can the sentry watching the street through the windows of my room have fallen asleep and my partner have stolen my eyes from him? Isn't seeing through my windows enough for him that he now also wants to see through my eyes? He would not hesitate to pry open a dead man's eyes to find out what's inside them. He is after those child's eyes, determined to pinpoint their mechanism as if the pieces of memory could be taken apart like a clock. The child stops in fright; his eyes blink on and off. He doesn't know yet—and it may already be too late for him ever to realize—that his images are random and incomplete: he has no notion of time and must have fused many hours and nights into one. He has confused the movements of different people, attributed the feelings of one to another and stumbled on charming discoveries. The eyes I now have know these things, but there are many other things they don't know. They don't know that the images feed on movement and live only in the sleeping self. My partner stops the images and the sleeping self wakes up; he nails them down with his eyes as if he were pinning butterflies in an album. Even when the child's images seem motionless, they feed on movement: someone makes them throb and pulse in the eye. And it is that someone whom the eyes I now have are betraying. When the child's eyes seize a part of something, they think it is the whole thing. (And the child cares no more than a dream does whether his images are complete or similar to those of real life: he simply proceeds as if they were.) When the child looked at Celina's bare arm he felt the whole of her was in that arm. The eyes I now have want to capture Celina's mouth, but they can't define the shape of her lips in relation to the rest of her face; they want to grasp a single feature and are left with none. The parts have lost their mysterious relationship to each other, they have lost their balance and natural proportion and seem disconnected, as if a clumsy hand had drawn them. If the hand tries to get the lips to articulate a word, their movements are as forced as those of a wind-up doll.

Only for a moment do the eyes I now have see well: the fleeting instant when they meet the eyes of the child. Then the eyes I now have reach avidly for the images, thinking they are still in time to linger on them. But an invisible innocence in the air of the world shelters the child's eyes. Nevertheless, the eyes I now have persist until they are tired. Even on the edge of sleep my partner tries to remember Celina's face, and when he stirs the waters of memory the images under the surface are deformed, as if seen in a cheap mirror with waves in the glass.

I realize the memory is over only when I feel an immediate physical discomfort in my eyes: a stinging as of tears drying on my eyelids.

A few days ago, in the evening, a strange and unprecedented event took place in me. Before, I could always find a precedent for an event, however strange: somewhere in my soul lay buried the first germ of it, at some point in my life there had been the hint of a scene or a plot that was a rehearsal for this final performance. But a few days ago, in the evening, the performance came unannounced. I don't know if the players were in the wrong theater, and whether it was by mistake or because they had deliberately broken in. If one were to call my condition that evening a sickness, I would say I didn't know I was predisposed to it, and if the sickness was a punishment, I would say it had fallen on the wrong person. It was not that I felt my partner take over: for hours I myself, all of me, was another person—such was the condition my sickness imposed on me. I was in the situation of someone who has assumed, all his life, that madness was one way, and, suddenly in its grip, discovers that it is not only different from the way he'd imagined it but that the person suffering from it is someone else, or has become someone else, and that this someone else is not interested in finding out what madness is like: he is simply immersed in it, or it has descended on him, and that's that.

While I hadn't quite ceased being who I was in order to become who I was meant to be, I was put through some very peculiar agonies. The person I had been and the man I was becoming would always have something in common: their memories. But as the memories were transferred to the man I was becoming, even while they remained within the same visual range and seemed factually unchanged, they were taking on a new soul. On this new man's face there was the hint of a moneylender's smile as the memories were appraised before being pawned. The moneylender's hands weighed the memories, not for their personal value, loaded with private feelings and associations, but for their intrinsic worth.

Then came another stage: the smile turned bitter because the pawned memories no longer weighed in the money-lender's hand: they were made of sand, suggesting age, that was all—the memories and times stolen by the moneylender were worthless. But there followed an even worse stage:

when the moneylender had smiled his bitter smile over his useless theft he still had a soul, but now he reached total indifference. His smile faded and he finally became what he was destined to be: an empty railway car, detached from life.

At first, that evening, when I started remembering and being someone else, I saw my past life as if it were in the next room. I had once been in that room, I had lived there; more than that: it had been my room. And now I saw it from another room, the room where I lived now, without quite knowing what distance separated the two rooms in time and space. In that room nextdoor I saw my poor lost self in the days when he was innocent. And I saw him not only seated at the piano in the lamplight with Celina, his mother and grandmother looking on, never suspecting his unrequited love, but with other loves as well. From all times and places I saw persons, furniture, feelings gather for the ceremony organized by the "inhabitants" of Celina's parlor. For a moment they were all jumbled and confused, as if bits of old movies were being mixed together, but then those that belonged in the same room recognized each other and began to form a separate group for each room: they seemed to have an unerring instinct for picking each other out, even if on reflection they proved to have been wrong. (Some nevertheless refused to regroup, but had to in the end, while others stonewalled and managed to stay together even if they were in the wrong place, and still others vanished as lightly as papers blown off a table by the wind. Some of those that blew off flitted around uncertainly, drawing our eyes after them, until they settled in some other familiar spot.) With these exceptions, I can say that all the places, times, and memories attending the ceremony, no matter what subtle threads or sympathies united them, were totally oblivious to others not of their same lineage. When a particular lineage was rehearsing its memories, it remained for some time in a spot next to the one from which I was observing it. Suddenly the performance would stop and the players would repeat a scene or go back to one that had happened long before. But the stops and abrupt changes of scene were muted, as if the missteps occurred in silk slippers. The players were never ashamed of having made a mistake and could repeat the same smile a thousand times before it wore out or looked strained. In the search for some scene's lost detail there was always a longing that brought everything back to life. When an extraneous detail introduced its own lineage, the previous lineage vanished, and if it reappeared in a while it showed no resentment toward the intruder.

The sympathy uniting these various lineages that totally ignored each other, never exchanging so much as a look, hovered over them: it was the innocent sky under which they all breathed the same air. In addition to being in the same room, at about the same time, to rehearse their memories, they had something else in common: the measured pace provided by the spectator's breathing. It was as if a single orchestra were playing for different ballets. But the spectator—me, in other words, just before I became someone else—sensed that the inhabitants of those memories, although directed by him and magically obedient to his every whim, were also capable of exercising a hidden but proud will of their own. It seemed as if on their way down the road in time between their first performance—when they were not yet memories—and now, they had run into someone who had turned them against me, and since then they had acquired a certain independence; and now, although they could not help being under my orders, they accomplished their mission in a distrustful silence. I could tell they weren't fond of me, that they wouldn't look at me and that, while resigned to the fate I was imposing on them, they did not even remember my appearance: if I had entered their sphere they probably would not have recognized me. In any case, their different mode of existence made it impossible for me to touch them, speak to them or be heard by them: I was condemned to being the person I now was, and if I tried to repeat those events they would never be the same. They were the events of another world and it would be useless to chase after them. But why couldn't I be happy watching those events live in their world? Could it be that my breath clouded or harmed them now because I was sick in some way? Might those memories be like children with a sudden instinct to reject and despise their parents? Would I have to renounce those memories as a bad father disowns his children? Unfortunately, something of the sort was going on.

The room I now occupied also contained memories, but they had no innocent sky overhead nor the pride of belonging to some lineage: they were inevitably attached to a man "with his tail between his legs," whose accomplices they had become. These memories did not arrive from distant places or know any ballet steps: they came from underground, loaded with remorse, and slithered around under a heavy sky, even during the brightest hours of the day.

The painful and confusing story of my life separates the child I was in the days of Celina from "the man with his tail between his legs."

Some women have seen Celina's child in the man while talking to him. I hadn't known the child was visible in the man until the child himself noticed it and told me he was visible in me, and that the women were seeing him and not me. Moreover, he was the first to attract and seduce them. The man later seduced them by appealing to the child. The man learned deceit from the child—who had much to teach him in that area—and practiced it the way children do. But he did not take into account his remorse or the fact that, although he practiced his deceit only on a few persons, they would multiply in the events and memories that haunted him night and day: which was why, fleeing his remorse, he wanted to be let into the room that had once been his, where the inhabitants of Celina's parlor were now gathered for their ceremony. And the sadness of being rejected and even totally ignored by those inhabitants increased when he remembered some of the persons he had deceived. The man had deceived them with the wiles of the child, but had then, in turn, been seduced by the child he had just used, when he had fallen in love with some of his victims. These were late loves become mythical or perverse with age—and that wasn't the worst of it. Worse still was the fact that the child had been able to attract and seduce the man he later became because his charms were more powerful than those of the man, and because life held more charm for him.

It was in the course of that same evening, when I discovered I had been shut out of the world of innocence and its ceremonies, that I started to become someone else.

First I had realized the inhabitants of that world did not look at me because I was on the other side of memory, the one where you carried a load of remorse on your back, as firmly attached as a camel's hump. Then I realized the two sides of memory were like the two sides of my body: I would lie on one and then the other, changing my position, as if I were having trouble going to sleep and couldn't predict which side luck would favor. But until I fell asleep I was at the mercy of my memories, like a spectator obliged to watch two very different companies perform without knowing what scene or which memories would light up first, how they would alternate, or what the relations between the actors would be, because the theater and producer were always the same, usually the same author was involved and the main characters were always a man and a child.

Then, when it was clear I couldn't do without the spectacle that, although vague and confused in its mixture of times, had such a lasting effect on the life I had to go on living into the future—then I started to be someone else, to change the present and the road leading into the future, to become the pawnbroker with nothing left in his hands to weigh, and to try to suppress the space where the performances took place. I had let my feelings languish: I was tired of suffering from those memories that treated each other like irreconcilable enemies. And since I had no feelings, I'd stopped being sad over myself and even over the uselessness of a stage emptied of its memories. I had also become as useless as if I'd been left guarding a fortress without soldiers, weapons, or supplies.

All that remained was my habit of pacing about and watching the thoughts arrive. They were like animals that kept returning to drink from a spot where there was no more water. None of them was burdened with feelings: they could be as sad as they pleased, they were only thoughts. Now I let them come as if I were lying under a tree and leaves were falling on me: I would see them and remember them only because they had fallen and piled on me. My new memories would be like a bundle of clothes piled on my head: as I walked I would feel their weight there but nothing else. I was like that stray horse I had seen in the street as a child. Now I was pulling a cart anyone could load with things: I wouldn't be taking them anywhere and I'd soon be tired.

That night, after lying in the bed for a while, I opened my eyes in the dark, which emptied them. But there were already skeletons of thoughts stirring—I don't know what worms had eaten the flesh off their ribs and calves. Meantime I seemed to be slowly, lazily unfolding an umbrella with no canopy.

That was how I spent the hours when I was someone else. Then I fell asleep and dreamed I was in a huge cage, surrounded by people I had known as a child. There were also a lot of calves going through a gate to the slaughterhouse. Among the calves was a little girl who was also headed for slaughter. The little girl kept saying she didn't want to go because she was tired, and the people were laughing at the innocent excuse she gave to escape death: they saw no point in worrying over something you couldn't get out of.

When I woke up I realized I had also seen the little girl in the dream as a calf. It was the feeling I'd had, as if her human appearance had been only a variation in form: that she was a calf and expected to be treated as such. Yet I'd been moved when she said she didn't want to go because she was tired—and my face was bathed in tears.

The tide of anguish sweeping over me during my dream had almost drowned me. But now it was as if I had been thrown out on a beach where I felt a great relief. My sense of well-being increased as my thoughts became receptive to my feelings again and I gradually recovered myself. Not only was I no longer someone else but I was more attuned than ever to what I felt: the least thought, even the idea of a jug of water, affected me deeply. I loved my shoes standing there alone, unlaced, always so fondly side by side. I felt capable of forgiving everything—and of being forgiven, even by remorse.

It was not morning yet. Things were clearing up in me a little before daylight. I had decided to start writing. Then my partner reappeared: he had also survived, thrown out on another part of the beach. Somehow I'd known he would be back the moment I sat down to write my memories.

At first he had made himself felt in the usual way, as a presence, not physically there but threatening to walk in off the street disguised as some ordinary person from the world of everyday reality. Because, until that morning, I had been in one place and the world in another. Between the world and me there was a layer of dense air. On very clear days I could see the world through that air and also hear the noises in the street and the murmur people make when they talk. My partner was the representative of the people living in the world. But he was not always an enemy who had come to steal my memories and speculate with them. Sometimes he appeared almost in the guise of a mother warning me of a danger and awakening my instinct for self-preservation. At other times he scolded me for not going out into the world—and then, as if he were my mother scolding me, I lowered my eyes and didn't see him—or he could appear as a friend advising me to write down my memories and appealing to my vanity. I felt closest to him when he evoked the presence of dear friends whose wise advice had helped me with my writing in the past. Sometimes I would even feel him put a hand on my shoulder. But at other times I didn't want his advice or his presence in any of its forms. That was when I was sick with my memories, especially in the stage of the sickness when I was watching the specters of remorse in their dramatic performance and trying to glimpse my fate in the relations between different memories from different times. If I had touched lonely depths of suffering with my remorse, afterward I felt entitled to a more or less extended period of relief: suffering was the best food to appease the beasts of remorse. And my greatest pleasure was searching through different memories to see whether they shared any secret and whether their different events all expressed a similar sense of being. Then I would rediscover a forgotten childish curiosity in myself, as if I were returning to a house in a corner of the woods where I had once lived, surrounded by people whose furniture I was now going through, uncovering secrets I hadn't suspected at the time, although everyone else may have known them. This was the task at which I most wanted to be left alone, because my partner would make so much noise coming in that he would scare off the silence that had settled on the objects in the house. Besides, my partner was a city man with city ideas: he would take many of the objects back to the city with him, changing their lives to make them serve those ideas; he would dust them off and dress them up in a new coat of paint, and they would lose their soul. But my greatest fear was for the things he would suppress, coldly wiping out their secrets until they had been stripped of all imprecision, like a dream emptied of everything that makes it fantastic and absurd.

That was when I ran from my partner—like a thief, deep into the woods, to be alone with my memories. When I thought there was no one near I would start going over the objects, trying to breathe an air of bygone days on them to bring them back to life. Then, having run all the way into the back of my mind, I had to push myself forward again. I wanted to make new sap flow through plants, roots, and tissues probably long dead or disintegrated. And the fingers of the mind delving down into itself not only found the old roots but discovered new connections, felt their way along new mosses branching out in new directions. But as the fingers sank through the waters in which the tips of the roots were submerged, it turned out they weren't sensitive enough to perceive endings so subtle that they melted into the water, and the fingers lost their way. Finally, the fingers broke off from the mind that was guiding them and continued the search on their own. I had no idea what old connections there might be between the delving fingers and the lost roots—whether the roots, back in those days of the past, might not have arranged to grow the fingers capable one day of the twists and turns along devious paths with which they were now feeling their way back to them. I couldn't think about this for long because I heard footsteps: probably my partner hiding in a tree, or behind it. Again I fled as if I were plunging deeper into the center of myself, shrinking from sight like a microbe contracting under a lens. But I knew I would never get away from my partner, who would soon be spinning around me, also changed into a microscopic body and drawn toward my center.

And while my partner kept circling me I also knew what he was thinking and how he was responding to my thoughts and actions: I could almost say my ideas attracted his like echoes. At times his ideas invaded me with such irresistible force that I thought of him as an enemy as inexorable as fate. The force of these ideas was also that of the world and its habits, which made me sad in so many ways. Yet that morning I felt at peace with my partner. I had my own lot of sad habits, and although they might not agree with those of the world, I had to try to combine the two. Because I wanted to be let into the world I decided to adjust to it and allow some of my affection to spill out over everything and everybody. Then I discovered that my partner was the world—it was useless to try to shake him off. I had received my daily bread and my words from him. Besides, when he was representing only one person at a time—not the whole world as now—while I wrote down my memories of Celina, he had been a tireless companion who had helped me turn my memories, including those burdened with remorse, into writing—and that had been a great relief to me. So I can forgive him for smiling when I refused to enclose my memories in a grid of space and time. And I can forgive him for tapping his foot impatiently over my scrupulous insistence on unraveling the tissue of memory down to the last thread, until its last wisps melted into the water and the last breath of movement was nowhere in space and left the air undisturbed.

On the other hand, I have to thank him for the times he followed me at night to the edge of a river where I went to see the water of memory flow. When I drew some water in a jug and was saddened at how little and how still it was, he would help me invent other containers for it and comfort me by showing me its different shapes in the different vessels. Afterward we invented a boat in which to cross the river to the island where Celina's house was. We would take along thoughts that fought hand to hand with our memories, knocking over or displacing many objects in the house. Some of the objects may have rolled under the furniture, and others we must have lost on our way back, because when we opened the bag with our hoard it was always down to just a few bones, and the small lantern we had been holding over the soil of memory dropped from our hands.

Yet the next morning we always turned what little we had gathered during the night into writing.

But I know the lamp Celina lit on those nights is not the same one that now lights up in memory. An immensity of time larger than the world separates her and the things lit up around her from me, blinding them to me. Caught in the air of that other time of theirs, under another sky, they have lost their memory, which is why they can't remember me. But I remember them all and have lived with them and breathed them in the air of many different times, roads, and cities. Now, with my memories hidden in the dark air of the night and only that lamp on, I realize once again that they don't recognize me and that their affection has become not only distant but oblivious of me. Celina and the other inhabitants of her room look at me sideways, or, when facing me, stare straight through me, as if there were someone behind me or I had never been in the room with them. Their looks are like the looks of mad people who have long forgotten the world. They are specters that don't belong to me. Could it be that Celina and her lamp and chairs and piano are angry at me because I never went back to that house? Yet it seems to me that the child I was took them with him when he left and they are all still living together somewhere, and that must be what they are remembering. Now I'm someone else and when I want to remember the child I can't: I don't know what he looks like from where I am now. Something of him is still in me and I have kept many of the objects that were in his eyes, but his way of seeing and being seen by the "inhabitants" of the room is lost to me.

No One Had Lit a Lamp

Once years ago I was reading a story in the parlor of an old house. A bit of sunlight had been filtering in through one of the shutters. Slowly it had enveloped the people in the room and spread to a table with pictures of dead "loved ones." I was having trouble bringing out my voice, as if squeezing notes from an instrument with a broken bellows. In the front chairs sat two widows, the ladies of the house. They were very old but still had thick hair done up in buns. I was reading listlessly, often raising my eyes. I tried not to look at the same person each time, but my eyes kept returning to the pale area between the collar and the bun of one of the widows. It was a settled face absorbed in a single memory that would still be with her for some time. At moments her eyes seemed like smoked glasses with no one behind them. Every now and then I remembered there were important people in the audience, and I did my best to breathe life into the story. One of the times my attention wandered I looked through the shutters and saw a statue with pigeons scrambling over it. Then, in the back of the room, I saw a young woman lean her head against the wall. Her wavy mane was spread out wide and I ran my eyes over it as if it were a plant growing along the wall of an abandoned house. It was too much of an effort for me to remember what I'd been trying to get across in the story, but sometimes the words alone and the habit of reading them in a certain way had an automatic effect and provoked unexpected laughter. I had already run my eyes a second time through the hair of the woman backed against the wall, and I wondered whether she had noticed. To avoid being indiscrete I looked out at the statue. While I went on reading I thought of the innocence with which the statue played a role it could not understand. Possibly it felt closer to the pigeons than to the self-important character it portrayed: it did not seem to mind having them flutter around its head or land on the scroll it held against its side. Suddenly I realized I was staring again at the head of the woman backed against the wall and that she had just closed her eyes. I struggled to recover the excitement I'd felt the first times I'd read the story: it was about a woman who went out on a bridge every night hoping to commit suicide but always met with some obstacle. The audience laughed when someone propositioned her one night and she was so frightened that she ran all the way home.

The woman against the wall was laughing too, turning her head right and left as if it lay on a pillow. By now I'd taught myself to shift my eyes from her head to the statue. I tried to imagine the character it portrayed but could think of nothing serious enough: perhaps he also had stopped taking himself as seriously as he used to in life and spent his time now playing with the pigeons. I was surprised when people smiled at my words again. I looked at the widows and noticed someone peering out the sad eyes of the one that seemed to be wearing smoked glasses. Once when I tore my eyes off the woman backed against the wall I didn't

look out at the statue but into another room where I
thought I saw flames on a table. Some eyes in the audience
followed mine, but it was just a vase with red and yellow
flowers that had caught a bit of sunlight.

When I finished reading, a busy crowd surrounded me
with questions and comments. A weighty gentleman started
to tell me a story about another woman who had committed suicide. He wanted to express himself properly but
couldn't find the right words and kept going into round-
abouts and digressions. I noticed the audience was growing
impatient: we all stood there not knowing what to do with
our hands. The young woman with the wavy mane came
up and joined us. I looked at her and then out at the statue.
I didn't want to hear the gentleman's story because his
clumsy hunt for words was painful to me: it was as if the
statue had started slapping at the pigeons. But there was no
way to get out from under the dull persistence with which
he droned on, as if he were trying to say: "I'm a politician
and can crank out a speech or a story to suit every
occasion."

Among the listeners was a young man with a strange
mark on his forehead: a dark smudge that followed his
receding hairline way back, like the shadow of a thick beard
that has just been shaved and powdered. I looked at the
woman with the wavy mane and to my surprise she was also
staring—at my hair. Just then the politician finished his story
and everyone clapped. I could not bring myself to congratulate him. One of the widows had already said: "Please sit
down." We all sat with a more or less general sigh of relief,
but I had to get up again when one of the widows
introduced me to the girl of the wavy mane, who turned
out to be her niece. I was invited to sit in the center of a
large sofa, between the niece and the young man with the

smudge on his forehead. The niece was about to speak, but the young man raised a hand to silence her. Addressing me, with his fingers still pointed upward like the ribs of an umbrella bent in the wind, he said:

"I'll bet you're the sort of lonely character who'd only make friends with a tree."

I wondered whether he had shaved his forehead to broaden his brow and, feeling mean, answered:

"Don't you believe it. You can't take a tree for a walk."

The three of us laughed. He threw his shaved forehead back and said:

"How true—a tree is the friend who's always where you left him."

The widows were calling their niece. She rose with a grimace, and as she walked away I suddenly realized she was heavyset and violent. I turned to meet another young man who was being introduced to me by the one with the shaved forehead. He had just combed and left droplets of water on the tips of his hair. Once when I'd combed my hair that way as a child my grandmother had asked me, "Cow lick you?" The newcomer sat in the niece's place and started to complain:

"Oh, that endless story! What an awful man! And so obstinate!"

"And you, my dear, so effeminate," I felt like saying, but instead I asked:

"What's his name?"

"You still talking about . . . ?"

". . . that obstinate man."

"Oh, I forget. He's from one of those old families. He's a politician and he's always on the juries of literary contests."

I caught the eye of the young man with the smudge on his forehead, who shrugged as if to say: "Such is life!"

The niece was back, pulling the effeminate young man off the sofa. While she tugged at his arm, shaking him so hard that he stood up with drops of water on his jacket, she was saying:

"Well, I don't agree with you . . ."

"Why not?"

". . . and I'm surprised you'd think a tree can't go for a walk with us."

"But how could it?"

"By repeating itself in long steps."

We praised her idea and she was encouraged:

"Repeating itself along an avenue, it shows us the way. Then all the trees of the avenue join heads to watch for us. And as we approach they open up to let us through."

She made it all sound like a joke so it wouldn't seem too romantic, blushing with pleasure and embarrassment.

The charm was broken by the effeminate young man:

"But at night in the woods the trees attack us from all sides. Some stagger and sway as if about to fall on us, and others trip us up or reach out and grab us with their branches."

The niece could not help exclaiming:

"Why, if it isn't Snow White!"

And while we laughed, she said she had been meaning to ask me a question, and we went into the next room, where I'd seen the vase with flowers. She leaned across the table toward me, with her hands deep in her hair, and said:

"Tell me the truth. Why did the woman in your story commit suicide?"

"I'm afraid you'd have to ask her."

"Couldn't you ask her for me?"

"No more than I could ask something of a figure in a dream."

She smiled and lowered her eyes, and I got a good look at her large mouth. It seemed the smile could go on stretching her lips forever, but I passed my eyes over their entire moist red surface with pleasure. Maybe she was watching me through her eyelids or wondering whether there wasn't something guilty in my silence, because she dropped her head on her chest and hid her face. Now she was showing me her full head of hair. Between two waves I could see a bit of scalp and it reminded me of the skin of a hen when the wind ruffles her feathers. I enjoyed thinking of that head as a big, warm human hen: it would give out a delicate warmth and the hair would be like very fine feathers.

One of the aunts—not the one with the smoked eyes—brought us two small glasses of liqueur. The niece raised her head and the aunt said:

"Watch out for this one, he looks sly as a fox."

I remembered the hen and said:

"As long as we're not in a henhouse!"

Alone with me again, as I tasted the liqueur—it was too sweet and turned my stomach—the niece asked:

"Aren't you ever curious about the future?"

She had puckered her mouth as if to tuck it into her glass.

"No, I'm more curious about what's going on at this moment inside another person or what I'd be doing right now if I were somewhere else."

"Tell me what you'd do if I weren't here right now."

"As a matter of fact, I'd pour my drink into this flower vase."

I was asked to play the piano. The two widows were huddled in the parlor, the one with the smoked eyes

PIANO STORIES

bending an ear to receive her sister's urgent whispers. The
creaky little piano was out of tune. I didn't know what to
play, and the minute I tried some notes the widow with the
smoked eyes burst into tears and we all fell silent. Her sister
and her niece helped her out of the room. A moment later
the niece came back in and said her aunt could not stand the
sound of music since the death of her husband: they had
been in love into dim old age.

Some of the guests were leaving, and the rest of us began
to lower our voices in the fading light. No one had lit a
lamp.

I was one of the last to go, stumbling over the furniture.
In the entrance hall the niece stopped me and said:

"Will you do something for me?"

But then she just leaned her head back against the wall,
holding on to my jacket sleeve.

The Balcony

I liked to visit this town in summer. A certain neighborhood emptied at that time of the year when almost everyone left for a nearby resort. One of the empty houses was very old; it had been turned into a hotel, and as soon as summer came it looked sad and started to lose its best families, until only the servants remained. If I had hidden behind it and let out a shout, the moss would have swallowed it up.

The theater where I was giving my concerts was also half empty and invaded by silence: I could see it growing on the big black top of the piano. The silence liked to listen to the music, slowly taking it in and thinking it over before venturing an opinion. But once it felt at home it took part in the music. Then it was like a cat with a long black tail slipping in between the notes, leaving them full of intentions.

After one of those concerts, a timid old man came up to shake my hand. The bags under his blue eyes looked sore and swollen. He had a huge lower lip that bulged out like the rim of a theater box. He barely opened his mouth to speak, in a slow, dull voice, wheezing before and after each word.

After a long pause he said:

"I'm sorry my daughter can't hear your music."

I don't know why I imagined his daughter was blind, although I realized at once that that would not have prevented her from hearing me, so that she was more likely deaf or perhaps out of town—which suddenly led to the idea that she might be dead. Yet I was happy that night: everything in that town was quiet and slow as the old man and I waded through leafy shadows and reflections.

Suddenly bending toward him, as if sheltering some frail charge, I caught myself asking:

"Your daughter couldn't come?"

He gasped in apparent surprise, stooped to search my face and finally managed to say:

"Yes, that's it. You've understood. She can't go out. Sometimes she can't sleep nights thinking she has to go out the next day. She's up early in the morning preparing for it, getting all excited. But after a while it wears off, she just drops into a chair, and she can't do it."

The people leaving the concert soon disappeared into the surrounding streets and we went into the theater café. He signaled the waiter, who brought him a dark drink in a small glass. I could only spend a few minutes with him: I was expected elsewhere for dinner. So I said:

"It's a shame she can't go out. We all need a bit of entertainment."

He had raised the glass to his big lip but interrupted the motion to explain:

"She has her own way of keeping entertained. I bought an old house, too big for just the two of us, but it's in good shape. It has a garden with a fountain and in her bedroom there's a door that opens onto a winter balcony. It's a corner room, facing the street, and you could almost say she lives in that balcony. Or sometimes she goes for a walk in the garden and on some nights she plays the piano. You can come and have dinner with us whenever you want and I'll be grateful to you."

I understood at once. So we agreed on a day when I would go for dinner and play the piano.

He called for me at the hotel one afternoon when the sun was still high. From a distance, he showed me the corner with the winter balcony. It was on a second floor. The entrance to the house was through a large gate on one side. It opened onto a garden with a fountain and some statuettes hidden in the weeds. Around the garden ran a high wall. The top of the wall was all splintered glass stuck in mortar. A flight of steps led up into the house, through a glassed-in corridor from which one could look out at the garden. I was surprised to see a large number of open parasols in the long corridor. They were different colors and looked like huge hothouse plants. The old man hastened to explain:

"I gave her most of the parasols. She likes to keep them open to see the colors. When there's nice weather she picks one and goes for a short walk in the garden. On windy days you can't open this door because the parasols blow away, we have to use another entrance."

We reached the far end of the corridor by going along the space left between the wall and the parasols. We came to a door and the old man rapped on the glass. A muffled voice answered from inside. The old man showed me in, and there was his daughter standing in the center of the winter balcony, facing us, with her back to the colored panes. We were halfway across the room before she left the balcony and came forward to meet us. Reaching out

-55-

through space she offered me her hand and thanked me for my visit. Backed against the darkest wall of the room was a small open piano. Its big yellowish smile looked innocent.

She apologized for not being able to leave the house and, pointing to the balcony, said:

"He's my only friend."

I indicated the piano and asked:

"How about this sweet soul? Isn't he your friend, too?"

We were lowering ourselves into chairs at the foot of her bed. I had time to notice many small paintings of flowers, all hung at the same height, along the four walls, as though parts of a frieze. The smile she had abandoned in the middle of her face was as innocent as the piano's, but her faded blonde hair and wispy figure also seemed to have been abandoned long ago. She was starting to explain why the piano wasn't as close a friend as the balcony when the old man left the room almost on tiptoes. She went on saying:

"The piano was a great friend of my mother's."

I made as if to go over and look at it, but she raised a hand and opened her eyes wide to stop me.

"I'm sorry but I'd rather you tried the piano after dinner, when the lights are on. Since I was a little girl I've been used to hearing the piano only at night. That was when my mother played it. She used to light the four candles in the candlesticks and play each separate note so slowly in the silence, it was as if she were also lighting up the sounds, one by one."

A minute later she rose and, excusing herself, went out on the balcony, where she leaned her bare arms on the panes as if she were resting them on someone's breast. But she came right back and said:

"When I see the same man go by several times through

the red pane, he usually turns out to be violent or hot-tempered."

I couldn't help asking her:

"Which pane did you see me through?"

"The green one. It usually means someone who lives alone in the country."

"I happen to like being alone among plants," I said.

The door opened and the old man came in followed by a maid who was so short that I couldn't tell whether she was a child or a dwarf. Her ruddy face shone over the little table she was carrying in her stubby arms. The old man asked me:

"What will you have?"

I was about to say "nothing," but I thought that would offend him, so I named the first drink that came to mind. He had the maid bring him a small glass with the same dark drink I'd seen him take after the concert.

As night fell we started for the dining room. We had to go through the corridor of the parasols. The girl rearranged a few of them and glowed when I praised them.

The dining room was below street level. Through the small barred windows one could see the feet and legs of the people going by on the sidewalk. A lamp with a green shade poured its light straight onto the white tablecloth, where old family treasures had gathered as if to celebrate happy memories. We sat down, without a word, and for a moment each object seemed like a precious form of silence. When our pairs of hands started to appear on the tablecloth it seemed as natural as if they'd always lived there. I couldn't stop thinking of the life in hands. Years back, hands had molded these objects on the table into certain shapes. After changing hands many times, the plates, glasses, and other small beings had found their home in a sideboard. Over the years they'd had to serve all sorts of hands. Any one of those hands could pile food on the plates' smooth bright faces, make the pitchers fill and empty their hips and the knives and forks sink into the meat, cut it up and bring the pieces to the mouth—after which the small beings were scrubbed, dried, and led back to their small dwellings in the sideboard. Some of these beings could outlive many pairs of hands, some of which would treat them lovingly and be long remembered, but they would have to go on serving in silence.

A while back, when we were in the girl's bedroom and she had not yet turned on the light—she wanted to enjoy every last bit of the evening glow coming from the balcony—we had spoken about the objects. As the light faded we could feel them nestling in the shadows as if they had feathers and were preparing for sleep. She said they developed souls as they came in touch with people. Some had once been something else and had another soul (the ones with legs had once had branches, the piano keys had been tusks). But her balcony had first gained a soul when she started to live in it.

Suddenly the ruddy face of the dwarf maid appeared over the edge of the tablecloth. Although she reached out confidently to grasp things in her tiny hands, the old man and his daughter slid their plates toward her. But when she handled them, the objects on the table lost their dignity. The old man also had a hasty, tactless way of grabbing the pitcher by the neck and wringing the wine out of it.

At first, conversation was difficult. Then a grandfather's clock made its presence felt by pounding out the time. It had been ticking against the wall behind the old man, but I had forgotten it was there. When we started up again the girl asked me:

"Aren't you fond of old clothes?"

"Sure I am! And going back to what you were saying about objects, clothes are the ones that have been in closest touch with us"—here I laughed but she remained serious—"and I wouldn't be surprised if they kept something more of us than just the shapes of our bodies and a whiff of our skin."

But she wasn't listening. Instead, she had been trying to interrupt, like someone watching others play jump-rope, waiting for her chance to cut in. No doubt she had asked the question thinking of what she would have answered. Finally she said:

"I make up my poems in bed"—she had already mentioned those poems in the afternoon—"and I have a white nightgown that has been with me ever since my first poems. Some summer nights I wear it in my balcony. Last year I wrote a poem for it."

She had stopped eating and did not seem to notice the dwarf's arms coming and going. Staring as in a vision she began to recite:

"To my white nightgown."

I braced myself to listen, at the same time observing the dwarf's hands. Her tiny stubby fingers were clenched as they approached things. They unbent only at the last moment, to clasp them.

At first I looked for different ways to show attention, but then I just nodded in time with the swinging motion of the clock's pendulum. This bothered me, adding to the agony I was already in, trying to think of something to say before the girl finished. Besides, the old man had a bit of chard dangling from his lower lip near the corner of his mouth.

The poem was corny, but she seemed to have kept count of her syllables. She'd found an unexpected rhyme for "nightgown": I would tell her it was fresh. Watching the old man, I had passed my tongue over my lower lip—but he was listening to his daughter. Now I began to feel the poem would never end. And then suddenly she rhymed "night" with "white" and it was over.

I sat there in serene contemplation, listening to myself, hoping to convey the impression that I was about to come up with something.

"I'm struck by the childish quality of the poem," I began. "It's very fresh and . . ."

The word "fresh" wasn't out of my mouth when she started to say:

"I have another one . . ."

I felt miserable . . . and treacherously concerned only with my own selfish needs. The dwarf was back with the next platter and I made a show of helping myself to a generous amount. All the glamour was gone from the objects on the table, the poem, the house overhead, even the parasols in the corridor and the ivy that grew up one whole side of the house. Wrapped up in myself, I gorged on the food, shamelessly. There wasn't a time the old man clutched the neck of the pitcher when my glass wasn't empty.

When she had finished her second poem I said:

"If this weren't so tasty"—and I nodded at my plate— "I'd ask to hear more."

The old man said at once:

"She ought to eat first. There'll be time for that later."

I was starting to feel cynical and at that moment I wouldn't have minded growing a huge paunch. But then something made me want to cling to the poor old man and be kind to him. So, pointing to the wine, I said I'd recently heard a funny story about a drunkard. I told the story and when it ended they both laughed desperately, so I told them some more stories. There was sorrow in the girl's laughter, but she begged me to go on telling my stories. Her mouth had stretched at the edges, into a painful gash. Her eyes, caught in their web of "crow's feet," were full of tears, and she was pressing her clasped hands between her knees. The old man was coughing so hard he had to put down the pitcher before filling his glass. The dwarf laughed, bending over as if to bow.

We had all been miraculously united and I felt not the least regret.

That night I did not play the piano. They begged me to stay and showed me to a bedroom on the side of the house where the ivy grew. As I started up the stairs I noticed a cord that ran from the grandfather clock all the way up the winding staircase. I followed it into the bedroom, up to the canopied bed, where it ended, tied to one of the slender bedposts. The room had ancient, paunchy furniture that shone yellowish in the lamplight. I put my hands on my stomach and eyed the old man's stomach. His last instructions that night were:

"If you can't sleep and want to know what time it is, pull on the cord. You'll hear the dining room clock from here. First it will give you the hour, then, after a pause, the minutes."

Suddenly he began to laugh and went out, waving good-night. He was probably remembering one of the stories, the one about the drunkard who talked to a clock.

He was still making the wooden stairs creak with his heavy steps when I started to feel alone with my body: it had absorbed all that food and drink like an animal swallowing other animals, and now it would have to struggle with it all night long. I stripped it naked and made it go barefoot around the room.

Later, in bed, I tried to figure out what I was doing with my life those days. I fished a few recent events out of my memory and thought of some people who were very far away. By then I was sinking into something like the bowels of silence, feeling sad and a bit lewd.

The next morning I looked back over my life with a smile, almost happily. It was very early. I dressed slowly and went out into a corridor built over the edge of the garden. On this side, too, there were weeds and tall, shady trees. I heard the old man and his daughter talking and realized they were on a bench right beneath me. I caught her words first:

"Ursula is unhappier now. She not only loves her husband less, but loves someone else more."

The old man asked:

"Can't she get a divorce?"

"No, because she loves her children and the children love her husband and not the other man."

Then the old man said timidly:

"She could tell the children that her husband has several mistresses."

She got up angrily:

"Just like you to say that! When will you understand Ursula? She would never say such a thing!"

I was very much intrigued. They couldn't be talking about the dwarf: her name was Tamarinda. Yet the old man had told me they lived completely alone. So where did this news come from? Could it have reached them during the night? After her burst of anger the girl had gone into the dining room. In a while she came back out into the garden carrying a salmon-colored parasol with white gauze ruffles. She did not come to the table for lunch. The old man and I ate and drank little. Afterward I went out to buy a book suitable for reading in an abandoned house among weeds, on a still night and a full stomach.

On my way back, just ahead of me, I saw a poor old black man limp past the balcony. He wore a green hat with a wide brim, like a Mexican. Just then a patch of white skin appeared in the balcony, behind the green pane.

That night, as soon as we sat down to eat, I started to tell my stories, and she did not recite her poems.

The belly laughs the old man and I let out covered up for the brutal amounts of food and drink we were putting away.

There was a moment when we fell silent. Then the daughter said:

"I want some music tonight. I'll go in ahead of you and light the candles on the piano. It's been a long time since they were lit. The piano will be happy, poor thing: it will think Mother is back."

Neither the old man nor I said another word. After a while Tamarinda came in to say the young lady was waiting for us.

When I was about to strike the first chord, the silence was like a heavy animal with a paw raised. The chord broke into rippling sounds like the wavering candlelight. I tried another chord, as if advancing one more step—and almost at once, before I could move on, a string snapped. The girl cried out. The old man and I leaped up. He bent over his daughter, who had her face in her hands, and tried to calm her, telling her the strings were old and rusted. But she would not take her hands off her face or stop shaking her head. I didn't know what to do: I had never snapped a string before. I asked to be excused, and on the way to my room I was afraid of stepping on the parasols in the corridor.

The next morning I slept late and missed part of the

conversation on the garden bench, but I was in time to hear the girl say:

"Ursula's love came wearing a big green hat with a wide brim."

I couldn't believe she meant the old black man I had seen limping by the previous afternoon, nor could I imagine who might have brought the news during the night.

At noon the old man and I had lunch alone again. It was my chance to say:

"There's a lovely view from my corridor. I was there earlier but didn't stay because you were discussing a certain Ursula and I was afraid to intrude."

The old man stopped eating and whispered:

"You heard us?"

I realized he wanted to confide in me, so I answered:

"Yes, I heard everything. But I don't see how Ursula can find that old black man handsome with his limp and that wide green hat."

"Oh, but you haven't understood," he said. "Since my daughter was knee-high she's been making me listen to her stories and take part in the lives of the characters she invents. And since then we've been keeping track of them as if they really existed and we kept hearing from them. She imagines them wearing and doing things she sees from the balcony. If yesterday she saw a man in a green hat go by, it's not surprising the hat turned up today on one of her characters. I'm too slow to keep up with her and she gets angry with me. Why don't you help her? If you want I'll . . ."

I didn't let him finish.

"I wouldn't think of it. I'd only invent things that would hurt her."

That evening, too, she was absent from the table. The old man and I ate, drank, and chatted until well into the night.

In bed, afterward, I heard a board creak; it wasn't the furniture. It took me a while to realize someone was coming up the stairs. The next moment there was a soft rap on my door. I asked who it was and the girl's voice answered:

"It's me. I want to talk to you."

I switched on the lamp and opened the door a crack, and she said:

"It's no use hiding behind the door. I can see you in the mirror, standing there without a stitch on."

So I shut the door and asked her to wait.

When I invited her in she walked straight across the room to another door I had not been able to open. She opened it with the greatest ease and groped her way into the darkness of some other room. She came right back out with a chair that she placed by my bed. She reached into a blue cape she was wearing, took out a notebook, and started to read poems from it. I had to make a great effort not to fall asleep. I tried to force my eyes open but all I could do was roll them back, so that I must have looked like I was dying. Suddenly she cried out, as she had done when the piano string snapped, and I jumped up in bed. In the middle of the room was a huge spider. By the time I saw it it was no longer walking: it had gathered up three of its hairy legs as if ready to pounce. I threw my shoes at it and missed. I got out of bed, but she told me to stay away or it would jump at me. So I took my lamp and edged along the walls of the room to the washbasin, from where I threw a brush, a cake of soap, and the lid of the soap dish. The soap dish finally hit it and it rolled up into a dark woolly ball. She asked me not to tell her father, who didn't like her to be up working or reading so late. When she had left I squashed the spider with the heel of my shoe and went back to bed without turning

-65-

out the light. As I was about to fall asleep I felt my toes curl. I thought the spider was in bed with me and I jumped up again.

In the morning the old man came in to apologize for the spider. His daughter had told him everything. I said it was nothing to worry about, and, to change the subject, I spoke of a concert I was about to give in a nearby town. He thought it was a pretext for leaving and I had to promise to return after the concert.

As we parted, I couldn't stop the girl from kissing my hand. I didn't know what to do. The old man hugged me and suddenly I felt him kiss me near my ear.

I never got to my concert. A couple of days later I received a phone call from the old man. After the first few words he said:

"Your presence is needed here."

"Has something serious happened?"

"I'd say a real tragedy."

"To your daughter?"

"No."

"To Tamarinda?"

"No, no. I can't tell you now. If you can postpone the concert, catch the four o'clock train and I'll meet you at the theater café."

"But your daughter is well?"

"She's in bed. Not ill, but she refuses to get up or face the light of day. She can only stand lamplight and has had all the parasols folded."

"All right, I'll be there."

The theater café was too noisy, so we moved elsewhere. The old man was depressed but eager to clutch at any hope I might offer him. He ordered his dark drink in the usual small glass and said:

"The day before yesterday there was a storm. We were sitting in the dining room in the evening when we heard a loud clatter. We realized at once it wasn't the storm. My daughter ran up to her room and I followed her. When I got there she had already opened the door to the balcony and all she saw was the sky and the light of the storm. She covered her eyes and fainted."

"You mean the light hurt her?"

"But, my dear friend! Don't you understand?"

"What?"

"That we've lost the balcony! It fell out! It wasn't the balcony light she saw."

"But a balcony . . ."

It was better to say nothing. He made me promise not to mention the subject to the girl. So what was I to do? The poor old man was counting on me. I remembered the orgies we'd had together and decided to simply wait and hope I'd be able to think of something when I met her.

It was distressing to see the corridor without the parasols.

That night we ate and drank little. Then the old man took me to his daughter's bedside and immediately left the room. She had not said a word, but as soon as he was gone she turned toward the door that opened into space and said:

"You see how he left us?"

"But I can't . . . Balconies don't fall out . . ."

"He didn't fall. He jumped."

"All right, but . . ."

"He loved me—as much as I loved him. I know because he'd already proved it."

I hung my head. I felt involved in an act of responsibility for which I was not prepared. She had started to pour her soul out and I didn't know how to receive it or what to do with it.

Now the poor girl was saying:

"It was all my fault. He got jealous the night I went to your room."

"You don't mean . . . ?"

"Who do you think I mean? The balcony, my balcony."

"Now, isn't that making too much of it? Remember how old he was. There are things that fall of their own weight."

She wasn't listening. She went on:

"That same night I understood the warning and the threat."

"Come on, now. You're not suggesting . . ."

"Don't you remember who threatened me? Who stared and stared at me, twitching those three hairy legs?"

"Yes, of course! The spider!"

"It's him all over."

She looked up at me. Then she threw off the covers and got out of bed in her nightgown. She headed for the balcony door and I thought she was going to jump out. I started to reach for her—but she was in her nightgown. While I hesitated she changed her course. Now she was going toward a small table next to the door that opened into space. On the small table, just before she reached it, I saw the notebook with the black oilcloth cover from which she read her poems.

She sat in a chair, opened the notebook and started to recite:

> "To a balcony
> from his widow . . ."

THE USHER

As soon as I grew up, I went to live in a big city. The city's downtown—where everyone rushed around among tall buildings—was near a river.

I was an usher at a movie theater, but the rest of the time I, too, scurried around like a mouse in old furniture. I knew holes everywhere with unexpected connections through which to reach my favorite places. And it gave me just as much pleasure to imagine the parts of the city I didn't know.

I had the late-afternoon shift at the theater. I rushed into my dressing room, polished my gold buttons, slipped my green tail coat on over my gray vest and trousers, and took up my post in the left aisle of the orchestra, where the gentlemen handed me the seat numbers and then fell in behind the ladies who followed my sinking steps down the red carpet. At each stop I did a minuet turn, bowed and put out my hand. I always expected to be surprised by the tip and knew how to bow at once with respect and contempt. I didn't care if people weren't aware of my superiority: I felt like an old rake with a flower in his buttonhole, wise to the ways of the world. I was happy watching the ladies in their different dresses and enjoyed the moment of confusion there was each time the screen lit up and the house darkened. Then I hurried back to the dressing room to count my tips, and afterward I set out to explore the city.

I got in tired, but on my way to my room, up stairs and along hallways, I hoped to see more sights through half-open doors. As soon as I turned on the light, the flowers of the wallpaper gave out a blaze of color: they were red and blue, on a black background. The ceiling light had been lowered on its cord until it almost touched the foot of the bed. I lay right under it to read, using a newspaper as a shade to block some of the glare and to dim the flowers a bit. At the head of the bed stood a table with bottles and other objects I watched for hours on end. Afterward I stayed awake with the light off until the sound of bones being sawed and hacked came in the window and I heard the butcher cough.

Twice a week a friend took me to a dining room where I could get a free meal. You went through an entrance hall that was almost as large as a theater lobby, into the silent luxury of the dining room. It belonged to a man who was going to go on offering those meals for as long as he lived because of a promise he had made when his daughter was saved from the river. The diners were foreigners sunk in memories. Each had the right to bring a friend twice a week. Once a month the host ate with them. He made a grand entry, like a conductor when the orchestra is ready to start playing, but the only thing he conducted was the silence. At eight o'clock sharp, a wing of the huge white double door at the far end of the room swung open on the dark emptiness of a neighboring room, and out of the darkness stepped a tall figure in black tails, his head cocked to the right and a hand raised to indicate we should remain seated. All faces turned toward him, but with blank stares, their eyes still on the thoughts inhabiting them at that moment. The conductor nodded a greeting as he sat and the players bent over their plates and sounded their instruments, each a professor of silence playing to himself. At first you heard pecking silverware, but then the noise took off and you no longer noticed it. To me it was just a meal, but to my friend, who was like the others, it meant the chance to spend a few moments remembering his country. Suddenly I felt confined to a circle the size of my plate, as if I had no thoughts of my own, surrounded by sleepers eating in concert, watched over by the servants. We knew we were finished with a plate when it was whisked away; soon we were cheered by the next one. Sometimes we had to divide our surprise between the plate and the neck of a bottle that came enveloped in a white napkin. At other times we were surprised at how the dark stain of the wine seemed to grow in the air, suspended in its crystal glass.

After a few such meals I had gotten used to the objects on the table and learned to play the instruments to myself alone, but the remoteness of the guests still troubled me. When the "conductor" made his appearance on the second month I no longer believed his generosity was because his daughter had been saved: I insisted on supposing she had drowned. In my wayward thoughts, a couple of long, nebulous steps carried me down the few blocks that separated us from the river, where I pictured the girl floating just below the surface. A yellowish moon shone on her but at the same time her gorgeous dress and the skin of her arms and face were all bright white—a privilege due perhaps to her father's wealth and his untold sacrifices on her behalf. I imagined the guests across the table from me, with their backs to the river, had also drowned: they hovered over their plates as if they were trying to come up to the surface from the bottom of the river. Those of us eating on my side of the table bowed in their direction but did not reach out to them.

Once during the meal I heard some words. A very fat guest said: "I'm dying," and immediately his head rolled forward, into his soup, as if he were trying to drink it without a spoon. All the other heads swiveled to look at the one served up in the soup plate, and all the silverware stopped clicking. Then there was the sound of scraping chair legs, the servants carried the dead man into the hat room and made the phone ring to call the doctor, and before the body was cold everyone was back in place clicking and pecking again.

In those days I had begun to slow down at my job, sick with silence. I was sinking into myself the way you sink into a swamp. My colleagues at work kept bumping into me—I had become an aimless obstacle. The only thing I did well was polish my gold buttons. Once I heard a colleague say: "Move it, hippo!" The word fell into my swamp, stuck to me, and sank in. It was followed by other insults that piled up in my mind like dirty dishes. By then everyone avoided me, changing direction to stay out of my swamp.

Some time later I was fired and my foreign friend got me another job in a less elegant theater. Here the women dressed badly and there were no big tippers. Still, I tried to hang on.

But on one of my most miserable days something appeared before my eyes that made up for all my ills. I had been catching glimpses of it now and then. One night I woke up in the dark silence of my room and, on the wall papered with purple flowers, I saw a light. I suspected at once that something extraordinary was happening to me and I was not frightened. I moved my eyes sideways and the spot of light shifted with them. It was like the spot you see in the dark when you put out a lamp, but it lasted longer and you could see through it. I lowered my eyes to the table and saw my bottles and other objects. There could be no doubt: the light was coming from my eyes and had been developing for some time. I stared at the back of my hand and saw my open fingers. Soon I felt tired: the light dimmed and I closed my eyes. In a minute I opened them again to make sure I was not imagining things. I looked at the electric lightbulb and it lit up with my light—so I was convinced. I smiled to myself: who else in the world saw with his own eyes in the dark?

The light grew stronger every night. In the daytime I stuck nails all over the wall and at night I hung glass and porcelain objects—the ones I could see best—from them. In a small cabinet engraved—before my time—with my initials I kept goblets with strings tied to their stems, bottles with strings around their necks, frilly saucers with looped edges, teacups with gold lettering, and so on. One night I was seized by a terror that almost drove me mad. I had gotten up to see if there was anything left in the cabinet, and, before I could turn on the electric light, I saw my face and eyes in the mirror, lit with my own light. I fainted, and when I woke up my head was under the bed and I saw the metal frame as if I were under a bridge. I swore never again to look at that face of mine with its otherworldly eyes. They were greenish yellow eyes in which some unknown disease gleamed triumphant: glowing round holes in a face broken into pieces no one could put together or understand.

I stayed awake until the sound of the bones being sawed and hacked came in the window.

The next day I remembered that as I had made my way

up the shadowy orchestra aisle a few nights before, a woman had caught my eye with a frown. On another night my foreign friend had made fun of my eyes, saying they shone like cat eyes. Now I began to watch for my face in dark store windows, where I could ignore the objects behind the windows. After much thought, I had decided I ought to use my light only when I was alone.

At one of the free dinners, before the host appeared in the white doorway, I saw the darkness through the half-open door and felt like penetrating it with my eyes. So I began planning a way to get into that room, where I had already detected glass cases loaded with objects that intensified the light in my eyes.

The hall leading from the street into the dining room was actually the back entrance to a house that stretched clear across the block and had its main entrance on another street. The only person you ran into in the back entrance at that time of day—by now I had seen him more than once on my walks up and down the street—was the butler, who had an apelike way of lumbering toward you with bow legs and flap arms, although seen from the side in his stiff tails he looked more like a stuffed bird. One afternoon, before dinner, I dared to address him. He watched me from under thick brows as I said:

"There's something I'd like to discuss with you. But I must ask you to keep it to yourself."

"At your pleasure, sir."

"It's just that"—now he waited, staring at his feet—"I have a light in my eyes that allows me to see in the dark."

"Indeed, sir, I understand."

"How could you understand?" I was annoyed. "You can't ever have met anyone capable of seeing in the dark."

"I said I understood your words, sir. But of course I find them amazing."

"Well, listen: if we go into that room—the hat room—and close the door, you can take any object from your pocket and put it on the table and I'll tell you what it is."

"But what if someone comes in, sir?"

"If by someone you mean the host, you have my permission to tell him everything. Do me the favor: it will only take a minute."

"But what for?"

"You'll soon find out. Put anything you want on the table when I close the door and I'll tell you . . ."

"Just make it quick, sir, please . . ."

He hastened in, straight to the table. I closed the door. The next moment, I said:

"That's only your open hand!"

"Alright, you've proved your point, sir."

"Now pull something from your pocket."

He produced his handkerchief and I laughed and said:

"What a dirty handkerchief!"

He laughed, too—but suddenly let out a squawk and made for the door. When he opened it he had a hand over his eyes and was trembling. I realized then he had seen my face—a possibility I had not anticipated. He was pleading:

"Go away, sir! Go away!"

And he started across the dining room, which was already lit but empty.

The next time the host ate with us I borrowed my friend's place near the head of the table, where the host sat: it was the area served by the butler, who would not be able to avoid me. In fact, when he was bringing in the first dish he felt my eyes on his, and his hands began to shake. While knives and forks made the silence throb, I kept up my pressure on him. Afterward I ran into him in the hall. He began:

"Please, sir, you'll ruin me."

"I certainly will if you don't listen to me."

"But what does the gentlemen want of me?"

"Only that you let me see, and I mean only see—you can search me when I come out—the glass cases in the room next to the dining room."

He gestured and grimaced wildly before he could get a word out. Finally he managed to say:

"Consider my years of service in this house, sir . . ."

I felt sorry for him, and disgusted at myself for being sorry. My craving to see made me regard him as a complicated obstacle. He was telling me the story of his life, explaining why he could not betray his master. I interrupted him to threaten:

"Save your breath—he'll never find out. But I'll scramble your brains if you don't obey, and then you really might do something you'd regret. Wait for me at two o'clock tonight. I'll be in that room until three."

"Scramble my brains, sir, kill me . . ."

"It'll be worse than death for you unless you do as I say."

As I left I repeated:

"Tonight, at two. I'll be at the door."

On my way out, trying to find an excuse for my behavior, I said to myself, "When he sees that nothing bad happens he won't suffer any more." I wanted to be let in that same night because it was the night when I ate there and the food and the wine excited me and made my light brighter.

During dinner the butler was not as nervous as I expected, and I thought he would not open the door, but when I went back at two o'clock he did. Following him and his candelabrum across the dining room I had the sudden notion that he had caved in under the mental torture of my threat and told the host everything and they had set a trap for me. The minute we were in the room with the glass cases I looked at him. He was staring at his feet, expressionless. So I said:

"Bring me a mattress. I can see better from the floor and I want my body to be comfortable."

He hesitated, hanging on to the candelabrum, but went out. Alone in the room, I started to look around me and it was like being in the center of a constellation. Then I remembered it might be a trap: the butler was taking his time. But he wouldn't have needed long to trap me. Finally he came in dragging a mattress with one hand, holding the candelabrum up with the other. In a voice too loud for a room full of glass cases he said:

"I'll be back at three."

At first I was afraid to see myself reflected in the huge mirrors or in the glass cases, but lying on the floor I was outside their range. Why had the butler seemed so calm? My light wandered over the universe of things around me but I felt no pleasure. After daring so much, I had no courage left to calm down. I could look at an object and make it mine by holding it for a while in my light, but only if I was at ease and knew I had the right to look at it. I decided to focus on a small area near my eyes. There was a missal in a tortoise-shell binding with a streaked surface like burnt sugar, except for a filigree in one corner, on which a flower had been pressed. Next to it, like a coiled reptile, lay a rosary of precious stones. Spread above those two objects were fans that looked like dancing girls flaring out their skirts. My light wavered a bit when it went over several with sequins and stopped on one showing a Chinaman with his face made of mother-of-pearl, his robe of silk. Only that Chinaman could stand being there alone in endless space: his impassiveness was as mysterious as stupidity. Yet he was the one thing I was able to make mine that night. As I left I tried to give the butler a tip, but he refused it saying:

"I'm not doing this for money, sir. You're obliging me to do it."

During the second session I focused on some jasper miniatures, but when I was scanning a small bridge with elephants crossing over it I realized there was another light in the room besides mine. I turned my eyes before turning my head and saw a woman in white advancing toward me with a blazing candelabrum. She had come out of the depths of the wide avenue bordered with glass cases. I felt my temples quiver and the quivers run like sleepy streams down my cheeks, then wrap around my head like a turban, and finally creep down my thighs and knot at my knees. The woman advanced slowly, her head rigid. I expected her to scream when her mantle of light touched my mattress. Every now and then she stopped and, before she started up again, I thought of escaping, but I couldn't move. In spite of the spots of shadow on her face I could tell she was beautiful: she seemed to have been made by hand after having been outlined on paper. She was coming too near, but I had decided to lie still to the end of time. She stopped by the edge of the mattress and then proceeded with one foot on the mattress and the other on the floor. I was like a dummy stretched out in a store window while she went by with one foot on the curb and the other in the street. I stayed there without blinking, although her light flickered strangely. On her way back she wove a winding path among the glass cases, the tail of her gown gently tangling in their legs. I had the feeling I had been asleep for a

moment before she reached the door at the far end of the
room. She had left it open when she came in and she went
out without closing it. Her light had not completely faded
when I became aware of another light behind me. Now I
was able to get up. I grabbed the mattress by a corner and
dragged it out after me. The butler was waiting, his whole
body and his candelabrum shaking. I couldn't understand
what he said because his dentures were chattering.

At the next session I knew she would return and I
couldn't concentrate on anything, all I could do was wait
for her. But when she appeared I calmed down. Everything
happened just as before: she had the same trancelike stare in
her hollow eyes; and yet, in some way I couldn't fathom,
each night had been different. At the same time, she was
already a fond habit I cherished. When she reached the foot
of the mattress I had a moment of anxiety. I realized she was
not going to walk along the edge but pass over me. Again
I was terrified thinking she would scream. She had stopped
by my feet, and now her first step came down on the
mattress, another on my knees—which shuddered and
parted, making her foot slip—the next, with the other foot,
on the mattress, another on the pit of my stomach, then one
more on the mattress, followed by a bare foot that landed on
my throat. And then I lost all sense of what was happening
in the delicate rustling of her perfumed gown as its tail
brushed over my face.

After that the nights blurred together. Although I had
different feelings each time, the events were so much alike
that in the end they fused in my mind, as if they had
happened in just a few nights. The tail of her gown erased
guilty memories, sweeping me into space on airs as gentle as
the ones stirred long ago by childhood bedsheets. Sometimes the tail settled on my face for a moment and then I

dreaded losing touch with her, under the threat of an unknown present, but when the airy feeling returned and I had cleared the abyss I thought of the interruption as an affectionate joke and breathed in as much of the tail as I could before it was whisked away.

Sometimes the butler would say:

"Haven't you seen everything by now, sir?"

But I would head back to my room, slowly brush down my black suit at the knees and waist, and then go to bed to think of her. I had forgotten about my own light—and would have given every bit of it to remember her more clearly in her mantle of candlelight. I went over her steps and imagined that one night she would stop and kneel by me and then it would not be her gown I'd feel but her hair and lips. I rehearsed the scene in different ways. Sometimes I put words in her mouth: "My darling, I've been lying to you . . ." But the words did not seem to fit her, and I would have to go back and start all over again. The rehearsals kept me awake and even found their way into my dreams. Once I dreamed she was going up the nave in church. There was the glow of candlelight against a background of red and gold. The brightest light fell on her wedding gown with the long train she slowly drew after her. She was about to get married but walked alone, with one hand clasped in the other. I was a woolly dog, shiny black, lying on her train. She dragged me along proudly, and I seemed to be asleep. At the same time I was being swept up in the crowd that followed the bride and the dog. In this version of myself I had feelings and ideas my mother could have had, and I tried to get as close to the dog as possible. He sailed along as calmly as if he were asleep on a beach, waking from time to time, wrapped in spray. I had transmitted an idea to him which he received with a smile. It was: "Let yourself go, but think of something else."

Then, at dawn, I would hear the meat being sawed and hacked.

One night, with few tips coming my way, I left the theater and went down to the street that ran along the river. My legs were tired but my eyes were aching to see. When I paused at a stall that sold used books I saw a foreign couple go by. He was dressed in black with a French beret; she wore a Spanish mantilla and spoke German. We had been walking in the same direction, but they were in a hurry and they left me behind. When they reached the corner, however, they bumped into a child who was selling candy, and spilled his merchandise. She laughed and helped the boy pick up his goods and gave him some coins before moving on—and when she turned for a last look back at him I recognized my woman in white and felt myself sinking into a hole in the air. I followed the couple anxiously and also barged into someone—a fat woman who said:

"Watch where you're going, you idiot!"

By then I was running and on the point of crying. They reached a seedy movie theater and while he bought the tickets she turned and looked at me with some insistence because of my frantic haste but did not recognize me. I was certain about her, though. I went in and sat a few rows ahead of them, and one of the times I looked back at her she must have seen my eyes in the dark because she whispered nervously in the man's ear. After a while I turned back again and again they exchanged a few words, out loud this time, then immediately got up and left, and I ran out after them. I was chasing her without knowing what I would do. She had not recognized me—besides, she was running off with someone else. I had never been so excited and—though I suspected it would end badly—I couldn't stop myself. I was convinced it was all a case of misplaced persons and lives, yet the man holding her arm had pulled his cap down over his ears and walked faster every minute. It was as if all three of us were plunging into the danger of a fire: I was catching up without a thought for what might happen. They stepped off the sidewalk and started to run across the street. I was going to do the same when another man in a beret stopped me from his car, honking and swearing at me. As soon as the car was gone I saw the couple approach a policeman. Without losing a beat I swung off in another direction. When I looked back after a few yards there was no one following me, so I started to slow down and return to the everyday world. I had to watch my step and do a lot of thinking. I realized I was going to be in a black mood and went into a dimly lit tavern where I could be alone with myself. I ordered wine and started to spend the tips I had been saving to pay for my room. The light shining on the street through the bars of an open window lit up the leaves of a tree that stood on the curb. I made an effort to concentrate on what had been happening to me. The floorboards were old planks full of holes. I was thinking the world in which she and I had met was inviolable, she could not just step out of it after all the times she had passed the tail of her gown over my face: it was a ritual governed by some fateful design. I would have to do something—or perhaps await some signal from her on one of our nights together. Meantime she seemed unaware of the danger of being awake and out in the street at night, in violation of the design guiding her steps when she walked in her sleep. I was proud to be nothing but a poor usher sitting in a dingy tavern and yet the only one to know—because even she did not know it—that my light had penetrated a world closed to everyone else. When I left the tavern I saw a man with a beret, then several others. I decided men with berets were everywhere but had nothing to do with me. I got on a trolley thinking I would carry a hidden beret with me the next time we met among the glass cases and suddenly show it to her. A fat man dropped his bulk into the seat next to me, and I couldn't think any more.

I took the beret into the next session, not knowing whether I would use it. But the moment she appeared in the depths of the room I whipped it out and waved it as if I were signaling with a dark lantern. Suddenly she stopped and, instinctively, I put the cap away; but when she started up I took it out and signaled her again. When she paused by the edge of the mattress I was afraid and threw the cap at her. It hit her on the chest and landed at her feet. It took her another few seconds to let out a scream. She dropped the candelabrum, which fell with a clatter and went out. Then I heard her body fall with a soft thud, followed by the louder sound of what must have been her head. I stood and reached out as if feeling for one of the glass cases, but just then my light came on and focused on her. She had fallen as if ready to slip into a happy dream, with half-open arms, her head to one side and her face modestly hidden under her waves of hair. I ran my light up and down her body like a thief searching her with a flashlight. I was surprised to find what looked like a large rubber stamp by her feet: it turned out to be my beret. My light not only lit her up but stripped something from her. I was pleased at the thought that the cap lying next to her belonged to me and to no one else. But suddenly my eyes began to see her feet turn a greenish yellow, like my face the night I had seen it in my wardrobe mirror. The color brightened in some parts of the feet and darkened in others, and soon I noticed little white bony shapes that reminded me of the bones of toes. By then horror was spinning in my head like trapped smoke. I ran my light over her body again and it looked changed, completely fleshless. One of her hands had strayed and lay across her groin: it was nothing but bones. I didn't want to go on looking and I tried to clamp my eyes shut, but they were like two worms turning and twisting in their holes until the light they projected reached her head. She had lost her hair and the bones of her face had the spectral glow of a far-off star seen through a telescope. And then suddenly I heard the butler's heavy step: he was switching on the lights and babbling frantically. She had recovered her full shape, but I could not bear to look at her. The host burst through a door I hadn't noticed before and ran to pick up his daughter. He was on his way out with her in his arms when another woman appeared. As they all left together the butler kept shouting:

"It was his fault, it's that fiendish light in his eyes. I didn't want to do it, he made me . . ."

Alone for a moment, I realized I was in serious trouble. I could have left, but I waited for the host to return. At his heel was the butler who said:

"You still here?"

I began to work on an answer, which would have gone something like this: "I'm not someone to just walk out of a house. Besides, I owe my host an explanation." But it took me too long—and I considered it beneath my dignity to respond to the butler's charges.

By then I was facing the host. He had been running his fingers through his hair, frowning as if in deep thought. Now he drew himself up to his full height and, narrowing his eyes, he asked:

"Did my daughter invite you into the room?"

His voice seemed to come out of a second person inside him. I was so startled that all I could say was:

"No, it's just that . . . I'd be in here looking at these objects . . . and she'd walk over me . . ."

He had opened his mouth to speak but words failed him. Again he ran his fingers through his hair. He seemed to be thinking: "An unforeseen complication."

The butler was carrying on again about my fiendish light and all the rest of it. I felt nothing in my life would ever make sense to anyone else. I tried to recover my pride and said:

"You'll never understand, my dear sir. If it makes you feel better, call the police."

He also stood on his dignity:

"I won't call the police because you have been my guest. But you have betrayed my trust. I leave it to your honor to make amends."

At that point I began to think of insults. The first one that came to mind was "hypocrite." I was looking for something else when one of the glass cases burst open and a mandolin fell out. We all listened attentively to the clang of the box and strings. Then the host turned and headed for his private door. The butler, meantime, had gone to pick up the mandolin. It was a moment before he could bring himself to touch it, as if he thought it might be haunted, although the poor thing looked as dried-out as a dead bird. I turned as well and started across the dining room with ringing steps: it was like walking inside a sound box.

The next several days I was very depressed and lost my job again. One night I tried to hang my glass objects on the wall, but they looked ridiculous. And I was losing my light: I could barely see the back of my hand when I held it up to my eyes.

EXCEPT JULIA

My last year in school I kept seeing a big curly head leaning back against a green wall. The boy's black curls—the green was oil paint—weren't that long, but they had spread like creepers, invading his pale brow, covering his temples and spilling over his ears and down his neck into the collar of his blue velour jacket. He always kept very still and almost never studied or did his homework. Once, when the teacher sent him home and she needed someone to go with him and ask his father to come in for a talk, I stood up and volunteered. She was surprised anyone would take on such an unpleasant task. Then she suspected the truth—that I had a plan to rescue him—and began trying to guess our intentions and impose conditions on us. But the minute we were out the door we headed for the park, swearing we would never go back to school.

One morning last year my daughter had me wait at a corner while she ran into a variety store. When she took too long I went in after her and discovered that the owner of the shop was my childhood friend. We started to chat and my daughter had to leave without me.

From the depths of the shop, up an aisle toward us, came

a girl carrying something. My friend was telling me he had spent most of his life in France. Over the years, he, too, had often remembered the ways in which we used to trick our parents into thinking we were in school. Now he lived alone, but four girls—in whom he took a fatherly interest— waited on him in the shop. The one coming up the aisle handed him a pill and a glass of water. He swallowed the pill and went on:

"They're very good to me. They don't mind my . . ."

His voice broke off and his hand fluttered around, not knowing where to settle, but his face had formed a smile.

I said, a bit in jest:

"Listen, if there's anything . . . strange bothering you, I know a doctor, a friend of mine . . ."

He didn't let me finish. His hand had landed on the edge of a jar. He raised his forefinger, which seemed about to break into song, and said:

"I love my . . . illness more than life. If I ever thought I might get well it would kill me."

"But . . . what is it?"

"Maybe some day I'll tell you. If you turned out to be one of those persons who can aggravate my . . . illness, I'd give you that chair with mother-of-pearl inlays that your daughter liked so much."

I looked at the chair—and for some reason I thought my friend's illness was seated on it.

The day he decided to tell me about his illness was a Saturday. He had just locked up for the weekend. We went to catch an out of town bus, followed by the four girls and a man with sideburns I had seen doing accounts at a desk in the rear of the shop.

"We're going out to my country place," he said. "If you

want to find out about the matter we were discussing, you'll have to stay overnight."

He stopped to give the others a chance to catch up and introduced them to me. The man with the sideburns was called Alexander. He kept his eyes lowered, like a lackey.

When we had left the city behind and the trip was becoming monotonous, I asked my friend for a preview . . .

He laughed and finally said:

"It all happens in a tunnel."

"Will you let me know when we're coming to it?"

"No, not one of those. This one's on my property. We'll walk through it. Later, at night. The girls will be waiting for us inside, kneeling on prayer stools along the left wall and wearing dark shawls. Along the right wall there'll be a long row of objects on an old counter. I'll touch the objects and try to guess what they are. I'll also touch the girls' faces, imagining I don't know them . . ."

He fell silent for a moment. He had held out his hands, as if expecting objects or perhaps faces to come within reach. When he became aware of his own silence he gathered up his hands in a way that reminded me of heads drawing back from a window. He seemed about to go on with his explanation but said only:

"You understand?"

I barely managed to say:

"I can try."

He gazed out at the scenery. I stole a look back at the girls' faces: they were innocent, evidently unaware of what we were discussing. A second later I nudged his elbow and said:

"If they're in the dark, why do they wear shawls?"

He answered absently:

"I don't know . . . I just like it that way."

And he went on staring at the scenery.

I, too, was looking out the window, but with an eye on his dark head, which hung suspended like a still cloud on the edge of the sky. I kept thinking of the places under other skies it had visited. Now that I knew of the tunnel it had in mind I understood it differently. Perhaps on those mornings in school when he rested his head against the green wall a tunnel was already forming on it. I wasn't surprised I hadn't known about the tunnel when we were playing hooky in the park. But, just as I had followed him then without understanding, I would have to do the same now. In any case, we still sympathized—and I hadn't yet learned much about human nature.

The noises of the bus and the sights going by outside the window distracted my attention, but every now and then I couldn't help thinking of the tunnel.

By the time he and I reached the property, Alexander and the girls were pushing open an iron gate. The leaves dropping from the tall trees had piled up on the bushes, which were like cluttered wastepaper baskets, and over gate and trees hung a sort of rusty dampness that seemed to be closing in on us. As we picked our way along paths between small plants an old house came into view, deep in the garden. When we approached it the girls let out cries of distress: next to the front steps lay a broken lion that had fallen off the terrace.

It was a house full of inviting corners, but to discover them I would have had to be alone and spend a long time in each place.

From the lookout tower I saw a trickling stream. My friend said:

"You see that closed shed with the large carriage door?

That's where the mouth of the tunnel is hidden. It runs in the same direction as the stream. And you see the arbor out back, near those other steps? That's where the tunnel comes out."

"And how long does it take you to go through it? I mean, when you're touching the objects and faces . . ."

"Oh, not long. In an hour it's swallowed us up and digested us. But afterward I stretch out on a couch and go over the things I remembered and the things that happened to me in there. I can't talk about it now: the light's too strong and spoils my picture of the tunnel. It's like when light enters a camera before the images are fixed. While I'm inside the tunnel I can't stand even a trace of this light: everything loses its magic, like theater sets the morning after."

We had come to a dark turn of the staircase. Below us, as we groped our way down, we saw the shadowy dining room. Floating in the middle of the room was an enormous white tablecloth that looked like a dead ghost riddled with objects.

The four girls sat at one end of the table, my friend and I and Alexander at the other. Between our two groups stretched several yards of empty white space, because the old footman was accustomed to setting the entire length of the table from the days when my friend used to live in the house with his large family. Only he and I spoke. Alexander sat with his thin face squeezed between his sideburns. I couldn't tell whether he was thinking: "I know my place" or: "I'm keeping my distance." At the far end the girls chattered and giggled without raising their voices. And at our end my friend was saying:

"Don't you sometimes need to be in complete solitude?"

I swallowed enough air to heave a deep sigh and said:

"I have two neighbors with radios across the hall and the minute they wake up they're inside my room with their radios."

"Why do you let them in?"

"No, I mean they play them so loud it's as if they were inside the room."

I had other stories to tell, but he interrupted me:

"You know, I used to hear a loud radio when I was strolling in the garden and it made me lose sight of the trees, of my whole life. It was a defilement that spoiled all my ideas: my own home no longer seemed mine, and more than once I decided I'd been born in the wrong century."

I could hardly keep from laughing because at that moment Alexander, still with downcast eyes—and bristling whiskers—let out a kind of burp, his cheeks puffing up as if he were blowing on a horn. I hastened to ask:

"And now the radio doesn't bother you any more?"

It was a silly conversation and I decided to concentrate on eating. But he was saying:

"You see, the man who made all that noise had to borrow some money and needed me as a guarantor . . ."

Alexander asked to be excused for a moment. He signaled one of the girls and as they left together another burp made his whiskers flare out like the black sails of a pirate ship.

My friend went on:

". . . so I told him: 'I'll not only guarantee your loan, I'll take care of the installments. In exchange, you'll turn off your radio on Saturdays and Sundays."

Then, nodding toward Alexander's empty chair:

"He's my man—he composes the tunnel like a symphony. He just got up because he didn't want to forget something. Before, I used to let a lot of his work go to waste: when I couldn't guess what a thing was, I asked him, and then he had to go to all the trouble of finding a new one to replace it. Now, if I can't make out an object, I leave it for the next session, and when I'm tired of touching it without being able to figure it out I stick a tag on it—I always have some in my pocket—and he takes it out of circulation for a while."

By the time Alexander returned we were well into the food and wines. Slapping my friend on the back, he said to me:

"You're looking at a great romantic, the Schubert of the tunnel. He's also shyer and he has more whiskers than Schubert. Imagine, he's been making love to a girl he's never seen—he doesn't even know her name. After ten at night he keeps books for a warehouse. He loves being alone in the silence and the smell of old wood. One night he jumped over his books because the phone rang: *she*'d dialed the wrong number, and has kept on dialing it ever since, every night. But he wouldn't dare *touch* her—except with his ears and intentions."

A deep blush was engulfing Alexander's black whiskers, and I began to like him.

After the meal Alexander and the girls went out for a walk while my friend and I napped on couches in his room. Then we also went out and spent the rest of the afternoon walking around. As the evening darkened my friend spoke less and his movements slowed. Now objects had to struggle to be seen in the fading light. It was going to be a very dark night: my friend was already feeling his way through the trees and plants. Soon we would be entering the tunnel with the memories of all the things the light had blurred before it went out. He stopped me at the carriage door.

Before he could speak I heard the trickling stream. Then he said:

"For now you're not to touch the girls' faces—they don't know you well enough. You may touch only the things along the wall to your right, on the counter."

I had already heard Alexander's footsteps. Keeping his voice low, my friend reminded me:

"Stay between us. Whatever happens, don't lose your place."

He shone a small flashlight on the first steps—dirt steps with bits of faded grass still growing on them. We came to another door and he switched off the light. Once again, he said:

"Remember, the counter is on your right, just ahead. Feel the edge of it, right here. And here's the first item—it's all yours. I could never figure it out."

I placed divining hands on a small square box with a round surface bulging out the top. I couldn't tell how hard the bulge was and I didn't dare stick my nail in it. I felt a smooth ridge, a grainy area, and bumps—or warts—on one side, near the edge of the box. It made my skin crawl and I drew my hands back. My friend said:

"Well, did you think of anything?"

"This doesn't interest me."

"I can tell from your reaction that you thought of something."

"I thought of the warty skin of some toads I used to see when I was a kid."

"All right, move on."

The next thing I touched felt like a mound of flour. I enjoyed sinking my hands in it. And he said:

"There's a cloth tacked to the edge of the counter so you can wipe off your hands."

I said, dropping a hint:

"I wish there were beaches made of flour."

"Well, go on."

Next was a cage shaped like a pagoda. I shook it to see if it had a bird inside. At that moment a light flashed—I couldn't tell where from or what it meant. I heard my friend's footstep and asked:

"What's going on?"

He, in turn, asked:

"Something the matter?"

"Didn't you see a light?"

"Oh, that—never mind. Since there are too few girls for such a long tunnel, they're spaced far apart, so each has a flashlight to let me know where she is."

I turned and saw the light flicker several times like a glowworm, just as my friend said:

"Wait here for me."

And, heading toward the light, he blocked it with his body. I imagined him scattering his fingers in the dark and gathering them up again on the girl's face.

Suddenly I heard him say:

"That's the third time you're first, Julia."

But a thin voice answered:

"I'm not Julia."

Whereupon I heard Alexander's approaching footsteps and I asked him:

"What was in that first box?"

He took a moment to say:

"A pumpkin rind."

My friend's angry voice jolted me:

"I would thank you not to ask Alexander any questions."

I swallowed hard to get his words down my throat and I put my hands back on the counter.

The rest of the session we were silent. The objects I had recognized were, in order: a pumpkin rind, a mound of flour, a cage without a bird, some baby boots, a tomato, a lorgnette, a woman's stocking, a typewriter, an egg, a burner grate from a Primus stove, a football bladder, an open book, a pair of handcuffs, and a shoebox with a plucked chicken inside. I thought Alexander had shown poor judgment in placing the chicken last: its cold pimply flesh left me with an unpleasant sensation.

As I came out of the tunnel, Alexander lit my way up the steps into the arbor. We reached a lighted gallery, where my friend patted me fondly on the neck, as if to apologize for the harshness with which he had come down on me earlier. At the same time, he turned away, as if to say: "But now I have something else on my mind and it's going to keep me busy for a while."

Motioning with his forefinger—which he then held to his lips, asking for silence—he had me follow him into his bedroom. There, he moved the couches around until they were back to back, so we'd be facing in opposite directions. Slowly he sank into one of the couches, and I into the other, letting my thoughts run on, promising myself I wouldn't stop until I had gotten to the bottom of things.

When he spoke, after a while, his deep voice startled me. He was saying:

"I'd like you to stay all day tomorrow. Unfortunately, I have to set one condition . . ."

I waited for a few seconds and answered:

"If I accepted, it would also have to be on one condition . . ."

At first he laughed. Then he said:

"Well, let's each of us write his condition down on a piece of paper—how does that suit you?"

"Just fine."

I took out a card, and, since our heads were almost touching, we exchanged messages over our shoulders. His paper read: "I need to be alone all day, out in the garden." And mine: "I'd like to spend the day shut up in a room." He laughed again. Then he got up and went out for a few minutes. When he came back he said:

"Your room is right above this one. Now let's go and have dinner. The food is on the table."

There I found an old acquaintance: the plucked chicken. After dinner he said:

"And now for some music. How about old Claude's quartet?"

I was amused at his familiarity with Debussy. We lay back on our couches. One of the times he got up to change a record he stood there holding it in midair and said:

"In the tunnel I can feel all sorts of ideas going by on their way to somewhere else."

The record had ended before he added:

"I've lived near other people and collected memories that don't belong to me."

He said nothing more that night. Alone in my room afterward, I walked up and down in a near rapture: I'd just discovered that he was the main object in the tunnel. I was admiring my idea when he rushed up the stairs, stuck his head in the door with a smile, and said:

"I can't stand your loud pacing. Remember I'm right beneath you."

"Oh, I'm sorry!"

As soon as he had left I took off my shoes and started to pace again, in my socks. The next moment he was back in the door:

"That's even worse, dear boy. Your steps are like heart

beats. I've felt my heart beat that way before. It's as if there were someone limping around inside me."

"How you must regret having offered me your hospital- ity!"

"On the contrary, I was thinking how unfortunate it will be to have an empty room after you've stayed in it."

I forced a smile and he backed out.

I fell asleep right away but soon woke up. There was distant thunder and lightning. I got up softly and went to open the window. I looked out at a dimly lit sky that was trying to unload its bloated clouds on the house. And suddenly I saw a man on a path in the garden. He was bent over some creepers, searching for something. He took several steps sideways, still crouching low, and I decided to alert my friend. The stairs creaked and I was afraid he would wake up and think I was the thief. The door to his room was open and the bed was empty. When I returned to my room the man had disappeared. I got into bed and went back to sleep.

Sipping my *mate* the next morning—the footman had brought up the *mate* service while I was downstairs washing—I remembered a dream I'd had. My friend and I were standing by a tomb and he said: "Do you know who's buried there? The chicken in her box." We had no sense of death: it was a quaintly shaped tomb, much like an icebox, and we knew the corpses it held were for eating.

I was remembering this, still sipping and gazing out the yellowish curtains at the garden, when suddenly I saw my friend cross one of the paths. I involuntarily drew back, like a spy. Then I decided not to look. Instead—since he couldn't hear me—I paced up and down the room. One of the times I came to the window, I saw him going in the direction of the carriage house. I thought he was headed for the tunnel and began to suspect all sorts of things. But then he took another path, up to some laundry that was hanging from a line, and placed one hand flat on a—probably—wet bedsheet.

We met only for dinner. At one point he said:

"When I'm in my shop I long for this day, and then when I'm here I feel horribly bored and depressed. But I need to be by myself, with no one near. Oh, I beg your pardon!"

I saw my chance and said:

"There must have been dogs in the garden last night . . . This morning I found some violets strewn on a path."

He smiled:

"That was me—I like to pick them out from between the leaves just before dawn." And with another, broader smile: "I had left my door open, but when I got back it was closed."

Now I smiled:

"I'd thought there was a thief and I'd gone down to warn you."

That night we went back to town. He was pleased with himself.

The next Saturday we were in the tower when suddenly one of the girls came up to me. I thought she wanted to tell me a secret and bent over to listen, but instead she planted a kiss on my cheek. It all seemed calculated, and my friend asked:

"What do you think you're doing?"

The girl answered:

"We're not in the tunnel now."

"But we're in my home," he said.

By then the other girls had arrived. They said they had

been playing forfeits and the kiss was a penalty. Trying to laugh it off, I said:

"Some penalty! You poor thing!"

And a little short girl answered:

"I wish it had been me!"

It all ended well. But it had been upsetting to my friend.

At the usual time we felt our way into the tunnel. I recognized the pumpkin rind, but my friend had already stuck a tag on it to have it removed from the counter. Then I began to sift through a mass of something like crumbling stone. It didn't interest me, and my mind wandered: I knew that soon the first woman would shine her light at us. Meantime I had forgotten my hands in the crumbling stone. Then I fingered some tasseled material, and suddenly I realized it was a pair of gloves. I wondered what the gloves meant to my hands: the surprise, I decided, was for them, not for me. When I touched a piece of glass, I suspected the hands wanted to try on the gloves. I was about to humor them, but held back, like a father who doesn't want to indulge his daughters' every whim. Then I began to suspect something else: my friend was too far advanced in that world of hands, perhaps encouraging an instinct for independence in them that allowed them to develop too much of a life of their own. I remembered the flour that had given them such pleasure in the previous session, and I said to myself: "The hands like raw flour." Doing my best to leave that idea behind, I returned to the glass I had touched before: it was on a stand. Could it be a portrait? How could I find out? Or—worse still—it might be a mirror. My imagination had been tricked, as if the dark were making fun of me. Almost at once, the first girl flashed her light. I don't know why, at that moment, I thought of the mass of crumbling stone I had touched at the beginning and knew it was the head of the lion that had fallen off the terrace.

My friend was asking one of the girls:

"What's this? A doll head? A dog? A chicken?"

I heard her answer:

"No, it's one of those yellow flowers that . . ."

He interrupted her:

"Haven't I told you not to bring anything in with you?"

The girl said: "Idiot!"

"What? Who are you?"

"I'm Julia," a firm voice said.

"Don't ever bring anything in your hands," my friend answered feebly.

Returning to the counter, he said to me:

"I like to know there's a yellow flower somewhere in the dark."

Just then I felt something graze my jacket. I immediately thought of the gloves, as if they could get up and walk, but also of a person, and said to my friend:

"Someone just went by."

"Impossible! All in your mind! Everyone imagines things in the tunnel."

And, when we least expected it, we heard a powerful wind blow. He shouted:

"What's that?"

Curiously, we heard the wind but did not feel it on our hands or faces, and Alexander said:

"It's a machine that imitates the sound of the wind. I borrowed it from a prop man in a theater."

"Fine," my friend said, "but it's not for the hands . . ."

He was silent for a minute and then suddenly asked:

"Who turned it on?"

"The first girl—she moved back after you'd touched her."

"There—you see?" I said. "She was the one who brushed by me."

That same night, while changing a record, my friend said:

"I enjoyed myself today. I got things mixed up, everything reminded me of something else and I had unexpected memories. As soon as I started to move my body in the dark I felt it was going to bump into something unusual, as if it lived differently in there and my head was ready for some important insight. And suddenly, when I turned my body from an object to touch a face, I realized who had swindled me in a business deal."

I went to my room and lay in bed thinking of a pair of kid gloves neatly filled out by a woman's slender hands. I was planning to peel off the gloves as if undressing the hands. But, as I fell asleep, the gloves turned into banana skins.

I must have been asleep for a long while when I felt hands touch my face. I woke up screaming, floated for a minute in the dark and finally realized I'd had a nightmare. My friend came running up the stairs to ask:

"What's the matter?"

I started to tell him:

"I had this dream . . ."

But I caught myself, afraid that if I mentioned the hands he might try to touch my face.

He backed out and I lay there, wide awake. But a few minutes later the door opened softly and I cried out in a failing voice: "Who is it?"—and heard paws pattering down the stairs.

Once more my friend appeared. I told him he had left the door open and a dog had come in. He started down the stairs again.

The following Saturday we were just inside the tunnel when I heard what I thought was a puppy whining for attention. One of the girls began to laugh and we all chimed in. My friend got worked up and started to rage at us, and we immediately broke off. But when he stopped to catch his breath the whining grew louder and we all laughed again, and suddenly he shouted:

"Out of here! Get going! All of you!"

Those of us near him heard him panting—until, in a muffled voice, as if hiding his face in the dark, he added:

"Except Julia."

I had an urge I could not resist: to stay in the tunnel. My friend waited for everyone to leave. Then, from way off, Julia started to signal him with her flashlight. The light blinked on and off regularly, like a beacon. He went toward her with heavy steps, unaware of me keeping step not far behind him. When I caught up Julia was saying:

"Are you reminded of other faces when you touch mine?"

He lingered over his answer, dragging out each word:

"Wellll . . . At the moment I'm reminded of a Viennese woman I knew in Paris."

"Was she a friend of yours?"

"Her husband was. But one day he was thrown by a wooden horse . . ."

"You can't be serious!"

"Let me explain. He'd always been weak and sickly, and a rich aunt in the provinces wanted him to exercise. She had brought him up. He kept sending her pictures of himself in sports clothes, but all he ever did was read. Soon after he got married he decided to have a picture taken on horseback. He was very proud of himself in his cowboy hat. But it was an old moth-eaten wooden horse and its leg broke, and he fell off and broke an arm."

Julia let out a short laugh, and he went on:

"So I visited him at home—that was how I met his wife . . . At first she had only a playful smile for me. He was surrounded with visitors, with his arm in traction. She brought him some broth, and he said he had lost his appetite since his fracture. All the visitors agreed that fractures did that to you. It sounded to me as if they'd all had fractures: I could see them waving swollen arms and legs in the darkened room, wrapped in white bandages."

(At that unlikely moment, we heard the puppy whine again, and Julia laughed. I was afraid my friend would go after the puppy and trip over me. But in a minute he went on with his story.)

"When he was able to get up he walked slowly, with his arm in a sling. Seen from behind, with one jacket sleeve on and the other dangling, he was like an organ grinder telling fortunes. He invited me down into the basement to fetch a bottle of his best wine. His wife wouldn't let him go alone. He led the way, with a candle, scattering spiders as the flame burned through the cobwebs. She was right behind him, and I was behind her . . ."

He stopped and Julia asked:

"Did you say that at first she had only a playful smile for you? And later on?"

He started to get annoyed:

"I never said I was the only one she was playful with!"

"You said she was at first."

"Well, and later on . . . nothing changed."

The puppy whined and Julia said:

"Don't think it bothers me. But . . . you've made my cheeks burn."

I heard the prayer stool being dragged aside, then their steps as they went out and shut the door. I ran to the door and banged on it and kicked it. My friend opened and asked:

"Who is it?"

When he saw it was me he sputtered:

"I don't want you in my tunnel ever again . . . you understand?"

He was going to add something more but instead he turned and left.

That night I caught the bus into town with Alexander and the girls. They rode in front and I in the rear. Not one of them looked back at me, and I felt like a traitor.

A few days later my friend called on me at home. It was late and I had gone to bed. He apologized for getting me up and for his outburst in the tunnel. I soon cheered up, but he still looked worried. And suddenly he said:

"Julia's father came to see me in the shop today. He won't have me touching his daughter's face any more, but he let on that he wouldn't object to an engagement. I glanced at Julia and she was looking down and scraping polish off a fingernail, and that was when I realized I loved her."

"Well, then," I said, "why don't you marry her?"

"I can't. She doesn't want me to touch any more faces in the tunnel."

He sat leaning his elbows on his knees, and suddenly he hid his face—a tiny lamb's face, it seemed to me at that moment. I reached out to put a hand on his shoulder and inadvertently touched his curly head. It felt like one of the objects in the tunnel.

The Woman Who Looked Like Me

A few summers ago I began to suspect I had once been a horse. At nightfall the thought would stir in me like a horse in a barn. As soon as I put my man's body down to sleep, my horse memory would begin to wander.

One such night I was plodding up a dirt road, stepping on the spots made by the shadows of the trees. The moon followed me on one side, my shadow dragged after me on the other. As I kicked up clods of earth, my shadow blotted out my crumbling tracks and was, in turn, swallowed up in the long shadows of the trees slowly stretching past me.

My tired flesh weighed on me and my fetlocks hurt. Sometimes I forgot to coordinate my front and hind quarters and I stumbled and almost fell.

Suddenly I would smell water—but it was just some stagnant pond nearby. My eyes, too, were ponds reflecting all sorts of things, big and small, near and far, on their sloped surfaces brightened with tears. I had nothing to do but watch for unfriendly shadows and threatening animals or humans. If I lowered my muzzle to nibble on a shoot of grass under a tree, then I also had to be careful to avoid prickly weeds, and when thorns stuck in my lips I had to work them loose.

In the early hours of the night, even when I was hungry, I never stopped. In the horse I'd found something very much like what I'd left behind in the man: a lazy well-being conducive to pleasant memories. I'd also realized that to get the memories going I had to wind them up, and the way to do that was by walking around. In those days I worked for a baker. I owed him what hopes for happiness I still had. He would put a sack over my eyes and yoke me to a pole that turned a sort of millstone, except that he used it for kneading; and, linked to this machine, circling without a stumble for hours on end with the pole, which was like a minute hand, listening to my steps and the sound of the gears, I would go over my memories.

We worked until late at night, and then he fed me, and grinding the corn between my teeth I let my mind run on.

(Right now, as a horse, I'm reminded of something that happened to me a short time ago, while I was still a man. One night I couldn't sleep because I was hungry. I remembered I had a packet of mints in the closet and started to eat them. But when I chewed on them it sounded like I was grinding corn.)

And now, suddenly, reality has brought me back to my sense of being a horse, my steps ringing out in the deep as I clomp over a long wooden bridge.

Along many different roads I've always had the same memories. Night and day they run through my mind like rivers through a land. Sometimes I watch them go by and other times they overflow.

As a young colt I hated the farm boy who looked after me. He was also a young colt. Once, after sundown, the little wretch whacked me across the nose, so hard that my blood boiled and I went wild and not only stood on my hands and threw him but bit his head and mangled his thigh. Then someone must have seen my mane fly as I wheeled around and finished him off with a couple of well-placed kicks.

The next day a lot of people left the wake to watch me receive my punishment from the men who were avenging the boy's death. They killed the colt in me, reducing me to a horse.

Soon after that I spent a very long night. I'd kept some of my "vices" from my early life and now I revived one of them: I jumped over a fence, onto the road. I'd barely managed to clear the fence and I was hurt.

From then on I felt free. But it was an unhappy freedom. Not only did my body weigh me down, but each of its parts wanted to live an independent life, without putting out any effort: they were like slaves fighting their owner by dragging their feet. When I was lying down and wanted to get up, I had to convince each separate part to cooperate, and at the last moment there were always unexpected groans and complaints. Hunger had a way of getting them to act together, but the strongest prod was the fear of being caught. When a mean owner beat one of the parts, they all joined forces to save the affected part from further damage—because none felt safe. I tried to pick owners with low fences and at the first beating I was off, and the hunger and the fear of being caught began again.

Once my owner was just too cruel. At first he used to beat me only when he was riding me and we went by his girlfriend's house, but then he started to place the load too far back in his cart, making me rear up so I couldn't get a foothold to press forward, and he flew into a rage and beat me on the head, legs, and belly. I ran off one evening and didn't stop for miles, until I could hide in the dark. I came to a shack near the edge of a village. A small fire was smoking inside and, hunched over it in the unsteady glow, I saw a man with his hat on. By then it was night out. But I had to keep going.

As soon as I was on my way again I felt lighter, as if some parts of my body had fallen behind or strayed in the night, and I tried to hasten my step.

In the distance I saw some trees with lights glinting through the leaves. Suddenly I realized there was a brightness at the end of the road. I was hungry but decided not to eat until I reached the brightness: it was probably a town. I drew the road in more and more slowly; it seemed I'd never reach the brightness at the far end. But gradually I realized none of my parts had deserted me: one by one they started to catch up, each hungrier and more tired than the one before. The first to arrive—and the hardest to trick—had been the parts in pain. I kept showing them the memory of the owner unsaddling them, his short flat shadow slowly circling my body. It was this man I should have killed as a colt, when I was still a single self, driven by the pain and anger that held me together.

I started to chew on a patch of grass near the first houses. I was easy to detect because of my large white and black spots, but it was late night now and no one was up. I kept snorting and raising dust—I couldn't see it but it got in my eyes. I reached a street with a hard surface and came to a wide gate. As soon as I went through the gate I saw pale spots moving in the dark. They were schoolchildren in their white smocks. They shooed me off and I went up a short flight of steps. Other children at the top of the stairs drove me on. My hooves clattered over a wooden floor and suddenly I came out in a small lit space facing an audience. There was an explosion of shrieks and laughter. The girls in long dresses who were in the small lit space scattered in every direction, and from the deafening audience, which was also full of children, voices rang out, "A horse! . . . A horse!" A boy with folds in his ears, as if he had forced a hat down on them, was shouting, "It's the Mendezes' pinto!" Finally the teacher came out on stage. She was also laughing, but asked for silence, saying the play was almost over and explaining how it ended. But she was interrupted when I sank down wearily on the rug and the audience burst into applause again and surged toward us. The rest of the performance was canceled. People climbed up on stage. A little girl, about three years old, broke from her mother, rushed up to me and put her open hand, like a tiny star, on my sweaty rump. When the mother dragged her away she was holding up her little open hand and saying: "Mommy, the horse is wet." Meanwhile, a gentleman with a knowing look was pointing his forefinger at the teacher, as if he were about to ring a bell, and insisting, "I can't believe you hadn't planned this surprise—but the horse came in ahead of time. Horses are very hard to train. Let me tell you about one I used to have . . ." And the boy with folds in his ears raised my upper lip, looked at my teeth, and said, "This horse is old."

The teacher was allowing the audience to think she really had planned the surprise. A childhood friend came up to congratulate her. The friend began to recall a quarrel they'd had when they were in school together, whereupon the teacher remembered what the friend had said to her during the quarrel—that she looked like a horse. To my surprise, it was true: the teacher looked like me. I still thought she might have shown more respect for a poor dumb beast than to bring this up in my presence.

When the applause and commotion were dying down, a young man made his way up the aisle and interrupted the teacher—who was still in conversation with her childhood friend and the man who had pointed his finger at her as if he were about to ring a bell—shouting:

"Tomasa—don Santiago says to move to the teashop, we're using too much light here."

"What about the horse?"

"You can't keep him here all night, sweetheart."

"Alexander will be along in a minute with a rope and we'll take him home with us."

The young man climbed on the stage and went on arguing with the three of them, against me:

"I don't think it looks right for Tomasa to take that horse home with her. I already heard the Zubiría girls saying it makes no sense for a woman to be alone in the house with a horse she has no use for, and Mother also says it's asking for trouble."

But Tomasa said:

"In the first place, I'm not alone at home because there's Candelaria, who helps out a bit. And in the second place, I could buy a buggy, if it's any of those spinsters' business."

Then Alexander—who turned out to be the boy with folds in his ears—came in and slipped a rope over my neck. But when they tried to get me up I couldn't move. The man who had been pointing his forefinger said:

"This animal is foundering. You're going to have to bleed him."

I was scared to death and, with great effort, I managed to stand up and walk, lame as a wooden horse. They led me out some back steps, into the courtyard. There, improvising a rope halter, Alexander jumped on my back and started kicking my sides and whipping me up. I limped all the way around to the front of the theater in incredible pain. But as soon as the teacher saw us she made Alexander get off.

Although my steps were dull thuds as we headed downtown, and in spite of my exhaustion, I couldn't fall asleep. Like a dinky street organ grinding out a single broken tune, I kept coming down on the same aching bones. The pain made me pay attention to each separate part of my body as it tried to keep pace with the rest. Now and then, out of step with my other movements, a chill ran down my back, but the next moment it was a shiver of anticipation at the thought of being alone later on, quietly going over my new store of memories.

The teashop was really a café with pool tables on one side and the tea room on the other. The two halves were divided by a thick wooden balustrade. On the railing stood two flowerpots wrapped in yellow crêpe, one with a rickety plant, the other without. Between them there was a large fishbowl with a single fish in it. The teacher's boyfriend was still arguing, probably over me. The moment I stuck my head in the door, the people on both sides of the room—I recognized many of the faces I'd seen in the theater—laughed, and the interest in me revived briefly. After a while the waiter came out with a pail of water. The pail smelled of soap and grease but the water was clean. The smell brought me wistful memories of a home that had once let me into its most intimate secrets, and I drank greedily. Alexander hadn't wanted to tether me outside or to go in with the others: he held my rope while I guzzled, tapping his foot as if marking time to music. A minute later the waiter brought me some dry grass and said:

"I know this pinto."

Alexander, laughing, put him straight:

"I thought he was the Mendezes' pinto, too."

But the waiter came right back with:

"No, the one I'm thinking of isn't from around here."

The three-year-old girl who had touched me on stage now appeared, leading another, older girl by the hand. In her tiny free hand she was carrying a few wisps of green grass that she tried to add to the pile I was chewing on, but she missed her throw and it fell on my head and into one of my ears.

Finally I was taken to the teacher's house and shut in the barn. She led the way in with a candle, shielding the flame with her hand.

The next day I couldn't get up. They slid open a window with a view of the sky and the man of the pointing finger bled me. Then Alexander came in, sat on a stool he had pulled up next to me and started to play the harmonica. When I was able to stand I looked out the window. Now I had a view down a slope to some trees, through which I saw a river in constant movement. From there they brought me water. They also gave me corn and oats. That day I didn't feel like remembering anything.

In the afternoon the teacher's boyfriend came. He seemed better disposed toward me, and I could tell from the way he stroked and patted my neck that he was a likable young man. She stroked me as well, but in an unpleasant way: she didn't know about horses and her light touch tickled me. One of the times she touched me on the forehead I wondered, "Does she realize that's where we're alike?" Then the boyfriend went around the outside of the barn and took a picture of us standing in the window. She put an arm around my neck and leaned her head against mine.

That night I had a big scare. I was at the window, gazing out at the sky and listening to the river, when I heard shuffling steps and saw a stooped figure go by. It was a woman with white hair. After a while she went by again in the opposite direction. And the same the next night and every night I lived in that house. Seen from behind, bent in two, with her square hips and crooked legs, she looked like a walking table. The day I was allowed out of the barn I saw her seated in the yard peeling potatoes. Her knife had a silver handle and she was black. At first I thought her white hair moved strangely as she bent over her potatoes, but then I realized there was smoke mixed in with it, from a short pipe that stuck out a corner of her mouth, clenched between her teeth. That morning Alexander asked her:

"Candelaria, do you like the pinto?"

And she answered:

"Owner'll be by for him soon."

I still didn't feel like remembering.

One day Alexander took me to school. The children went wild. But there was a boy who kept staring at me without a word. He had big flap ears, spread like wings about to fly off. He also wore huge glasses—but his squint eyes stuck close to his nose. The moment Alexander wasn't watching, he kicked me hard in the stomach. Alexander ran to tell the teacher. When he returned, a little girl with a pot of red ink was painting over a white spot on my stomach with the cork stopper. Alexander ran back to the teacher:

"And that girl painted a heart on his belly."

During recess another girl showed us a large doll and said

that after school she was going to have it baptized. Alexander and I left the minute classes ended, and not the same way we had come. He led me around the back of a church, to the sacristy, called the priest and asked:

"Hey, Father, how much would you charge to baptize the horse?"

"Baptize a horse, son? What an idea!"

The priest's huge belly shook with laughter.

But Alexander insisted:

"You remember that prayer card of the Virgin where she's riding a donkey?"

"Yes."

"So, if you can baptize a donkey, why can't you baptize a horse?"

"But the donkey wasn't baptized."

"You mean the Virgin was riding a donkey that hadn't been baptized?"

The priest was laughing so hard he couldn't talk.

Alexander went on:

"You blessed the picture, and the donkey was in the picture."

We left with heavy hearts.

A few days later we ran into a little black boy and Alexander asked him:

"What'll we call the horse?"

The black boy seemed to be searching his mind for something. Finally, he said:

"What was that word the teacher said to use for something that's pretty?"

"Wait, I know," said Alexander. "Additive."

That night Alexander was perched on the stool, next to me, playing his harmonica, when the teacher came in:

"Go on home, they must be waiting for you."

"Hey, Miss, you know the pinto's name? Additive."

"In the first place, it's *adjective*. And in the second place, that's not a name, it's a . . . an adjective!" the teacher said, after hesitating for a moment.

One afternoon when we got home I was pleased with myself because I'd heard a voice behind a shutter say:

"There goes the teacher with her horse."

Shortly after leaving me in the barn—Alexander was off that day—the teacher came for me and, unexpectedly—I'd never been so amazed—took me into her bedroom. She tickled me in that unpleasant way of hers and said, "Please don't start neighing." Then, right away, for some reason, she left. Alone in the bedroom, I started to wonder, "What does this woman really want of me?" There were jumbled clothes strewn on the chairs and bed. Suddenly I looked up and stared straight at myself, with my poor old forgotten horse head hanging mournfully. The mirror also showed parts of my body: my white and black spots were like more rumpled clothes. But it was my head that struck me most, and I began to raise it, higher and higher. I was so overwhelmed I had to shut my eyes for a moment to remember the self with which I had imagined my horse self before seeing it.

There were other surprises. At the foot of the mirror was the picture that Tomasa's boyfriend had taken of us standing in the window. And suddenly my legs buckled, as if they had recognized the voice I heard talking outside before I did. I couldn't make out what "he" was saying, but I caught Tomasa's answer:

"He's run away again. Just like he ran away from you.

When they went to feed him this morning the barn was as empty as it is now."

The voices moved away and, as soon as I was alone, all the thoughts I'd been having before came tumbling down on me and I didn't dare face myself in the mirror. To think a horse could have such impossible dreams! Who would have believed it! It took her a long time to come back. And when she began to tickle me again it was painful. But even more painful to me was her innocence.

One afternoon, a few days later, Alexander was playing the harmonica next to me when he remembered something. He got off his stool and, putting the harmonica away, reached into his pocket and pulled out the picture of Tomasa and me in the window. He held it up to one of my eyes, then to the other, first close up, then—when I didn't react—a bit farther away, and finally straight ahead, at a distance of about three feet. I sank into my guilty thoughts, bitterly.

One night, absorbed in listening to the river, I started at the sound of Candelaria's steps, which I hadn't recognized, and kicked over the pail of water. As she went by, the black woman said:

"It's all right—your owner'll be back for you soon."

The next day Alexander took me swimming in the river. He was on my back, happily riding his warm boat. I felt my heart begin to shrink, and almost at once I heard a whistle that froze my blood. I pricked my ears right and left, like periscopes. Finally "his" voice reached me. "He" was shouting:

"That horse is mine!"

Without a word, Alexander yanked me out of the water and we galloped home. My owner came running right behind us so there was no time to hide me. I was stuck in my body as if I were wearing an oak wardrobe.

The teacher offered to buy me, and "he" said:

"When you have sixty bucks, which is what he cost me, come and get him."

Alexander removed my head straps and bit, which belonged to him, and the owner put his on me. The teacher went into her bedroom and the last I saw of Alexander the corners of his mouth were bending down at right angles as he burst into tears. My legs were shaking, but "he" lashed me hard across the nose and I started to walk. Only then did I remember that I hadn't cost him sixty bucks: he'd gotten me in exchange for a junky blue bicycle without tires or a pump. Now he had begun to vent his fury by beating me steadily and as hard as he could. I had to gasp for breath because I was very fat—Alexander had taken such good care of me! But I was also remembering the success that had led to my being welcomed into the teacher's home and the happiness I had known there, even when it provoked guilty thoughts in me. Now an uncontrollable anger was stirring in my guts. I was very thirsty and I remembered we would soon be crossing a stream under a tree that stuck a dry arm out almost into the middle of the road. It was a moonlit night and from a distance I saw the pebbles in the stream shining like fish scales. Just before reaching the stream I slowed down. He knew what was coming and started to beat me again. For a few seconds I struggled with conflicting impulses: they were like enemies hurriedly sniffing each other over, probing in the dark. Then I aimed straight for the tree with the dry arm sticking out at us. He barely had time to latch on to the branch as I bolted out from under him, and the next moment it snapped and they fell into the water together, rolling over the pebbles and wrestling. I

turned and ran back to him just when he was coming out
on top, and I managed to trample on him while his body
still lay sideways. My hoof slipped on his shoulder, but I got
a good bite out of his throat and then a grip on the nape of
his neck. I held on with the force of madness and waited
without moving. In a moment, after twitching an arm,
he also stopped moving. I felt the sour taste of his flesh in
my mouth and his beard made my tongue prickle. I had
begun to taste blood when I saw the water and the pebbles
redden.

I crossed the stream several times, back and forth, not
knowing what to do with my freedom. In the end I decided
to return to the teacher's house—but not before going back
over my steps one more time to drink some water near the
body.

I set out slowly because I was very tired. But my freedom
made me fearless. How happy Alexander would be to see
me! And what would *she* say? I used to feel so guilty when
Alexander showed me our picture! But wouldn't I have
loved to have it with me now!

Trudging along I reached the house. I was on my way to
the barn—but I heard people arguing in Tomasa's bedroom. I
recognized the boyfriend's voice: he was carrying on about the
sixty bucks she wanted to waste on me. I had just begun to
cheer up at the thought that now I wouldn't cost them a cent
when I heard him talking about marriage, all steamed up until,
finally, beside himself and already halfway out the door, he
shouted:

"It's either the horse or me!"

At first I let my head hang until it rested on her red
windowsill. But, a minute later, I decided my life: I'd have
to go. I had reached noble heights and didn't want to
breathe an air that would grow dirtier every day. If I stayed

I would soon become an undesirable horse: even she would begin to have doubts about us.

I'm not too sure how I got away. But my one big regret at not being a man was not having a pocket so I could take our picture with me.

My First Concert

The day of my first concert I went through strange agonies and may have been granted some unexpected insights into myself. I had gotten up at six in the morning, which was unusual for me because I not only played in a café at night but had trouble falling asleep afterward. Some nights, late as it was when I reached my room—where the small black piano reminded me of a coffin—I couldn't face going to bed and went out for a walk. I had taken one of those late walks the night before but nevertheless hurried out early in the morning to spend the day shut up in an empty theater—the one reserved for the concert. It was a fairly small theater with a balcony encased in short brass balusters painted white. The aging black piano was already on stage, between red and gold paper walls representing a parlor. A few dusty rays of sunlight shone through holes in the set, and cobwebs billowed in the hot air overhead. I distrusted myself that morning and started going over my program like someone counting his money because he suspects it has been stolen from him during the night, and I soon found out I didn't have as much as I had thought I did. I had first suspected this some days before, the moment I had given

the owners of the theater my word: I had felt strangely hot
in the stomach and sensed imminent danger. My reaction
had been to sit right down and study. But with several days
ahead of me, I had fallen into my usual habit of overesti-
mating what I could do with the time on my hands, and
now I had realized I was so far from the goal I'd set myself,
because of all the compromises I'd made along the way, that
even if I spent another year studying I would never reach it.
My memory was giving me the most trouble: no matter
what passage I tried or how slowly my fingers groped for it,
I simply couldn't remember the notes. Desperate, I went
out into the street. Rounding a corner I saw my name
written large on two huge posters stuck on either side of a
cart, and felt even more miserable. If the letters had only
been smaller, perhaps less would have been expected of me.
I returned to the theater, determined to keep calm and
figure out what to do. Seated in an orchestra seat, I watched
the stage, where the solitary piano awaited me with its black
lid raised. Near me were the seats usually occupied by two
brothers who were friends of mine, and behind them sat a
family that had recently greeted a concert by some local girls
with such loud jeers that in the middle of the show the girls
had run out like frightened hens, clutching their heads. It
was while recalling this incident that I had the sudden idea
to rehearse the theatrical aspect of my performance. First I
checked out the whole theater to make sure no one could
see me, then I started to practice my entrance, crossing the
set from the wing to the piano. On my first try I sped in like
a delivery boy rushing to plop the meat on the table—that
wouldn't do. I had to exude weight and authority, like
someone giving the twenty-fourth performance in the
nineteenth concert season, almost bored with myself, not
driven headlong by frightened vanity but carelessly bearing

a mysterious something all my own, grown in unknown depths. I began a slow entrance, imagining all eyes on me, so vividly that I could hardly walk, and the more I concentrated on my steps the less control I had over them. So then I tried to imagine I was casually strolling somewhere else, far from the theater, and to imitate my own steps. At moments I caught myself acting almost natural—but even when I thought I was perfectly relaxed and unselfconscious I was mimicking different walks: swaying my hips like a bullfighter, stiff as a waiter carrying a loaded tray, or rocking from side to side like a boxer.

My next big problem was my hands. I had always disliked the way some pianists dangled and swung their arms like pendulums when they came out and bowed. I tried to keep my arms in time with my steps—but that seemed more appropriate for a military parade. Then I thought of something that for a long time I was to find strikingly original: I'd come out with my left wrist clasped in my right hand, as if fastening my cufflink. (Years later an actor told me it was a cheap affectation known as "the ballet pose." And, laughing, he imitated some dance steps, switching back and forth between clasping his left wrist in his right hand and his right wrist in his left hand.)

I barely had lunch, and spent the whole afternoon rehearsing. In the evening the electrician arrived and we practiced dimming and heightening the lights in the room and onstage. Then I tried on the tuxedo a friend had given me: it was too small and held me so tight it would have frustrated all my attempts at ease and naturalness, if it didn't burst on me first. In the end I decided to wear street clothes: that would make everything seem more natural . . . although, at the same time, looking too familiar would not be right either: I would have liked to invent something strange. But I was very tired and still sore under the arms from the chafing of the tuxedo. So I went and sat in the shadows of the orchestra to wait until it was time for the concert. But whenever I managed to keep still for a moment, my obsession with remembering the notes of some piece came back with such irresistible force that the only relief was to get up and look up the notes in the score.

A while before the concert, the two brothers who were my friends showed up, with the tuner. I asked them to wait for a minute while I shut myself in the dressing room, knowing that if I didn't finish going over the passage I had in my mind I wouldn't have a moment's peace, but that afterward I could relax because once I got into conversation my attention would be distracted and I wouldn't start remembering any more passages. The theater was still empty. One of my friends stood in the door to the set, staring at the black piano as if it were a casket. Then they both lowered their voices around me as if I were the dead person's closest relative.

When the people started to trickle in, we peeked out at them from backstage through slits in the paper walls, crouching as if we were in a trench. From certain angles, the piano—like a huge cannon—blocked much of our view of the orchestra. I moved from peephole to peephole like a commander instructing his troops. I was glad for the small audience, which meant news of the coming disaster would not spread so fast—and also, I hoped, that critical expectations would be lower, in which case the "theatrics" I had been rehearsing for people who weren't too knowledgeable about the music would work in my favor, perhaps making even those with some critical sense doubt their judgment . . . It was all going to my head and I had even begun to put on airs with my friends and complain:

"You see! There's just no interest in these events! It's unbelievable! After so much sweat and sacrifice!"

But then more people arrived and my heart sank, although I kept rubbing my hands and saying, "That's more like it!"

My friends seemed frightened, too, and at one point—after pretending not to notice for a while—I started haranguing them in a loud voice:

"So, what's the matter? You're not worried for me, are you? If you think it's the first time I've played in public and it's like being led to torture . . . you're in for a surprise! I've kept this to myself until now, but I was just waiting for my chance to show those music teachers over there that a 'café pianist'"—I had come to town hired to play in the café—"can give concerts. Because what those chattering ladies don't know is that in this country the opposite can happen: a concert pianist may well end up playing in a café."

Although my voice did not carry beyond the stage, they tried to calm me down.

It was time to begin. I gave orders to ring the bell and sent my friends to their seats in the orchestra. Before leaving they promised to come back afterward and bring me the audience's comments. I signaled the electrician to lower the lights and, reminding myself of the steps I had rehearsed, took my left cufflink in my right hand and made for the stage as if sailing into the glare of a fire. Although I was watching my steps from above, from my eyes, I put all my energy into picturing my walk from the audience's point of view. My thoughts were like mad birds beating loud wings in my face—but I trod on firmly, measuring each step across the set.

I had reached my bench and still there was no applause.

Finally it rippled out and I had to take a bow, interrupting
the motion with which I had started to sit down. In spite of
this minor setback, I was ready to carry on with my plan. I
cast a more or less general and unfocused look over the
audience, but made out the brittle shapes of whitish faces in
the dark, pale as eggshells. And over the velvet-topped
railing of the balcony with the short brass balusters painted
white were sprinkled many pairs of hands. I put mine on the
piano, pounded out several chords in quick succession and
settled back. Next, according to my plan, I had to fix my
eyes on the keyboard for a minute as if to concentrate my
thoughts and await the arrival of the muse or the composer's
spirit (which must have been a long way off, because it was
Bach). But more people were coming in and I had to break
off communications. The unexpected reprieve was welcome: when I looked out at the audience again, I didn't
seem to be in such an impossible world. A few seconds later,
however, I felt the fear I thought I had left behind catching
up with me again. I tried to remember the keys involved in
the first chords—but knew at once that if I proceeded along
that road it would only lead to some forgotten chord. So I
decided to attack the first note. It was a black key, and when
I put my finger on it, before pressing down, I had time to
realize the big moment had come: I was ready and further
delay would be useless. The audience withdrew into a
silence that was like the hole opening under you just before
an accident you can't avoid. The note rang out and it was
like a stone falling down a well. Dazed by what I'd done, on
blind impulse, I spread my hand out flat in a chord that
sounded like a slap in the face. Wrestling hard I went on and
got through the first bars. Suddenly I hunched forward,
dampened the sound and started to peck out a *pianissimo* in
the upper register. I liked the effect and decided to

improvise a few more. In no time I was plunging my hands into the mass of sound and shaping it as if I were molding warm clay. At moments I would draw it out, lengthening the tempo, trying to give the mass a different shape, until it started going cold, and then I worked faster and felt it warm up again. It was like being in a magician's den. I couldn't guess what substances the magician had combined to start the fire, but I followed his every inspiration. At times I would settle into a slow tempo and the flame would become a steady glow. Then I would tilt my head back over one shoulder as if kneeling at a shrine. I felt the audience's eyes on my right cheek, where they seemed to raise blisters. My last note was greeted with a burst of applause. I got up and bowed soberly, but I was euphoric. When I sat down again, the hands spread along the balcony railing were still clapping.

Everything went smoothly until I came to a "Music Box." I had slid my bench a bit toward the upper register so I could play more comfortably and was sprinkling out the first notes like raindrops, certain that I was doing no worse than before, when suddenly there were murmurs in the theater and I even thought I heard some laughter. I started to shrink like a worm, feeling clumsy and unsure of myself. It seemed to me I had also seen a long shadow slide across the stage. When I managed to sneak a glance I found there really was a shadow, but now it was motionless. I went on playing and the murmurs continued. Now I could tell, without looking, that the shadow was moving. I wasn't about to imagine a monster or even a joke at my expense. During a relatively easy passage I saw the shadow stretch out a long paw. I looked and it wasn't there. But when I looked again I saw a black cat. I was near the end of the piece and the laughter and murmurs grew louder. I realized the cat

was grooming his face—and what was I supposed to do?
Pick him up and take him out? A ridiculous idea. I got
through the piece and when I stood for the applause I felt
the cat brush against my trouser leg. I was bowing and
smiling. I sat down again and found myself stroking the cat.
I had let more time than was prudent go by before starting
on my next piece and I still didn't know what to do with
him. I would have looked insane chasing him around the
stage in front of the audience. So I decided to let him sit
next to me while I played. But now I couldn't think of any
more shapes to mold or ideas to run after—my mind was on
the cat. Then I was seized by a terrifying thought: halfway
through my next piece there was a spot where I had to claw
out the notes with my left hand. The cat was on that side
and might well spring up on the keyboard. But when I was
coming to the spot I said to myself: "If the cat jumps they'll
blame *him* for my bad playing." So I decided to take my
chances and really let myself go. The cat did not jump and
I wound up with a flourish, and that ended the first part of
the concert. I looked all around the stage during the
applause, but the cat was gone.

My friends came to see me during intermission. They had
not been able to wait until the concert was over to tell me
of the praise I had been receiving from the family that sat
behind them, the same one that had been so critical of the
previous concert. They had spoken to other people, too,
and decided to give a small lunch for me afterward.

All ended well, with two encores. And on my way out I
heard a girl in the crowd say:

"*He*'s the music box!"

THE DARK DINING ROOM

For some months my job was to play the piano in a dark dining room. An elderly lady was my only audience. She didn't care who played for her—and I can't say my heart was in my playing. But during the pauses between pieces— when neither of us spoke—the silence set my mind to working in unusual ways.

I had landed the job through the Pianists' Association. The boys there had often helped me find work with pop music bands. Recently they had even sponsored one of my concerts. Then, one afternoon, the director had called me aside:

"Hey, I've got a little something for you. It's not much, but, who knows"—I had already noticed the wicked gleam in his eye—"it could lead to bigger things. A rich widow wants you to play for her twice a week. The sessions are to last an hour each and she'll pay a buck and a half a session."

He broke off and slipped out for a moment because they were calling him from the next room.

He had expected I would find it depressing to work for such low wages and had spoken half-jokingly, but also cajolingly, because work was scarce and I would be wise to grab the first opportunity that came along.

I would have loved to be able to tell him how happy the offer made me, but it would have been difficult for me to explain, and for him to understand, why entering unknown homes was so important to me.

When he returned I was on a cloud, all puffed up at the thought that the widow must have heard my concert, or my name, or seen my picture or articles about me in the papers, and I asked him:

"Did she say it had to be me?"

"Not really. She just wanted a pianist."

"To play good music?"

"I don't know. You can discuss that with her. Here's the address: ask for Miss Moppet."

It was a two-story house with marble balconies. I was impressed by the oversized entrance hall with walls of even finer marble than the balconies, their shades of color indistinct, as if they weren't really living there but were still in their faraway country of origin.

A pair of beveled windows watched me. It was the double door to the patio, with twin panes extending far down the slight frame: I thought of a lady in a low-cut or low-waisted dress. The curtains on the door were so flimsy it seemed I had surprised it in its underwear. Through the curtains I could see a swaying fern almost as tall as a palm.

A good while after I had rung the bell, an enormous woman emerged from the depths of the patio. Until she had opened the door I could not quite believe she had a cigarette dangling from her lips. Without greeting me, she asked:

"You the one from the *Pie*anists' Association?"

When I nodded she let me in, turned on her heel and led

the way back across the patio. The image of her talking mouth stuck with me: I kept seeing the lit cigarette twisting between her fleshy lips. We had reached a corner of the patio that was invisible from the entrance hall. Lowering myself into an armchair to which she had directed me with a look through half-shut eyes, I asked:

"Are you Miss Moppet?"

"If Miss Moppet heard you call me that she'd fire us both. But never mind, I was expecting you."

She opened the door to the dining room. Its glass had a scene with storks etched on it. Her blonde head was at a level where it coincided with the head of a stork that was about to swallow a fish it held in its beak.

I barely had time to look around the wide patio full of plants and lined with colorful glazed tile when the big blonde reappeared with a dessert plate. She sat in a chair next to my armchair, laying the plate on another chair, and said:

"She won't be long. I've taught her to ring the bell whenever she comes in from the street. I told her if she left the door open she'd have thieves."

For a long moment I couldn't find my voice, as if I had to search my pockets for it, until I managed to say:

"With her good taste, no wonder . . ."

She didn't let me finish.

"It's not *her* taste—a real cultured gent used to live here, a *doctor*. He lost his daughter and sold *her* the house when she was still a young girl—but already a widow and rich."

She flicked her cigarette ash on the dessert plate, nearly knocking it off the chair.

"What the doctor didn't have was a *pie*ano. *She* bought that—and lived to regret it, I can tell you."

I looked at her wide-eyed and possibly open-mouthed as

well. She seemed to like my way of listening because the standoffishness she'd shown at first had disappeared and she chattered away until the lady of the house arrived. Her favorite topic was anything connected with Miss Moppet: no matter what else she might be talking about, it seemed she couldn't help gradually and almost inadvertently falling back on it.

I asked her:

"Is Miss Moppet as tall as you?"

She laughed.

"When we moved into this house she made me lower all the mirrors—too bad if I have to stoop to see myself."

Suddenly, and irrelevantly—as if she had left a pot simmering and it was time to stir it again—she returned to the topic of the *pie*ano.

"She lived to regret it, all right. She bought it so a boyfriend she had could play it. He wrote a tango and called it 'Moppet' in her honor. Then, one night, he left for Buenos Aires. He hadn't wanted her to see him off, but she insisted on going. I couldn't stop her and went along. He was late for the boat . . . and when he showed up he had another woman on his arm and they ran up the gangway together."

I started to reach out to catch the dessert plate, which seemed about to fall again. She saw my arm twitch and told me not to bother. But just then the bell rang and she swept up the plate and vanished through the scene of the glass storks.

A few seconds later I made out a purple shadow pressed against the door to the entrance hall and heard nails rapping impatiently on the glass. The big blonde opened the door and a short woman stepped right in and started talking about the butcher. I had the impression that one of the short woman's eyes was fixed on me. I saw her in profile, and, although elderly, she did not seem ugly. But I remember what happened when she began to turn her face slowly toward me: it was such a narrow face that it gave me a shock. I had felt the same effect coming around to the front of a house built at a sharp angle, on a diagonal: it could almost have been said that face existed only in profile, with no front except for the bit of space between the eyes, which were skewed, the left one aimed straight ahead, the right one to the right. To compensate for the face's narrowness, her hair was done up in a promontory that displayed its various colors—black, several shades of brown and strands of dirty white—and ended in a tight knot where all the colors combined.

Her eye fastened on me all the way, she crossed the patio without a word, until she stood before me:

"So you're the pianist? You want to come in?"

She carried her promontory toward the dining room door. In spite of all that hair, the top of her head barely reached the foot of the stork with the fish in its beak. When we pulled the chairs back from the large table, the sound they made echoed like a roar. It was a dark room with dark furniture and its own dark silence—in which her voice sounded like a desecration.

"In my family," she was saying (now both her eyes strayed, so I didn't know which one to look at because I couldn't tell which one was looking at me), "in my family we've always respected music. And I want music played in this house twice a week."

She was called away because the butcher had arrived. She got up swinging a long gold chain that hung over her breast in several loops and a final coil tied to the left side of her waist.

On the sideboard, facing the patio, stood two oval trays that still caught a bit of evening light. A painting of fish that hung over the sideboard also gave off a dim glow. I felt my hand going numb from running my palm over the table cover, which was turning a dark green. When Miss Moppet returned I tried to get down to business.

"What kind of music would Madam like me to play?"

"What do you mean what kind of music? The kind everyone plays—whatever is in fashion."

"All right. Can I try the piano?"

"You should have done that already."

"Where is it?"

"In the corner, right behind you. Don't you see it?"

"I'm sorry, Madam, there isn't much light."

She drew up a footlamp, grumbling as she tripped over it. When she managed to plug it in, its light fell on a small cherry red piano. After trying it and saying "all right" again, I remembered to ask:

"At what intervals do you want the pieces?"

"What's that about intervals?"

"How long do you want the pause to last between one piece and the next?"

"The same as in the Japanese Café."

I said my last "all right" and took my leave after fixing the date when I was to begin.

Again, when I arrived that afternoon for my first session, the lady was out. The big blonde showed me in to the dining room, where she kept me entertained with her chatter. Her name was Dorothy, but ever since she was a child she'd had people call her Dolly, after an unhappy heroine who had thrown herself into the sea in a film that was popular back in those days. Later I found out neither she nor the lady of the house knew that their names meant the same thing, and, for some mysterious reason, I was afraid to enlighten them on the subject. Now she was telling me about a brother of Miss Moppet's. The lady had made him find a job, promising that if he "behaved" she would transfer a property she had—a small house in the Prado, next to a summer home also owned by her—to his name.

By then the palm of my hand had fallen asleep: I had been stroking the embossed leather of a chair next to me.

When Miss Moppet rang the bell I moved my chair to the piano, put my music on the stand and waited for instructions. She came in reaching for the left side of her waist to draw out a tiny watch that hung from the end of her long chain—a combination as disproportionate as if she'd had a lapdog on a well chain—and said: "You may begin." She sat at the far end of the table, for some reason running her hand over the table cover, just as I had done.

I started to play a tango. But the big blonde appeared in the middle of the piece, raising her voice over the sound of the piano:

"Miss Moppet, dear, where did you put the teapot?"

Miss Moppet had a different notion of what was going on: she was paying for the music and took it seriously, as if she had hired a theater company for a private performance, and here was this creature interrupting the show and spoiling the dignity and aristocratic refinement she wanted for her home. She stood up angrily and said:

"Don't ever come in like that, screeching and interrupting the music."

The big blonde wheeled around and left the room, but almost at once Miss Moppet called after her:

"Dolly!"

The big blonde's voice answered:

"Miss Moppet?"

"Fix the *mate*. The pot's in the bathroom."

I had finished the tango and was looking around at the furniture, remembering the doctor. There was something about the house that made me think of a sacred tomb hastily abandoned and then invaded by these two women who desecrated its most hallowed memories. On the sideboard stood a gaping package of *mate*, and the crystal goblets in a glass cabinet had been crowded back indecently to make room for a bottle of ordinary table wine.

Dolly brought the *mate* in silence. I started to play a "sentimental waltz" and no one said another word. Miss Moppet sipped her *mate*, gazing out at the patio. Like the oval trays, she seemed to be there only to reflect the dying light. I didn't ask to have the footlamp turned on. I played a few pieces from memory. During the intervals I let my thoughts wander. Miss Moppet not only seemed unaware of the music: she had left her *mate* on the table, her hand resting motionless by it.

The next sessions they had everything ready when I arrived, and after Miss Moppet had drunk her first *mates* and I had played my first tangos she sat motionless and I followed my thoughts.

I had been working there for over a month when it happened once again that Miss Moppet's *mate* wasn't ready. She came up to me a bit nervously and said she would be listening as usual, but from another room. Again, that afternoon, she ordered Dolly to prepare her *mate*, reminding her the pot was in the bathroom.

When Dolly returned and saw the lady wasn't in the room she seized on her chance to tell me:

"Today it's been exactly two years since we saw Miss

Moppet's boyfriend run up the gangway with the other woman on his arm, so you'd better watch it, *pet*."

I didn't appreciate being *petted* by her and was about to object when the lady came in. All afternoon, Miss Moppet kept appearing and disappearing, like a drizzle between sunny skies.

A few days later they sent for me from the Pianists' Association and the director told me:

"Miss Moppet was here to ask for another pianist. She says you're the gloomy type and your music doesn't cheer her up. I said: 'He's the best we have, lady,' and tried to convince her you'd change your repertory and liven things up a bit."

I hated going to the next session, depressed at the thought of having to "liven things up" and also having to tell Dolly not to *pet* me. But a surprise awaited me in the dining room: Miss Moppet's brother was visiting and he turned out to be someone I knew. He stood up at once to shake my hand and said:

"How are you, Maestro? Congratulations on your concert—I know it was a big success. I saw the articles and pictures in the papers."

Miss Moppet's eyes shot looks right and left, as if their defect made them naturally suspicious, and her voice burst on us:

"What? Why didn't someone tell me you were in the papers?"

Her brother went on:

"That's right! We were even in the same paper once, only two columns apart. It was when I was named secretary of the club."

"And the president congratulated you," Miss Moppet broke in. And then she said: "Come on, this way."

I had kept my eyes lowered modestly, and first I saw her purple skirt go out the door, and, right behind it, her brother's black trousers.

Then I started to remember the café where I had been playing when I met the young brother. They called him Spider in those days, I don't know why, or why he put up with the name, considering his mean temper. And now I was intent on fitting Miss Moppet, with her purple dress, into the story of this young man. She was a latecomer to the idea I had of him, and, although it might not be the best moment for such an enterprise, I couldn't help reviewing everything I knew about him in the light of this sister I had not imagined before. And it seemed she, too, was straining to enter the picture, as if pushing her way onto a crowded bus.

The café was hidden behind some trees, in a building with overhanging balconies. Anyone trying to go in had to contend with the door, which had a large black knob shaped like a tailor's iron. The moment you put your hand on the knob it spun without catching in either direction. It seemed the door was laughing at you. If someone inside happened to be sitting close enough—which meant no more than a few feet away—to be seen through the dirty glass, he might signal you with a gesture that meant "Come on! Push!" Then, if you gave a shove, the door would complain but let you through—although as soon as you had your back to it, it got its revenge by bouncing on its spring and slamming on you.

The smoke in the room swallowed up most of the dim lamplight and the colors people wore. It also enveloped the thin columns holding up the balcony where we played. There were three of us: a violin, a flute, and I. It was the smoke, it seemed, that had raised us in our balcony, almost to the white ceiling, as if to a heaven from where we had been hired to send down—through the clouds of smoke—the music no one seemed to be listening to. As soon as we finished a piece we were invaded by the murmur of the crowd. It was a loud, steady murmur, and in winter we were in a sleepy haze. From our seats we would lean over the edge of the balcony and let our eyes roam over the vague shapes below. Occasionally we would focus on a group of heads gathered into the white circle of a marble table, with small dark spots that were cups of coffee held up to their noses. One of the waiters was nearsighted and followed behind his thick glasses, which slowly advised him of an object's location and then guided him to it, his nose pointing right and left like a compass needle until it had found its target. On one hand he balanced a tray, and with the other he groped his way through the crowd. He had been divorced and remarried and had a house full of children. Seen from above, he was like a small boat making its way between islands, running aground half the time and unloading everything at the wrong ports.

All this happened at night. During the evening show, though, things were different, and not only because one knew it was evening instead of night or because there was a different audience that ordered different drinks. At that time of day the members of a political club with headquarters above the café came down and filled two tables in the rear. They were Spider's friends and admirers, and had come to see him. Before engaging him in conversation they watched him for a long while from their far corner, waiting for him to finish mixing the cocktails behind the bar. By then a bright light had come on: it shone on his white vest, white shirt, and very white teeth. Opposed to all that whiteness was the black of his tie, brows, eyes, and decidedly black hair. In his face the opposite combined: it was olive-colored—or a shade darker in spots, especially above the brows, which would have seemed immense if he hadn't shaved them down to two shoestring lines.

Nothing stirred in that face during the mixing ceremony, nor could you have told at what precise moment he picked up a bottle or put it down: the eye wasn't quick enough to register the split second it took an object to respond to one of his movements. It seemed the bottles and glasses, as well as the ice and strainers, had a life of their own and had been given complete freedom of action. It didn't matter if they did not obey him at once: they knew their responsibility and would act in good time. The only moment one could satisfy the base need to measure cause and effect was when he was tossing the mix vigorously in the cocktail shaker. At one such moment I happened to go by one of the tables in the rear and I heard someone say: "Shows he's a man of character!"

Spider knew which cocktail would be most in demand at any given time, so he prepared enough for several glasses. After shaking a mix he distributed it in the glasses with quick flips of his wrist. It was a gesture of such precision it seemed to embody some secret of nature: each drop fell into its glass home as if by family instinct. After relieving the shaker of its first load—which might be of some dark race—he prepared another—of a white race this time—and distributed the new families of drops just as he had the previous ones. Then came the moment we had all been eagerly awaiting: he took a tall spoon, spun the families in each glass around with a few deft strokes until they blended, and, lo and behold, the glasses began to sing, each with its own sound, producing unexpected combinations. And that was the one surprise of the day: the unpredictable way in which apparently similar glasses combined the music of mysteriously different sounds.

Suddenly, Spider would slip into his trim black jacket, and, donning his flat-brimmed hat, which sat stiff and sharp as a razor, he would circle around to the front of the bar, where the owner himself—his friend and coreligionist—would serve him a brandy. By then the politicians at the table in the rear were leaving for the club, where they would be expecting him. On several occasions, as I watched them go, I remembered something I knew about him. He had once had a girlfriend who had asked his permission to go to a dance and insisted on going even when the permission was denied. He had soon found out and broken off with words that were like loud hard slaps. One afternoon the girl had come in looking for him, but he'd had the waiter throw her out, and shortly afterward she had poisoned herself.

At first he had been very friendly toward us, but then one day he had dropped us. There was a row of colored lights on the balcony railing and he was in charge of turning them on when the orchestra struck up. The violin had noticed Spider was in the habit of turning them on just as we sounded the first chord of our opening piece, and one night we decided to play a joke on him: we suddenly struck out a chord at random. The blast combined with the burst of light caught people's attention and there was some applause, but Spider paced furiously back and forth behind the bar, as if about to spring on us. He stopped talking to us—but years later, when I was no longer playing in the café, he saw me in the street one day and came over with a big open smile to say hello, and we ended up friends again.

Now he was just as friendly when he came back through the dark dining room on his way out to say good-bye and assured me:

"You can relax. Your job is safe in this house."

I was relieved—my concert had helped, after all. But I knew something was still bothering me, although I couldn't think what it was. Soon I remembered: I had to tell Dolly not to *pet* me. And just then she ran in on tiptoes, holding out her hand: I couldn't avoid shaking it. After a breathless moment she said:

"Good for you, *pet*," and ran out.

During the next sessions Miss Moppet sat silently in the room again, sipping her *mate*, and I was able to let my thoughts roam at will.

Starting that day when my position in the house had been assured, it was a long time before Miss Moppet interrupted my thoughts. She sipped her *mate* until the water went cold and then her eyes stopped straying and she, too, settled in to gaze at her memories. But one evening near the end of the session, when the room was very dark, she spoke to me. At that moment she was the farthest thing from my mind, and when her words struck me and the silence collapsed I made an awkward move and kicked the piano. While the sound box was still reverberating she let out a coarse laugh. Then she asked, for the second time:

"What did you say was the name of that nice little tango you just played?"

My first impulse was to tell her, but then I decided the title—"Hello and Goodbye"—might sound like an allusion to the boyfriend who had shipped out with another woman, and instead I switched on the light, intending to hand her the score so she could see for herself. But she read my mind and stopped me before I could get up:

"No, just say it."

I did, in a strangled voice.

She made me repeat it and then said:

"Heavens! And it isn't even Carnival!"

I hadn't wanted the title of the song to bring back her bad memories, but I was drawn to the tragedies in other lives and one of the purposes I had been hoping to achieve with my concert was to make new acquaintances who would help me find my way into unknown homes.

One afternoon when I was thinking about people's tragedies I caught the pungent smell of roast suckling in the dark dining room and said to Dolly:

"What a stink! Can't you get that thing out of here? It's a shame, in such a nice dining room . . ."

She was annoyed:

"Why, *pet*, don't you think suckling is a dining room smell? Would you rather have it in the living room?"

There it was, on the sideboard, in a blue enameled serving dish, covered with a white cheesecloth. Dolly had left the room in a huff, but soon she came back in and said:

"I know what's eating you, *pet*: you'd like a piece."

I protested vigorously, but she kept shushing me, trying to stifle my voice and grab my hands. While I waved them around and she reached after them, we drew groping figures in the air and I felt the wind raised by the four hands blow on my hot face. Finally, I put my hands behind my back, resigned to hear her say:

"Listen, *pet*, come around the back way tonight at ten o'clock. There's a tree in the street with thick branches reaching to the kitchen window. I can't let you in the front door because there'd be gossip and I'm engaged to be married."

I tried to interrupt but she had managed to trap one of my hands, and while I snatched it back and then wondered about my violent gesture, she was explaining:

"Just climb the tree and come in—at ten. I'll have the suckling ready, with a bottle of wine, and we'll have some fun."

Finally I was able to say:

"What if Miss Moppet catches me? Do you think I want to lose my job over a piece of meat?"

She watched me for a moment in silent disbelief, then she said:

"By nine thirty I'll have put her to bed sound asleep and I won't even need to undress her until morning."

"You mean she's such a heavy sleeper?"

At that she laughed so hard she collapsed in a chair. She kicked off her red shoes, curled her bare feet around the legs of the chair, and said:

"The moment you leave, she starts drinking wine. She drinks some more with her dinner, goes on drinking after her dessert, and when she's dead drunk I put her to bed."

What she saw in my face emboldened her and she went on:

"There she is with her fancy ways, carrying on about what's right and proper, forbidding me to talk to her visitors, even her brother, and then she goes and gets drunk as a pig."

I hung my head and she asked:

"So, how about it, *pet*? You want suckling tonight or don't you?"

I started to make up clumsy excuses, one of the lamest being that I was afraid of falling off the tree. She understood and stepped back into her shoes, curling her lip as she left, saying:

"Go on, poor baby—and remember to wipe your nose."

One afternoon, a short time later, Dolly didn't come out to receive me. Instead there was a bewhiskered footman in a vest and striped sleeves, who handed me an envelope with my wages and a letter from Miss Moppet informing me that my services were no longer needed.

After that I spent some time without work, and was even on the point of climbing the tree into Dolly's room.

One summer morning I was very depressed, thinking about all my failures. My concert not only hadn't brought me money, it had not fulfilled any of my expectations or even opened the doors of any unknown homes to me, except for the one with the dark dining room, where I had caught only the faintest whiff of tragedy in Miss Moppet's drinking and none at all in Dolly.

I was dragging these thoughts along, strolling up an avenue in the Prado with my hands clasped behind my back, when someone tickled one of my palms. I swung around and it was Dolly. She said:

"I saw you go by my window and I followed you."

"So you're no longer at Miss Moppet's?"

"That old bag of bones? She'll remember me for the rest of her life. One afternoon I told her: 'You can start looking for someone else—I'm leaving tomorrow.' She was stunned and asked: 'What did I do now?' So I let her have it: 'It's not you but me, dear. I'm getting married . . . to your brother.' She started to shake all over and foam at the mouth, because that very morning she'd put the little house where we're living in her brother's name."

We had been walking along, but when she mentioned

Spider and the house I stopped to look at her. She took my hand and said:

"Come on, I'll show you the house. Spider's always at work at this time."

I freed my hand and said:

"Maybe some other day."

She flew into a rage, just like when I had refused to climb her tree, and, curling her lip at me, said:

"Get out of here, you poor *pie*anist."

The Green Heart

Today, in this room, for several hours, I've been happy. So what if I've left the table full of pinpricks. If only I didn't have to change the newspaper spread out on it: it's been there for a while and I've grown fond of it. It's a greenish color, with orange headlines over a picture of some quintuplets.

Toward evening, as the heat died down, I was on my way home, tired after a long walk. I had gone out to pay an installment due on the overcoat I bought last winter. I was a bit disappointed with life but careful not to get run over by a car. Thinking of my room, I remembered the bald heads of the quintuplets, which reminded me of fingertips. Back at my table, with my bare arms on the green paper and a round spot of light shining on the books I've been underlining in colors, I opened my pencil box and took out my tiepin. I turned the pin over between my fingers until they were numb, absently poking holes in the quintuplets' eyes.

Once the head of that pin had been a small green stone worn by the sea into the shape of a heart, then the heart had been attached to the pin on a mount embedded—like a filling—in a square the size of a horse's tooth. At first, when I turned the pin over between my fingers, it brought nothing special to mind, but suddenly I began to think of my mother, then a horse-drawn tram, the lid of a candy jar, a trolley, my grandmother, a French lady who wore a paper hat and was always sprinkled with tiny feathers, her daughter Ivonne who had a hiccup as loud as a scream, a dead man who used to sell chickens, a doubtful neighborhood in a city in Argentina where I slept on the floor one whole winter under layers of newspapers, an elegant neighborhood in another city where I slept like a king under a pile of blankets, and, finally, an ostrich and a cup of coffee.

All these memories lived in some part of me that was like a small lost town known only to itself, cut off from the rest of the world. For many years no one had been born or died there. The founders of the town had been my childhood memories. Then, years later, some foreigners had arrived: my memories of Argentina. This afternoon I had the feeling I was in that town for a rest, as if misery had granted me a holiday.

During much of my childhood in Montevideo, we lived on the Hill. The people climbing the street toward my house carried their bodies bent forward, as if looking for something among the stones, and going the other way they bent backward, although it meant tripping over the stones, as if they were too proud to look down. In the afternoons my aunt took me to a high knoll near the old fortress. From there you could see the ships at dock with their many tall and short masts like fishbones. When the fortress cannon was fired at sundown, we started home.

One afternoon my mother said she was taking me to visit a grandmother who lived in the port area, and that I'd see a trolley. And yet I had misbehaved that morning: I'd been sent to the store to get a box of starch but instead I'd bought loose starch, and gotten scolded. A bit later I'd been sent with some change to buy *mate*, and since I'd insisted it had to be in a box, the grocers—who were friends of the family—had put it in a shoebox, but I'd done something else wrong: I'd come home with the change and gotten scolded for not paying. Next I'd been sent with paper money for some noodles and I'd remembered to pay—but I hadn't accepted the change so I wouldn't be scolded again. At home they were alarmed when I didn't have the change and they had sent me back for it. The grocers scribbled my mother a note, which had seemed to calm her, at last. I had peeked and it said: "The change is in the noodles."

That afternoon all the women in the house tried to fasten a big starched collar on me. The only one who could handle the metal buttons that attached it to my shirt was another grandmother—not the one who lived in the docks and wore the pin with the green heart on her breast. This grandmother had hot, pudgy fingers, and when she stuck them inside the collar to fasten it, she pinched my neck and I choked a couple of times and nearly threw up.

Out in the street, the sun made my patent leather shoes shine and I hated scuffing them on the stones as I hopped along after my mother, who was leading me by the hand, almost running. But I was happy, and when she didn't answer my questions I answered them myself, until suddenly she said:

"Will you stop your chattering! You sound like the loony with the seven horns."

A moment later we passed the loony's place. It was an ancient house with crumbling walls. Tied with wires to a window grille were some cans through which the loony bellowed at the people who went by. He was a large fat man in a checkered shirt. Sometimes his tiny, thin wife could be seen trying to make him shut up, but in a minute he was clinging to the bars again, shouting himself hoarse.

Then we went by the butcher shop, where I spent entire mornings waiting in lines, in a silence broken only by a loud thrush that kept singing the same boring song.

At the foot of the Hill was the street where you caught the horse-drawn tram. It came blowing its horn, with a clatter of hooves, rattling chains and the sound of the long whip snapping over the horses' heads. I used to kneel on one of its two long benches to look out the window. After a long while I had to hold my nose as we went by the packing houses near a stream. Sometimes, rumbling over the bridge, I forgot to hold my nose and caught a whiff of the smell. That afternoon we got off at the Paso Molino stop and went into a candy shop, where my mother chatted with the lady who owned the place. After a long while, the lady said:

"Your boy's looking at the candy."

And, pointing to the different jars, she asked me:

"Would you like one of these? How about these here?"

I told my mother I wanted the lid of a candy jar. They both laughed and the lady brought me the lid of another jar that had broken recently. My mother didn't want me to carry it in the street, but the lady wrapped it up and tied it with a string to which she attached a small wooden handle.

It was evening when we left the shop, and in the middle of the street I saw a lit gallery. As my mother led me toward it, I admired its colored windows. She was telling me it was a trolley, but coming on it from behind I went on thinking it was a gallery. At that moment a bell clanged and the "gallery" let out a loud sigh and slowly heaved forward. At first it barely moved and the people I could make out inside sat still as dummies in a show window, but we didn't reach it in time and soon it was far away, slipping around a bend between some trees.

My grandmother's house was on a street near the docks. We crossed a long patio, after which we had to climb some stairs, and then we went through the dining room, where there was a table with a platter full of pastries. My mother had instructed me not to ask for one, so I told my grandmother:

"If you'll give me one I'll ask, if not I won't."

My grandmother was amused, and one of the times she hugged and kissed me I saw the green heart on her breast and asked her for it, but she didn't give it to me. Before dinner I was allowed to play with a little girl named Ivonne. The girl's mother wore a hat made of newspaper and her face and kerchief were sprinkled with tiny white feathers.

That night before going to sleep I saw a small bright ladder climbing the wall by the bed: it was the light coming in the slats of the shutters. Then I slept through the noise that got everyone else up in the middle of the night, when the lid of the candy jar slipped out from under my pillow and crashed on the floor. The next morning, while I drank my milky coffee, I kept hearing a strange screech and I was told it was Ivonne hiccuping—she seemed to do it on purpose. After breakfast she invited me to see a dead man in a room across the back patio. Her mother didn't want to let her go because of her hiccups. I looked at the mother's paper hat: the feathers, that morning, were purple. Then I thought of the dead man. Ivonne was saying:

"He's all right, Mom, we know him. It's that little old man who used to sell chickens."

She led me by the hand and I hung on, afraid to let go. The little old man was alone, under a white sheet. Ivonne not only went on hiccuping and screeching but wanted to blow out all the candles around the coffin. Suddenly her mother came in, grabbed her by the arm, and dragged her out at top speed and me with her, still clutching her hand.

That same morning my grandmother gave me the green heart—and a few years ago these old memories were joined by some new events.

I was in a city in Argentina where the man in charge of organizing my concerts had done everything wrong from the beginning, until in the end nothing could be done. Meanwhile I'd had time to sample the downtown hotels from top to bottom and landed in a doubtful neighborhood in a suburb, where a friend rented a room. My friend's parents had sent him a bed, and he let me have the top mattress. The nights were very cold and I had spent most of my money buying old newspapers, which I spread over a thin blanket and covered with an overcoat lent to me by the concert organizer. One night I woke my friend with a wild shriek. I also woke up and found myself holding a pillow against the wall: I'd been dreaming there was a hole in the wall and a smiling loony had stuck his head through it, wearing a hat made of newspaper. After thinking about it for a while, forcing myself to stay awake—I was afraid of going back to sleep and having the nightmare return—I remembered the hat worn by Ivonne's mother.

I was so depressed, a few evenings later, strolling through the lights downtown, that suddenly I decided to pawn the green heart and go to a movie. After the show that night, I worked up the courage to write another friend I had in Buenos Aires asking for a loan. I already owed this friend a lot of money, but I could risk it because now the arrange-ments for my next concert, in a neighboring town, were looking good. That same night I thought of the lady with the newspaper hat again and decided to find out from my mother, who might know, what the hat meant and why the lady was always sprinkled with feathers. In my letter I mentioned remembering the lady always picking at something on her lap, as if plucking a bird.

When the money came I redeemed the green heart and moved on to the neighboring town, where everything went well from the start and I was able to stay in a comfortable hotel. I had been given a room with three beds, a double and two singles, all to myself, with permission to choose my bed. So, after a somewhat excessive dinner, I took the double bed and piled all the blankets from the other beds on it. The furniture in the room was dark with age and the mirrors were blurred and almost blind to the light.

The concert ended early and afterward I had time— before the stores closed—to buy books, colored pencils for underlining, and an indexed notebook I'd find some use for later on. As soon as I'd had dinner and taken the books to bed with me I thought of the movies and couldn't resist the temptation: I got dressed again and went to see an old film in which a couple exchanged long kisses. I was very happy and didn't want to go to bed, so I sat in a café where there was an ostrich. It was a very tame ostrich which wandered around with slow steps among the tables. I was staring at it absently, turning my tiepin over between my fingers, when suddenly it lunged toward me, plucked the pin from my hand and swallowed it. I watched in horror as the pin worked its way down the bird's throat like a bulge in a sock. I would have liked to squeeze it back up, but the waiter arrived with my coffee and said:

"Never mind, sir."

"Not at all! It's only an heirloom!"

"If you'll allow me, sir," the waiter was saying, raising a

hand like a policeman stopping a car. "The ostrich has swallowed all sorts of things before and always returned them. So, rest assured—tomorrow or the next day you'll have your pin back, good as new."

The next day the newspapers carried the reviews of my concert. But one of them appeared under a front-page headline that said: "Pianist's stay depends on ostrich," and was full of jokes.

That same day I received a letter from my mother in which she said Ivonne's mother made powder puffs, that the swan down she used for them came in all colors, and that her plucking must have been when she was picking at the down in its envelope, because sometimes it was packed in very tight.

The following day the waiter at the cafe brought me my pin and said:

"What did I tell you, sir? It's a very reliable ostrich—it always gives everything back."

The next time I come to this little lost town for a rest, maybe the number of inhabitants will have increased with new memories. But the old greenish newspaper is almost sure to be here, as well as the quintuplets and the holes poked in their eyes with the pin.

"LOVEBIRD" FURNITURE

The publicity for this furniture took me by surprise. I had been spending a month's vacation at a nearby resort, not wanting to know what was going on in town. When I got back it was very hot and that same night I went to the beach. I returned to my room fairly early and in a bit of a bad mood because of what had happened to me on the trolley. I had caught the trolley at the beach and found a spot on a bench facing the aisle. Because it was still very hot, I had folded my jacket on my lap, and—since I was wearing a short-sleeved shirt—my arms were bare. Suddenly one of the persons going by in the aisle leaned over me and said:

"With your permission, please . . ."

I said at once, "It's yours."

But by then—already too late—I was frightened. In a flash several things had happened. The first was that even before he had finished asking for my permission or I'd had a chance to answer, the man was already rubbing something cold—for some reason it felt like spit—on my bare arm. And by the time I'd finished saying "It's yours," I had felt a needle prick and seen the large syringe with letters on it. At the same time, a fat woman across the aisle had said:

"I'm next."

I must have jerked my arm because the man with the needle said:

"Careful or it'll hurt. Just hold still . . ."

In a minute he withdrew the needle and—the passengers all around me were smiling: they had seen my face—he started rubbing on the arm of the fat woman, who watched appreciatively. I noticed the large syringe squirted only a small amount of liquid, the plunger bouncing right back out. Then I read the yellow letters down the side: LOVEBIRD FURNITURE. I was too embarrassed to ask what the injection was for and decided to find out the next day from the newspapers. But the moment I got off the trolley I thought, "It can't be a tonic—it has to be something with an immediate visible effect if it's really a promotional stunt." I still couldn't figure out how it would work, but I was very tired and made up my mind to ignore it. In any case, I was confident the Lovebird people wouldn't be allowed to dope the public with some drug. Before going to sleep I wondered whether they might be trying to induce a state of physical pleasure or well-being. I was still awake when I heard a birdsong inside me. It didn't have the quality of a remembered sound or one reaching you from the outside. It felt abnormal, like a new disease, but with an ironic twist to it as well, as if the disease were happy and had started to sing. These sensations soon wore off and were followed by something more concrete: a voice—also ringing in my head—that said:

"Hello, hello, this is your Lovebird station . . . Hello, and welcome to our special broadcast. The persons sensitized to these transmissions. . . ." and so on.

I heard all this standing barefoot by my bed, without daring to turn on the light. I had jumped out of bed and frozen on the spot: I couldn't believe the sounds were in my head. I dropped back in bed, waiting to see what would happen next. The voice was giving instructions for buying Lovebird Furniture on the installment plan. Then suddenly it said:

"And now stay tuned for our first selection, the tango . . ."

Desperate, I pulled a heavy blanket over my head, but that only made the sound worse because the blanket muffled the street noise and I could hear what was going on inside my head more clearly. So I threw off the blanket and started to walk up and down the room, which helped a little—until I caught myself listening in secret, as if perversely determined to go on feeling sorry for myself. I got back into bed and, hanging on to the bedstead, heard the tango again, even louder than before.

When I'd had enough, I went out searching for other sounds to block the ones in my head. I thought of buying a newspaper, looking up the radio station's address and finding out how to neutralize the effects of the injection. But a trolley went by and I got on, and soon we were going over a rough spot in the rails and the clatter and jangle relieved me of the next tango. Then, suddenly, looking around the trolley, I saw another man with a syringe: he was injecting some children in the seats facing forward. I went up and asked him what I could do to neutralize the effects of an injection I had received an hour earlier. He stared at me in amazement and said:

"You don't like our programming?"

"Absolutely not."

"If you wait a few minutes you'll catch a soap opera."

"I couldn't bear it," I said.

He went on with the injections, shaking his head and

smiling. The tango was over and the voice was back with another sales pitch. Finally, the man of the injections said:

"Sir, haven't you seen the ad for Lovebird pills? It's in all the papers. If you don't like our programming, you simply take a pill and that's the end of it."

"But all the drugstores are closed at this time and I'm losing my mind!"

Just then I heard the announcer say:

"And now for a poem entitled 'My Favorite Armchair.' It's a sonnet composed specially for Lovebird Furniture."

Whereupon the man of the injections drew up close to me and whispered in my ear:

"I can fix things for you—another way. I'll only charge you a buck: you look like I can trust you. If you give me away I'll lose my job, because the company would rather have people buy the pills."

I pressed him to reveal his secret and he extended his hand and said:

"Let's have the buck first."

And after I had given him the money:

"Go soak your feet in hot water."

THE TWO STORIES

On the 16th of June, just before dark, a young man sat down at a small table where there were some writing materials. His intention was to capture a story and confine it in a notebook. For days he had been looking forward to the thrill of sitting down to write. He had promised himself to write the story very slowly, putting the best of himself into it. Finally, that afternoon, the moment had come. He worked in a toy shop and, while gazing at a slate board with red and blue beads strung across it on wires, he had suddenly realized he was ready to begin. He remembered another afternoon when he had been pondering a detail of the story and the manager of the shop had called him to account for not paying attention to his work; but his mood allowed him to efface all such ugly memories as soon as they appeared and go on with the thoughts that made him so happy. In the street, after work, these thoughts had also made him clumsy: his spirit freed, the minute he was out the door of the shop, he had delegated only a minimal part of himself to deal with the external world and get him home. While letting himself be drawn along by the small force to which he had entrusted the task of guiding him, he had concentrated heart and soul on his beloved story. At times the very intensity of his happiness had allowed him to abandon his happy thoughts for a moment to observe things in the street and try to find them interesting; but soon he returned to his story, still drawn along by the small force to which he had entrusted the task of guiding him.

In his room at last, he thought tidying up a bit before he got started might help him settle down. On the other hand, it seemed he would only keep stumbling over things, with his eyes, nose and forehead bumping into doors and walls. So in the end he decided to sit right down at the small table, which had short legs and was stained in walnut. After sitting down, he still had to get up once more to fetch a notebook in which he had written the date when the story began.

"The 16th of May was a Saturday and it must have been about nine in the evening when I met her. A moment ago I was remembering the person I was that night and the indifference I felt. I was also imagining that if the person I am now had told the person I was then, on the way out of her house, to note the date because it marked a great event, that other person would have accused this one of being decadent and falling into the trap of the commonplace. Nevertheless, the person I am now laughs at the one I was then, without stopping to ask himself whether the other would have been right or not. Moreover, he tries to recall even the smallest details relating to the other in order to laugh harder and to determine when and how the other started to be him. Further: he in interested in recalling the other because in that way he can also remember her. And not only that, if the truth be known: most of all, he is interested in writing this story so as to concentrate on her, and if he has made a note of the date when he met her, as the most commonplace lover would have done, it is because in this matter, even more than in everything else, he is not ashamed of not being original. A final warning: I worked out the date of that night with the help of a great friend who accompanied me that night and every other night until we were both convinced she loved me and not him."

When he finished this paragraph he stopped, got up, and started to pace back and forth. The room was very cramped. He could have set the small table aside for more space, but he liked to bend over it and read what he had written. He could also have gone on with his task, but he felt a secret anguish: in order to write, which meant bringing back the events of the past, he had to distort his memories, and he was too fond of those events to allow himself to distort them. He had sat down with the purpose of telling everything exactly as it had happened—and soon realized that this was impossible. And that was when his vague and secret anguish began.

If distorting his memories provoked such anguish in him, even deeper and more secret was the reason why, the next day, his anguish was gone. The reason was the same one that made writing the story necessary for him and more intensely pleasurable than he could explain. Just as his mind had erased the ugly memory of the toy shop manager rudely breaking into his most cherished thoughts, so now it hid from him his deepest and most desperate reason for wanting to write the story. His mind was able to hide the reason from him in spite of himself, using the interminable arguments he had developed in the passage he was writing, but he knew what it was: that she no longer loved him.

"The person I was before meeting her was too worn out to feel anything but indifference. If we had met years before I would have consumed my energies in loving her, but, not having found her then, I had consumed all my energies in thinking: I had done so much thinking that I had discovered how vain and false thought is when it regards itself as the preeminent force directing our lives. And yet, despite knowing this, I had gone on thinking, wasting my energies in thought, until I felt unpleasantly worn out. The person I am now can find rest in the anxiety of loving as he pleases, but between the 19th of May—three days after our story began—and the 6th of June—the day I myself interrupted the story because early the next morning I had to leave the town where she lived—in the space of the eighteen days between those two dates, I found rest as well in her large blue eyes. There was a wide space, too, between those eyes and their brows, and from this vaporous blue vault with its dab of light blue shadow seemed to come whatever it was in her eyes that released me from my thoughts and made me love her and reach out toward her with my whole being."

Although his mind hid the reason for writing the story from him, he may have felt something like a breath of misfortune following close behind him. It was, after all, his own mind that was preventing the impression that she no longer loved him from entering his thoughts, not only by burying it under the arguments with which he explained his motives for writing the story but also by clinging to the dates, as if securing them could also secure time and ensure her love for him. But that night of the 6th of June, after he had been with her, when he was in the hotel room with me, there was a moment when I detected the small burden of doubt still covertly weighing on his mind. It happened when he was telling me about her, wondering how long it would be before he saw her again, and, looking at the calendar, he noticed the number 6, which marked the day we were on, and said, "What a strange 6! It's like an animal sitting there . . . with its tail curled around it." That was when I saw the small burden of doubt still covertly weighing on his mind, and it must have been when he felt the breath of misfortune following close behind him.

Many years before, when his thinking had begun to torture him, he had found rest in another pair of blue eyes. From among the things he wrote then I have chosen the ones that best gave me the feeling for what he knew about himself. They were three fragments: *The Visit*, *The Street* and *The Dream*.

The Visit

Last night I was forced to attend to some thoughts. At moments they tired me and then I wanted to ignore them, if only for a few seconds, but I knew how important they were and that I couldn't overlook them. I allowed myself to rest only if someone interrupted me to ask me something; doing anything to distract myself would have been cheating. It was all right when some spontaneous event interrupted my thoughts, but I mustn't be lying in wait for the opportunity, on the contrary: even if the opportunity presented itself and I was glad for the rest, I had to regret the interruption. Something similar used to happen to me as a child when I had to recite a lesson I didn't know: if I needed to cough I was glad because it postponed the torment and, meantime, something important might happen to get me off the hook, but if I coughed on purpose the teacher caught on. Back in those days it would have seemed incredible to me that now, as a grownup, I'd oblige myself to do something as if the teacher were inside me.

Late in the night, my sisters brought a friend home with

them: a blonde girl with a big, clear, happy face. Before the night was out I told the girl that, looking at her, I had found rest from some thoughts that had been torturing me, and that I hadn't even realized when the thoughts had left me. She asked me what the thoughts had been like, and I told her they had been useless thoughts, that my head was like a gym where the thoughts were exercising, and that when she'd come in the thoughts had jumped out the windows.

The Street

Today I was remembering something that happened to me a few nights ago. That night I had met a woman and we were walking along a deserted street with forbidding white walls—factory or warehouse walls—on either side. The sidewalks seemed to have been born from the foot of the walls and were pleasant and friendly, but the streetlamps, which also seemed to have been born of the walls, wore little white hats and looked ridiculous. Since it was a moonless night, the lamps provided the only light, and it seemed that all they lit up was the air and the silence.

We were walking slowly. I had asked her not to speak to me for a while because I wanted to think about something. But I couldn't concentrate on that thought because my head was busy anticipating the moment when we'd leave one spot of light only to be caught up in the next one waiting to welcome us with the same stupid glow.

Suddenly I stopped and turned to look back at a train going by, several blocks behind us. She took a few more steps before stopping. I don't know what went through her mind. I had always been interested in the spectacle of the train going by, perhaps that was why I had turned to have another look at it; but, as it happened, that night I didn't feel like seeing it and hadn't meant to turn: it seemed as if at that moment I'd had someone else inside me who had come out without my consent, awakened by the clatter of the train. But then I became aware of yet another character, also sprung from me, who had gone on looking in the direction in which I had been walking and who was trying to impose his will on the previous one and pull me forward. If neither of these characters made sense and both wanted to break away from me, it was because I, my central character, was lost in my own complications. When I discovered this I tried to banish them both, get a grasp on reality and do something positive: so I looked at my hands. Then, on an impulse—it was another way of acting normal, coming back up to the surface of things—I caught up with her, and, since the street was still deserted, I kissed her. But her face was so strange when I kissed her that I realized it had been the same as with the train: I hadn't felt like kissing her, she had been kissed by the character who had turned to look back. And when I recovered and tried to be positive once more and took her arm to go on walking, I felt it was the character pulling straight ahead who had taken over again. After proceeding a few steps, I stopped to consider what was happening to me. I reached for a cigarette, put it between my lips, and, since the emery of the matchbox was worn and I couldn't get a spark, I left her in the middle of the street and went to strike my match on a wall.

When we had left the street behind and I was still thinking about what had happened to me there, I decided it wasn't the same street now as before, because my match had left a scar on a wall and gone on burning after I'd dropped it on the sidewalk born of that wall. Later, as if awakening from a dream and understanding what had happened in it, it seemed to me that the forbidding white walls had exchanged a look across the silent air lit by the lamps with the ridiculous little hats. Yet I can't say what the air or the silence was like that night in that street.

In spite of everything, I seem to be getting better all the time at writing about what happens to me. Too bad I'm also doing worse.

The Dream

In a dream that stretched on and on, I was in a bedroom, at night, seated in a chair next to a large bed. In the bed, under the covers, sat a girl. She was at the uncertain age between the child and the young woman. She was busy playing with some things that she seemed to think interested me, in constant motion, arranging the things around her. I found it hard to believe she could be so absorbed in her play, like any little girl busily engaged in the sort of activity that makes little girls happy, and at the same time feel the almost purely spiritual pleasure of a deep love like the one I knew she felt for me. At times she seemed to be reading my thoughts and carrying on intentionally: she liked to show off for me. But then suddenly she would stop playing and put her face very close to mine, with imploring eyes in which there was a hint of precocious sadness and pain. And suddenly she would slip me a quick kiss and go on playing as before, and I was convinced again that she was almost entirely absorbed in that game of hers which I couldn't figure out, with things I couldn't name, but which I pretended to watch with great interest, the way one feigns interest in a child's play when what one is really interested in is the child. At such moments she was just a child to me and I forgave her for what she was doing, the way one forgives a child who doesn't realize what a bother he's being. Her constant movement disturbed me by causing flickering interruptions in the waves of light and shadow coming from the footlamp with a green shade that stood opposite me, across the bed. There was also a touch of malice and premeditation in my forgiveness, because I knew that after indulging her for a while by showing an interest in her play I would ask for a kiss and she would cover me with hugs and kisses. Yet the minute I found myself kissing her, I felt I didn't love her, that I had been less than honest with myself, and that I was only trying to make the best of a complicated situation I had gotten myself into. Then I kissed her on the cheeks, trying to avoid the big tears pouring down them, because when I came in contact with them I felt obliged to lick them away and they were getting heavier and saltier all the time.

At moments, it seemed, I was in the chair pulled up very close to the bed, at other moments at some indefinite distance from the bed, watching myself seated on the chair in a light suit. When I was in the chair, with her next to me, I felt the reality of things without being aware that I felt it and I was in anguish, knowing I would catch myself either staring at her or doing things I hadn't meant to do. At other times she was playing so far away from me that not a sound came from any of her movements, which were like the gestures in silent movies shown without music. But then I became aware of that silence, and my own, and realized I couldn't say a word because the person sitting in the chair next to her probably wasn't me but someone else: her boyfriend, whom her parents knew and therefore allowed into her room to talk to her.

When I was far from the bed, watching myself seated in the chair, wearing my light suit, I was less anguished because she and "I"—the "I" at an indefinite distance from me—were much more in harmony with each other.

One of the times I was next to her, she had a baby's body and a very large head. She was playing with a sheet of paper, wrapping it around her shoulders or sometimes her entire tiny self. The paper made a loud crackling sound. Her parents, who were in the next room, leaned over the foot of their bed to watch us through the connecting door, which was open. Suddenly the mother appeared before me in her nightgown and said, "I never would have expected this victory of you." How those words made me suffer! . . . I felt my betrayal and the pain of the person betrayed as she yielded the victory to me . . . I looked for my hat, which was in a different place each time I reached for it: I couldn't get hold of it or leave. But then—suddenly I thought of this lie—I said. "My dear lady, the fact is that I'm very much in love with one of your daughter's girlfriends and I've stopped by to ask your daughter about the woman I love. I was going past the house and I saw the light on inside, so I was encouraged to ring the bell and she let me in." No sooner had I spoken than the girl was crying her eyes out and what I had said was beginning to come true . . .

"As usual, I understood only when I woke up. Then I began to put things together and it was like the pieces of a puzzle falling into place: her parents had been awakened by the crackling of the paper, she had cried because she knew I loved another woman, and so on. But what most amazed me when I woke up was to realize that her mother was really my mother.

"I was thinking about physical and human laws when I remembered an impression I'd had just before falling asleep and, again, as I came out of the dream: that I was watching my desires go by like clouds in a checkered sky. As the dream unfolded, the pattern had broken up, but I had gone on thinking and feeling as if it were still whole, the fragments somehow held together, forming a picture so well disguised behind another picture that my mother could be hidden in hers . . ."

The young man does not want to relate events in the order in which they occurred, nor does he want to speak about the characters connected with the woman he loved, not even the members of her family. Instead, he feels like doing something ridiculous, like describing her nose:

"Often while living at her side I concentrated all my attention and my adoration on her nose. It seemed to me, as well, that many strange thoughts drifting by in the air got into my head and came out my eyes to settle on her nose. I was convinced, then, that the way she sat, perfectly upright, the way she raised her head, sticking out her chin, and everything else that was physically and spiritually beautiful in her was a trick her nature played on the mind and soul to incline them toward adoring her nose.

"Her nose stood out in her face like a passionate desire not openly declared, rather, just barely insinuated and perhaps even taken back a little after having been insinuated, not without malice. When I looked her full in the face and her big blue eyes were half closed, her nose showed how sensitive it was to the tears streaming from those eyes and drying on it, their traces still faintly visible in the two tiny pale bumps shining on the very tip of the nose.

"When I was the one insinuating passionate desires—with words, now: clumsy words coming out to be heard like grotesquely shy men stepping out to dance for the first time—it was her nose that seemed to be listening and—since her eyes were almost shut—even looking at me. And when she leaned out the window to see what was going on in the street, it seemed her nose was waiting for the opera glasses that would slowly settle on it."

"I can't spend time thinking why I need to explain the horrible thought floating around in my mind today. The fact is that right now I feel like spreading it out on this page.

"First I sat on the bed and gazed at the little table with the walnut stain, then I looked around at the number of other things in my room . . . I realize I feel like saying what all the things in my room are like so I can put off remembering exactly how the thought came to me, but I won't torture myself all that much over it, since it's only the first time I have to remember it . . . Suddenly I felt a clear space inside my mind, where a sort of airplane was floating. I'll assume my eyes were looking outward as well as inward and that, being round, when they moved looking inward they also moved looking outward, which explains why I was—if only vaguely—aware of the objects in the room. But I was focusing my attention on the airplane floating in the clear space inside me.

"Then it happened that the part of my eyes absently looking outward came—as the most commonplace lover's eyes might have come—on a picture of her which stood on the little table with the walnut stain, and at that point I shifted my attention from the airplane inside me to the picture outside. When I tried to return to the airplane it had vanished into the clear space. I told myself, 'It'll be back in a while—the delay is because it's being loaded.' But when it reappeared it didn't just seem loaded—it wasn't the same airplane. And it seemed to be headed straight toward me, toward my stupid self of that moment, and all I could think of doing was to pull out a cloth from some other part of my mind and try to wave it past . . . But instead I must have flagged it down because it came and smashed right into me, blowing up my head and all the hidden places of my stupid self."

I think it will be a long time before I can get over my amazement at what happened to me today: I spoke to the young man of the story and he told me he doesn't want to go on writing it and may never feel like taking it up again.

Too bad he feels that way, because after gathering so much information that I find interesting I won't be able to make use of it for this story. But I'll be sure to keep these notes, because they will always tell another story—the one that took shape in reality when a young man tried to capture the one in his mind."

THE DAISY DOLLS

I

To María Luisa

Next to a garden was a factory, and the noise of the machines seeped through the plants and trees. And deep in the garden was a dark weathered house. The owner of the "black house" was a tall man. At dusk his slow steps came up the street into the garden, where—in spite of the noise of the machines—they could be heard chewing on the gravel. One autumn evening, as he opened the front door, squinting in the strong light of the hall, he saw his wife standing halfway up the grand staircase, which widened out into the middle of the courtyard, and it seemed to him she was wearing a stately marble gown, gathered up in the same hand that held on to the balustrade. She realized he was tired and would head straight up to the bedroom and she waited for him with a smile. They kissed and she said:

"Today the boys finished setting up the scenes . . ."

"I know, but don't tell me anything."

She saw him up to the bedroom door, ran an affectionate finger down his nose and left him to himself. He was going to try to get some sleep before dinner: the dark room would divide the day's worries from the pleasures he expected of the night. He listened fondly, as he had since childhood, to the muffled sound of the machines, and fell asleep. In a dream he saw a spot of lamplight on a table. Around the table stood several men. One of them wore tails and was saying: "We have to turn the blood around so it will go out the veins and back through the arteries, instead of out the arteries and back through the veins." They all clapped and cheered, and the man in tails jumped on a horse in the courtyard and galloped off, through the applause, on clattering hooves that drew sparks from the flagstones. Remembering the dream when he woke up, the man in the black house recognized it as an echo of something he had heard that same day—that the traffic, all over the country, was changing from left- to right-hand driving—and smiled to himself. Then he put on his tail coat, once more remembering the man in the dream, and went down into the dining room. Approaching his wife, he sank his open hands in her hair and said:

"I always forget to bring a lens to have a good look at the plants in the green of your eyes. I know how you get your complexion, though: by rubbing olives in your skin."

She ran her forefinger down his nose again, then poked his cheek, until her finger bent like a spider leg, and answered:

"And I always forget to bring scissors to trim your eyebrows!"

As she sat down at the table he left the room, and she asked:

"Did you forget something?"

"Could be . . ."

He came right back and she decided he had not had time to use the phone.

"Won't you tell me where you went?"

"No."

"Then I won't tell you what the men did today."

He had already started to answer:

"No, my dear olive, don't tell me anything until after dinner."

And he poured himself a glass of the wine he imported from France.

But his wife's words had dropped like pebbles into the pond where his obsessions grew, and he could not get his mind off what he expected to see later that night. He collected dolls that were a bit taller than real women. He had had three glass cases built in a large room. In the biggest one were all the dolls waiting to be chosen to compose scenes in the other cases. The arrangements were in the hands of a number of people: first of all, the caption writers (who had to express the meaning of each scene in a few words). Other artists handled settings, costumes, music, and so on. Tonight was the second show. He would watch while a pianist, seated with his back to him, across the room, played programmed works. Suddenly the owner of the black house remembered he must not think of all this during dinner. So he took a pair of opera glasses out of his pocket and tried to focus them on his wife's face.

"I'd love to know if the shadows under your eyes are also plants."

She realized he had been to his desk to fetch the opera glasses, and decided to humor him. He saw a glass dome, which turned out to be a bottle. So he put down the opera glasses and poured himself some more wine from France. She watched it gurgle into his glass, splashing black tears that ran down the crystal walls to meet the wine on its way up. At that moment, Alex—a White Russian with a pointed beard—came in, bowing at her, and served her a plate of ham and beans. She used to say she had never heard of a servant with a beard, and he would answer that it was the one condition Alex had set for accepting the job. Now she shifted her eyes from the glass of wine to the man's wrist, where a tuft of hair grew out of his sleeve, crawling all the way down his hand to his fingers. As he waited on the master of the house, Alex said:

"Walter" (the pianist) "is here."

After dinner, Alex removed the wineglasses on a tray. They rang against each other, as if happy to meet again. The master, half-asleep—in a sort of quiet glow—was pleasantly roused by the sound and called out after him:

"Tell Walter to go to the piano. He mustn't talk to me as I come in. Is the piano far from the glass cases?"

"Yes, sir, on the other side of the room."

"Good. Tell Walter to sit with his back to me, to start on the first piece in the program and keep repeating it without stopping until I flash the light at him."

His wife was smiling. He went up to kiss her and for a moment rested his flushed face on her cheek. Then he headed for the little parlor off the big show room. There he started to smoke and sip his coffee, collecting himself: he had to feel completely isolated before going in to see the dolls. He listened for the hum of the machines and the sounds of the piano. At first they reached him in what seemed like watery murmurs, as if he were wearing a diver's helmet. Then he woke up and realized some of the sounds were trying to tell him something, as if he were being singled out from among a number of persons snoring in the room. But when he tried to concentrate on the sounds, they scattered like frightened mice. He sat there puzzled for a moment, then decided to ignore them. But suddenly he realized he was not in his chair any more: he had gotten up without noticing it. He remembered having just opened the door, and now he felt his steps taking him toward the first glass case. He switched on the light in the case and through the green curtain he saw a doll sprawled on a bed. He opened the curtain and mounted the podium, which was actually a small rolling platform on rubber casters, with a railing. From there, seated in an armchair at a little table, he had a better view of the scene. The doll was dressed as a bride and her wide open eyes stared at the ceiling. It was impossible to tell whether she was dead or dreaming. Her arms were spread in an attitude of what could be either despair or blissful abandon. Before opening the drawer of the little table to read the caption, he wanted to see what his imagination could come up with. Perhaps she was a bride waiting for the groom, who would never arrive, having jilted her just before the wedding. Or perhaps she was a widow remembering her wedding day, or just a girl dressed up to feel like a bride. He opened the drawer and read: "A moment before marrying the man she doesn't love, she locks herself up, wearing the dress she was to have worn to her wedding with the man she loved, who is gone forever, and poisons herself. She dies with her eyes open and no one has come in yet to shut them." Then the owner of the black house thought, "She really was a lovely bride." And after a moment he savored the feeling of being alive when she was not. Then he opened the glass door and entered the scene to have a closer look. At the same time, through the noise of the machines and the music, he thought he heard a door slam. He left the case and, caught in the door to the little parlor, he saw a piece of his wife's dress. As he tiptoed over to the door, he wondered whether she had been spying on him—or maybe it was one of her jokes. He snatched the door open and her body fell on him. But when he caught it in his arms it seemed very light . . . and he recognized Daisy, the doll who resembled her. Meantime his wife, who was crouching behind an armchair, straightened up and said:

"I wanted to give you a surprise, too. I just managed to get her into my dress."

She went on talking, but he did not listen. Although he was pale, he thanked her for the surprise: he did not want to discourage her, because he enjoyed the jokes she made up with Daisy. But this time he had felt uneasy. So he handed Daisy back to her, saying he did not want too long an intermission. Then he returned to the show room, closing the door behind him, and walked toward Walter. But he stopped halfway and opened another door, which gave onto his study, where he shut himself in, took a notebook from a drawer, and proceeded to make a note of the joke his wife had just played on him with Daisy, and the date. First he read the previous entry, which said: "July 21. Today, Mary"—his wife's name was Daisy Mary, but she liked to be called Mary, so when he'd had a doll made to look like her they had dusted off the name Daisy for the doll—"was in the balcony, looking out over the garden. I wanted to put my hands over her eyes and surprise her. But before I reached her I saw it was Daisy. Mary had seen me go to the balcony—she was right behind me, laughing her head off." Although he was the only one to read the notebook, he signed each entry with his name, Horace, in large letters and heavy ink. The entry before last said: "July 18. Today I opened the wardrobe to get my suit and found Daisy hanging there. She was wearing my tail coat, which looked comically large on her."

Having entered the latest surprise, he was back in the show room, heading for the second glass case. He flashed a light at Walter for him to go on to the next piece in the program and started to roll up the podium. In the pause

Walter made before taking up the new piece, he felt the machines pounding harder, and as the podium moved the casters seemed to rumble like distant thunder.

The second case showed a doll seated at the head of a table. Her head was tilted back and she had a hand on each side of her plate, on a long row of silverware. Her posture and the way her hands rested on the silverware made her look as if she were at a keyboard. Horace looked at Walter, saw him bowed over the piano with his tails dangling over the edge of the bench, and thought of him as a bird of ill omen. Then he stared at the doll and had the sudden feeling—it had happened to him before—that she was moving. The movements did not always begin right away, nor did he expect them when the doll was dead or lying down, but this time they started too soon, possibly because of her uncomfortable position. She was straining too hard to look up at the ceiling, nodding slightly, with almost imperceptible little jerks that showed the effort she was making, and the minute he shifted his gaze from her face to her hands, her head drooped noticeably. He in turn quickly raised his eyes to her face again—but she had already recovered her stillness. He then began to imagine her story. Her dress and surrounding objects suggested luxury, but the furniture was coarse and the walls were of stone. On the far wall there was a small window, and behind her a low, half-open door, like a false smile. She might be in a dungeon in a castle. The piano was imitating a storm and every now and then lightning flashed in the window. Then he remembered that a minute ago the rolling casters had reminded him of distant thunder and the coincidence unsettled him. Also, while collecting himself in the little parlor, he had heard those sounds that had been trying to tell him something. But he returned to the doll's story: maybe she was praying, asking God to liberate her. Finally, he opened the drawer and read: "Second scene. This woman is expecting a child soon. She is now living in a lighthouse by the sea. She has withdrawn from the world, which has blamed her for loving a sailor. She keeps thinking, 'I want my child to be alone with himself and listen only to the sea.'" He thought, "This doll has found her true story." Then he got up, opened the glass door, and slowly went over her things. He felt he was defiling something as solemn as death. He decided to concentrate on the doll and tried to find an angle from which their eyes could meet. After a moment he bent over the unhappy girl, and as he kissed her on the forehead it gave him the same cool, pleasant sensation as Mary's face. He had hardly taken his lips off her forehead when he saw her move. He was paralyzed. She started to slip to one side, losing her balance, until she fell off the edge of the chair, dragging a spoon and a fork with her. The piano was still making sea noises, and the windows were still flashing and the machines rumbling. He did not want to pick her up and he blundered out of the case and the room, through the little parlor, into the courtyard. There he saw Alex and said:

"Tell Walter that's enough for today. And have the boys come in tomorrow to rearrange the doll in the second case."

At that moment Mary appeared:

"What's the matter?"

"Nothing: a doll fell—the one in the lighthouse . . ."

"How did it happen? Is she hurt?"

"I must have bumped into the table when I went in to look at her things . . ."

"Now let's not get upset, Horace!"

"On the contrary, I'm very happy with the scenes. But where's Daisy? I loved the way she looked in your dress!"

"You'd better go to bed, dear," answered Mary.

But instead they sat on a sofa, where he put his arms around her and asked her to rest her cheek on his for a moment, in silence. As their heads touched, his instantly lit up with memories of the two fallen dolls, Daisy and the girl in the lighthouse. He knew what this meant: the death of Mary. And, afraid his thoughts might pass into her head, he started to kiss her ears.

When he was alone again in the darkness of the bedroom, his mind throbbing with the noise of the machines, he thought of the warning signs he had been receiving. He was like a tangled wire that kept intercepting calls and portents meant for others. But this time all the signals had been aimed at him. Under the hum of the machines and the sound of the piano he had detected those other hidden noises scattering like mice. Then there had been Daisy falling into his arms when he opened the door to the little parlor, as if to say: "Hold me, for Mary is dying." And it was Mary herself who had prepared the warning, as innocently as if she were showing him a disease she did not yet know she had. Just before, there had been the dead doll in the first case. Then, when he was on his way to the second case, the unprogrammed rumble of the podium, like distant thunder, announcing the sea and the woman in the lighthouse. Finally, the woman slipping out from under him, falling off her chair, condemned to be childless, like Mary. And, meantime, Walter, like a bird of ill omen, with his flapping coattails, pecking away at the edge of his black box.

I I

Mary was not ill and there was no reason to think she was going to die. But for some time now he had been afraid of losing her and dreading what he imagined would be his unhappiness without her. So one day he had decided to have a doll made to resemble her. At first the result had been disappointing: he had felt only dislike for Daisy, as for a poor substitute. She was made of kidskin that attempted to imitate Mary's coloring and had been perfumed with Mary's favorite scents, yet whenever Mary asked him to kiss her he expected to taste leather and had the feeling he was about to kiss a shoe. But in time he had begun to notice a strange relationship developing between Daisy and Mary. One morning he saw Mary singing while she dressed Daisy: she was like a girl playing with a doll. Another time, when he got home in the evening, he found Mary and Daisy seated at a table with a book in front of them. He had the feeling Mary was teaching a sister to read, and said:

"It must be such a relief to confide in someone who can keep a secret!"

"What do you mean?" said Mary, springing up and storming out of the room.

But Daisy, left behind, held firmly in place, tipped over the book, like a friend maintaining a tactful silence.

That same night, after dinner, to prevent him from joining her on their customary sofa, Mary sat the doll next to her. He examined Daisy's face and disliked it once more. It was cold and haughty, as if to punish him for his hateful thoughts about her skin.

A bit later, he went into the show room. At first he strolled back and forth among the glass cases. Then, after a while, he opened the big piano top, removed the bench, replaced it with a chair—so he could lean back—and started to walk his fingers over the cool expanse of black and white keys. He had trouble combining the sounds, like a drunk trying to unscramble his words. But meantime he was remembering many of the things he had learned about the dolls. Slowly he had been getting to know them, almost without trying. Until recently, Horace had kept the store that had been making his fortune. Alone, after closing time every day, he liked to wander through the shadowy rooms, reviewing the dolls in the show windows. He went over their dresses, with an occasional sidelong glance at their faces. He observed the lighted windows from various angles, like a stage manager watching his actors from the wings. Gradually he started finding expressions in the dolls' faces similar to those of his salesgirls. Some inspired the same distrust in him, others the certainty that they were against him. There was one with a turned-up nose that seemed to say, "See if I care." Another, which he found appealing, had an inscrutable face: just as she looked good in either a summer or a winter dress, she could also be thinking almost anything, accepting or rejecting him, depending on her mood. One way or another, the dolls had their secrets. Although the window dresser knew how to display each of them to her best advantage, at the last moment she always added a touch of her own. It was then that he started to think the dolls were full of portents. Day and night they basked in covetous looks and those looks nested and hatched in the air. Sometimes they settled on the dolls' faces like clouds over a landscape, shadowing and blurring their expressions, and at other times they reflected back on some poor girl innocently happening by, who was tainted by their original covetousness. Then the dolls were like creatures in a trance, on unknown missions, or lending themselves to evil designs. On the night of his quarrel with Mary, Horace had reached the conclusion that Daisy was one of those changeable dolls who could transmit warnings or receive signals from other dolls. Since she lived in the house, Mary had been showing increasing signs of jealousy. If he complimented one of his salesgirls, he felt Mary's suspicion and reproach in Daisy's brooding look. That was when Mary had started nagging him until she got him to give up the store. But soon her fits of jealousy, after an evening in mixed company, had reached the point where he had also had to give up visiting friends with her.

On the morning after the quarrel he had made up with both of them. His dark thoughts bloomed at night and faded in the daytime. As usual, the three of them had gone for a walk in the garden. He and Mary carried Daisy between them—in a long skirt, to disguise her missing steps—as if gently supporting a sick friend. (Which had not prevented the neighbors from concocting a story about how they had let a sister of Mary's die so as to inherit her money, and then, to atone for the sin, had taken in a doll who resembled her, as a constant reminder of their crime.)

After a period of happiness, during which Mary prepared surprises for him with Daisy and he hastened to enter them in his notebook, had come the night of the second show, with its announcement of Mary's death.

Horace had then hit on the idea of buying his wife a number of dresses made of durable material—he intended these memories of her to last a long time—and asking her to try them on Daisy.

Mary was delighted, and he also pretended to be, when, at her urging—but in response to his subtle hints—they had some of their closest friends to dinner one night. It was stormy out, but they sat down to eat in a good mood. He kept thinking of all the memories the evening was going to leave him with and tried to provoke some unusual situations. First he twirled his knife and fork—like a cowboy with a pair of six-shooters—and aimed them at a girl next to him. She went along with the joke and raised her arms, and he tickled her shaved armpits with the knife. It was too much for Mary, who burst out:

"Horace, you're being a brat!"

He apologized all around and soon everyone was having fun again. But when he was serving his wine from France, over dessert, Mary saw a black stain—the wine he was pouring outside the glass—growing on the tablecloth, and, trying to rise, clutching at her throat, she fainted. They carried her into the bedroom, and, when she recovered, she said she had not been feeling well for days. He sent at once for the doctor, who said it was nothing serious but she had to watch her nerves. She got up and saw off her guests as if nothing had happened. But, as soon as they were alone, she said:

"I can't stand this life any more. You were messing with that girl right under my nose."

"But, my dear . . ."

"And I don't just mean the wine you spilled gaping at her. What were you up to in the yard afterward when she said, 'Horace, stop it'?"

"But, darling, all she said was 'a boring topic.'"

They made up in bed and she fell asleep with her cheek next to his. But, after a while, he turned away to think about her illness. And the next morning, when he touched her arm, it was cold. He lay still, gazing at the ceiling for several grueling minutes before he managed to shout: "Alex!" At that moment the door opened and Mary stuck her head in—and he realized it was Daisy he had touched and that Mary had put her there, next to him, while he slept.

After much reflection, he decided to call his friend, Frank, the doll manufacturer, and ask him to find a way to give Daisy some human warmth.

Frank said:

"I'm afraid it's not so easy, dear boy. The warmth would last about as long as a hot-water bottle."

"All right, I don't care. Do what you want, just don't tell me. I'd also like her to be softer, nicer to touch, not so stiff . . ."

"I don't know about that, either. Think of the dent you'd make every time you sank a finger in her."

"Well, all the same, she could be more pliant. And, as for the dent—that might not be such a bad idea."

The day Frank took Daisy away, Horace and Mary were sad.

"God knows what they'll do to her," Mary kept saying.

"Now then, darling, let's not lose touch with reality. After all, she was only a doll."

"Was! You sound as if she were dead. Anyway, you're a fine one to talk about losing touch with reality!"

"I was just trying to comfort you . . ."

"And you think dismissing her like that is the way to do it? She was more mine than yours. I dressed her and told her things I've never told anyone, do you realize? And how she brought us together—have you ever thought of that?"

He was heading for his study, but she went on, raising her voice:

"Weren't you getting what you wanted with our surprises? Wasn't that enough, without asking for 'human warmth'?"

By then he had reached the study and slammed the door behind him. The way she pronounced "human warmth" not only made him feel ridiculous but soured all the pleasures he was looking forward to when Daisy returned. He decided to go for a walk.

When he got back, Mary was out, and when she returned

they spent a while hiding the fact that they were unexpectedly glad to see each other.

That night he did not visit his dolls. The next morning he
was busy. After lunch he and Mary strolled in the garden.
They agreed that Daisy's absence was temporary and should
not be made too much of. He even thought it was easier
and more natural to have his arm around Mary instead of
Daisy. They both felt light and gay and enjoyed being
together. But later, at dinnertime, when he went up to the
bedroom for her, he was surprised to find her there alone.
He had forgotten for a moment that Daisy was gone, and
now her absence made him strangely uneasy. Mary might
well be a woman without a doll again, but his idea of her
was no longer complete without Daisy, and the fact that
neither she nor the house seemed to miss Daisy was like a
kind of madness. Also, the way Mary drifted back and forth
in the room, apparently not thinking of Daisy, and the
blankness of her expression, reminded him of a madwoman
forgetting to dress and wandering naked. They went down
to dinner, and there, sipping his wine from France, he stared
at her in silence, until finally it seemed he caught her with
Daisy on her mind. Then he began to go over what the two
women meant to each other. Whenever he thought of
Mary, he remembered her fussing over Daisy, worrying
about how to get her to sit straight without sagging, and
planning to surprise him with her. If Mary did not play the
piano—as Frank's girlfriend did—it was because she expressed herself in her own original manner through Daisy.
To strip her of Daisy would be like stripping an artist of his
art. Daisy was not only part of her being but her most
charming self, so that he wondered how he ever could have
loved her before she had Daisy. Perhaps in those days she
had found other means or ways to express that side of her

personality. Alone in the bedroom, a while back, without Daisy, she had seemed insignificant. Yet—Horace took another sip of his wine from France—there was something disquieting about her insignificance, as if Daisy had still been there, but only as an obstacle she had put up for him to trip over on his way to her.

After dinner he kissed Mary's cool cheek and went in to look at his glass cases. One of them showed a Carnival scene. Two masked dolls, a blonde and a brunette, in Spanish costumes, leaned over a marble balustrade. To the left was a staircase with masks, hoods, paper streamers and other objects scattered on the steps with artful neglect. The scene was dimly lit—and suddenly, watching the brunette, Horace thought he recognized Daisy. He wondered whether she had been ready sooner than expected and Mary had sent for her as a surprise. Without looking again, he opened the glass door. On his way up the staircase he stepped on a mask, which he picked up and threw over the balustrade. The gesture gave the objects around him phys-ical reality and he felt let down. He moved to the podium, irritated because the noise of the machines and the sound of the piano did not blend. But after a few seconds he turned to the dolls again and decided they were probably two women who loved the same man. He opened the drawer and read the caption: "The blonde has a boyfriend. He discovered, some time ago, that he preferred her friend, the brunette, and declared his love to her. She was also secretly in love with him but tried to talk him out of it. He persisted, and, earlier on this Carnival night, he has told the blonde about her rival. Now the two girls have just met for the first time since they both learned the truth. They haven't spoken yet as they stand there in a long silence, wearing their disguises." At last he had guessed the meaning of one of the scenes: the two girls in love with the same man. But then he wondered whether the coincidence was not a portent or sign of something that was already going on in his own life and whether he might not really be in love with Daisy. His mind flitted around the question, touching down on other questions: What was it about Daisy that could have made him fall in love with her? Did the dolls perhaps give him something more than a purely artistic pleasure? Was Daisy really just a consolation in case his wife died? And for how long would she lend herself to a misunderstanding that was always in Mary's favor? The time had come to reconsider their roles and personalities. He did not want to take these worries up to the bedroom where Mary would be waiting for him, so he called Alex, had him dismiss Walter, then sent him for a bottle of wine from France and sat for a while, alone with the noise of the machines. Then he walked up and down the room, smoking. Each time he came to the glass case he drank some wine and set out again, thinking: "If there are spirits that inhabit empty houses, why wouldn't they also inhabit the bodies of dolls?" He thought of haunted castles full of spooked objects and furnishings joined in a heavy sleep, under thick cobwebs, where only ghosts and spirits roam, in concert with whistling bats and sighing marshes . . . At that moment he was struck by the noise of the machines and he dropped his glass. His hair stood on end as it dawned on him that disembodied souls caught the stray sounds of the world, which spoke through them, and that the soul inhabiting Daisy's body was in touch with the machines. To shake off these thoughts he concentrated on the chills going up and down his spine. But, when he had settled in his armchair, his thoughts ran on: no wonder such strange things had happened on a recent moonlit night. They were out in the garden, all three of them, and suddenly he started chasing his wife. She ran, laughing, to hide behind Daisy—which, as he well realized, was not the same as hiding behind a tree—and when he tried to kiss her over Daisy's shoulder he felt a sharp pinprick. Almost at once he heard the machines pounding, no doubt to warn him against kissing Mary through Daisy. Mary had no idea how she could have left a pin in the doll's dress. And how—he asked himself—could he have been so foolish as to think Daisy was there to grace and adorn Mary, when in fact they were meant to grace and adorn each other? Now, coming back to the noise of the machines, he confirmed what he had been suspecting all along: that it had a life of its own, like the sound of the piano, although they belonged to different families. The noise of the machines was of a noble family, which was perhaps why Daisy had chosen it to express her true love. On that thought he phoned Frank to ask after Daisy. Frank said she was nearly ready, that the girls in the workshop had found a way to . . . But at this point Horace cut him off, saying he was not interested in technical details. And, hanging up, he felt secretly pleased at the thought of girls working on Daisy, putting something of themselves into her.

The next day, at lunchtime, Mary was waiting for him with an arm around Daisy's waist. After kissing his wife, he took the doll in his arms, and for a moment her soft warm body gave him the happiness he had been hoping for, although when he pressed his lips to hers, she seemed feverish. But he soon grew accustomed to this new sensation and found it comforting.

That same night, over dinner, he wondered: "Why must the transmigration of souls take place only between people and animals? Aren't there cases of people on their deathbed who have handed their souls over to some beloved object? And why assume it's a mistake when a spirit hides in a doll who looks like a beautiful woman? Couldn't it be that, looking for a new body to inhabit, it guided the hands that made the doll? When someone pursues an idea, doesn't he come up with unexpected discoveries, as if someone else were helping him?" Then he thought of Daisy and wondered whose spirit could be living in her body.

Mary had been in a vile mood since early evening. She had scolded Daisy while dressing her, because she would not hold still but kept tipping forward—and now that she was full of water, she was a lot heavier than before. Horace thought of the relationship between his wife and the doll and of the strange shades of enmity he had noticed between women who were such close friends that they could not get along without one another. He remembered observing that the same thing often happened between mother and daughter . . . A minute later, he raised his eyes from his plate and said:

"Tell me something, Mary. What was your mother like?"

"May I ask the reason for your question? Do you want to trace my defects to her?"

"Of course not, darling. I wouldn't think of it!"

He had spoken in a soothing voice, and she said:

"Well, I'll tell you. She was my complete opposite. Calm as a clear day. She could spend hours just sitting in a chair, staring into space."

"Perfect," he said to himself. Although, after pouring himself a glass of wine, he thought: "On the other hand, I can't very well have an affair with the spirit of my mother-in-law in Daisy's body."

"And what were her ideas on love?"

"Do you find mine inadequate?"

"Mary, please!"

"She had none, lucky for her. Which was why she was able to marry my father to please my grandparents. He was wealthy. And she made him a fine wife."

Horace, relieved, thought: "Well, that's that. One thing less to worry about."

Although it was spring, the night turned cold. Mary refilled Daisy, dressed her in a silk nightie and took her to bed with them, like a hot water bottle. As he dropped off to sleep, Horace felt himself sinking into a warm pond where all their legs tangled, like the roots of trees planted so close together he was too lazy to find out which ones belonged to him.

III

Horace and Mary were planning a birthday party for Daisy. She was going to be two years old. Horace wanted to present her on a tricycle. He told Mary he had seen one at the Transportation Day fair and he was sure they would let him have it. He did not tell her the reason for using this particular device was that he had seen a bride elope with her lover on a tricycle in a film years ago. The rehearsals were a success. At first he had trouble getting the tricycle going, but as soon as the big front wheel turned it grew wings.

The party opened with a buffet dinner. Soon the sounds from human throats and necks of bottles mixed in an increasingly loud murmur. When it was time to present Daisy, Horace rang a school bell in the courtyard and the guests went out holding their glasses. They saw him come tearing down a long carpeted hallway, struggling with the front wheel. At first the tricycle was almost invisible beneath him. Of Daisy, mounted behind him, only her flowing white dress showed. He seemed to be riding the air, on a cloud. Daisy was propped over the axle that joined the small back wheels, with her arms thrust forward and her hands in his trouser pockets. The tricycle came to a stop in the center of the courtyard, and, acknowledging the cheers and applause, he reached over with one hand and stroked her hair. Then he began pedaling hard again, and as the tricycle sailed back up the carpeted hallway, gathering speed, everyone watched in breathless silence, as if it were about to take flight. The performance was such a success that Horace tried to repeat it, and the laughter and applause were starting up again when suddenly, just as he reached the yard, he lost a back wheel. There were cries of alarm, but when he showed he was not hurt there was more laughter and applause. He had fallen on his back, on top of Daisy, and was kicking his legs in the air like an insect. The guests laughed until they cried. Frank gasped and spluttered:

"Boy, you looked like one of those wind-up toys that go on walking upside down!"

Then they all went back into the dining room. The men who arranged the scenes in the glass cases surrounded Horace, asking to borrow Daisy and the tricycle to make up a story with them. He turned them down, but he was so pleased with himself that he invited everybody into the show room for a glass of wine from France.

"If you wouldn't mind telling us what you feel watching the scenes," said one of the boys, "I think we could all learn something."

He had started to rock back and forth on his heels, staring at his guests' shoes. Finally he made up his mind and said:

"It's very difficult to put into words, but I'll try . . . if you promise meantime to ask no more questions and to be satisfied with anything I care to say."

"Promised!" said one who was a bit hard of hearing, cupping a hand to his ear.

Still, Horace took his time, clasping and unclasping his hands. To quiet the hands, he crossed his arms and began:

"When I look at a scene . . ." Here he stopped, then took up the speech again, with a digression: "(It's very important to see the dolls through a glass, because that gives them the quality of memories. Before, when I could stand mirrors—now they're bad for me, but it would take too long to explain why—I liked to see the rooms that appeared in them.) So . . . when I look at a scene, it's like catching a woman in the act of remembering an important moment in her life, a bit—if you'll forgive the expression—as if I were opening a crack in her skull. When I get hold of the memory, it's like stealing one of her undergarments: I can use it to imagine the most intimate things and I might even say it feels like a defilement. In a way, it's as if the memory were in a dead person and I were picking a corpse, hoping the memory will stir in it . . ." He let his voice trail off, not daring to describe the weird stirrings he had seen.

The boys were also silent. One of them thought of emptying his glass of wine at a swallow and the others imitated him. Then another said:

"Tell us something more about yourself—your personal tastes, habits, whatever."

"Ah, as for that," said Horace, "I don't think it would be of any help to you in making up your scenes. For instance, I like to walk on a wooden floor sprinkled with sugar. It's that neat little sound . . ."

Just then Mary came in to ask them all out into the

garden. It was a dark night and the guests were requested to form couples and carry torches. Mary took Horace's arm and together they showed the way. At the door that led into the garden, each guest picked a small torch from a table and lit it at a flaming bowl on another table. The torchlight attracted the neighbors, who gathered at the low hedge, their faces like shiny fruit with watchful eyes among the bushes, glinting with distrust. Suddenly Mary crossed a flowerbed, flicked a switch, and Daisy appeared, lit up in the high branches of a tall tree. It was one of Mary's surprises and was greeted with cheers and exclamations. Daisy was holding a white fan spread on her breast. A light behind the fan gave her face a theatrical glow. Horace kissed Mary and thanked her for the surprise. Then, as the guests scattered, he saw Daisy staring out toward the street he took on his way home every day. Mary was leading him along the hedge when they heard one of the neighbors shout at others still some distance away, "Hurry! The dead woman's appeared in a tree!" They staggered back to the house, where everyone was toasting the surprise. Mary had the twins—her maids, who were sisters—get Daisy down from the tree and change her water for bed.

About an hour had gone by since their return from the garden when Mary started looking around for Horace and found him back in the show room with the boys. She was pale, and everyone realized something serious had happened. She had the boys excuse Horace and led him up to the bedroom. There he found Daisy with a knife stuck under one breast. The wound was leaking hot water down her dress, which was soaked, and dripping on the floor. She was in her usual chair, with big open eyes. But when Mary touched her arm she felt it going cold.

Collapsing into Horace's arms, Mary burst out crying:

"Who could have dared to come up here and do such a thing?"

After a while she calmed down and sat in a chair to think what was to be done. Then she said:

"I'm going to call the police."

"You're out of your mind," he said. "We can't offend all our guests just because one of them misbehaved. And what will you tell the police? That someone stuck a knife in a doll and that she's leaking? Let's keep this to ourselves. One has to accept setbacks with dignity. We'll send her in for repairs and forget about it."

"Not if I can help it," said Mary. "I'm going to call a private detective. Don't let anyone touch her—the finger-prints must be on the knife."

Horace tried to reason with her, reminding her the guests were waiting downstairs. They agreed to lock the doll in, as she was. But, the moment Mary had left the room, he took out his handkerchief, soaked it in bleach, and wiped off the handle of the knife.

IV

Horace had managed to convince Mary to say nothing about the wounded doll. The day Frank came for her, he brought his mistress, Louise. She and Mary went into the dining room, where their voices soon mixed like twittering birds in connecting cages: they were used to talking and listening at the same time.

Meantime, Horace and Frank shut themselves in the study. They spoke one at a time, in undertones, as if taking turns at drinking from a jug.

Horace said, "I was the one who stuck the knife in her so I'd have an excuse to send her in to you . . . without going into explanations." And they stood there in silence, with their heads bowed.

Mary was curious to know what they were discussing. Deserting Louise for a minute, she went to put her ear to the study door. She thought he recognized her husband's voice, but it sounded hoarse and blurred. (At that moment, still mumbling into his chin, Horace was saying, "It may be crazy, but I've heard of sculptors falling in love with their statues.") In a while, Mary went back to listen again, but she could only make out the word "possible," pronounced first by her husband, then by Frank. (In fact, Horace had just said: "It must be possible," and Frank had answered, "If it's possible, I'll do it.")

One afternoon, a few days later, Mary realized Horace was acting strangely. He would linger over her, with fond eyes, then abruptly draw back, looking worried. As he crossed the courtyard at one point, she called after him, went out to meet him and, putting her arms around his neck, said:

"Horace, you can't fool me. I know what's on your mind."

"What?" he said, staring wildly.

"It's Daisy."

He turned pale:

"Whatever gave you that idea?"

He was surprised that she did not laugh at his odd tone.

"Oh, come on, darling . . . After all, she's like a daughter to us by now," Mary insisted.

He let his eyes dwell on her face, and with them his thoughts, going over each of her features as if reviewing every corner of a place he had visited daily through many long happy years. Then, breaking away, he went and sat in the little parlor to think about what had just happened. His first reaction, when he suspected his wife had found him out, had been to assume she would forgive him. But then, observing her smile, he had realized it was madness to suppose she could imagine, let alone forgive, such a sin. Her face had been like a peaceful landscape, with a bit of golden evening glow on one cheek, the other shaded by the small mound of her nose. He had thought of all the good left in the innocence of the world and the habit of love, and the tenderness with which he always came back to her face after his adventures with the dolls. But in time, when she discovered not only the abysmal nature of his more than fatherly affection for Daisy but also the care with which he had gone about organizing his betrayal, her face and all its features would be devastated. She would never be able to understand the sudden evil in the world and in the habit of love, or feel anything but horror at the sight of him.

So he had stood there, gazing at a spot of sun on his coat sleeve. As he withdrew his arm, the spot had shifted, like a taint, to her dress. Then, heading for the little parlor, he had felt his twisted insides lump and sag, like dead weights. Now he sat on a small bench, thinking he was unworthy of being received into the lap of a family armchair, and he felt as uncomfortable as if he had sat on a child. He hardly recognized the stranger in himself, disillusioned at being made of such base metal. But, to his surprise, a bit later, in bed with the covers pulled up over his ears, he went straight to sleep.

Mary was on the phone to Frank, saying:

"Listen, Frank, you'd better hurry with Daisy. Horace is worrying himself sick."

Frank said:

"I have to tell you, Mary, it's a bad wound, right in the middle of the circulatory system. We can't rush it. But I'll do my best, I promise."

In a while, Horace woke up under his pile of blankets. He found himself blinking down a kind of slope, toward the foot of the bed, and saw a picture of his parents on the far wall. They had died in an epidemic when he was a child. He felt they had cheated him: he was like a chest they had left full of dirty rags instead of riches, fleeing like thieves in the dark before he could grow up and expose the fraud. But then he was ashamed of these monstrous thoughts.

At dinner, he tried to be on his best behavior.

Mary said:

"I called Frank about hurrying Daisy."

If only she had known the madness and betrayal she was contributing to by hastening his pleasure! he thought, blindly casting right and left, like a horse trying to butt its way out.

"Looking for something?" asked Mary.

"No, here it is," he said, reaching for the mustard.

She decided that if he had not seen it standing there in front of him, he must not be well.

Afterward he got up and slowly bent over her, until his lips grazed her cheek. The kiss seemed to have dropped by parachute, onto a plain not yet touched by grief.

That night, in the first glass case, there was a doll seated on a lawn, surrounded by huge sponges, which she seemed to think were flowers. He did not feel like guessing her fate, so he opened the drawer with the captions and read: "This woman is sick in the head. No one has been able to find out why she loves sponges." "That's what I pay them for, to find out," he said to himself, and then, bitterly: "The sponges must be to wipe away her guilt."

-201-

In the morning he woke up rolled into a ball and remembered the person he had become. It seemed to him even his name had changed, and if he signed a check it would bounce. His body was sad, as it had been once before, when a doctor told him he had thin blood and a small heart. But that other time he had gotten over the sadness. Now he stretched his legs and thought: "Formerly, when I was young, I had far stronger defenses against guilt: I cared much less about hurting others. Am I getting weak with age? No, it's more like a late flowering of love and shame." He got up, feeling better. But he knew the dark clouds of guilt were just over the horizon, and that they would be back with night.

V

The next days, Mary took Horace for long walks. She wanted to get his mind off Daisy. Yet she was convinced it was not Daisy he missed but the real daughter she could never have.

The afternoon Daisy was returned, Horace did not show any particular affection for her, and again Mary feared she was not the reason for his sadness. But, just before dinner, she noticed him lingering over Daisy with restrained emotion, and felt relieved.

After that, for several nights, as he kissed his wife before going in to see his dolls, he watched her face intently, with searching eyes, as if to make sure there was nothing strange hidden anywhere. He had not yet been alone with Daisy.

Then came a memorable afternoon when, in spite of the mild weather, Mary replenished Daisy's hot water, packed

Horace comfortably into bed with her for his nap, and went out.

That evening he kept scanning every inch of her face, watching for the enemy she would soon become. She noticed his fidgety gestures, his stilted walk. He was waiting for the sign that he had been found out.

Finally, one morning, it happened.

Once, some time ago, when Mary had been complaining of Alex's beard, Horace had said: "At least he's not like one of those twin maids of yours that you can't tell apart."

She had answered: "Why, do you have anything special to say to either of them? Has there been some mix-up that has . . . inconvenienced you?"

"Yes, I was calling you once—and who do you think turned up? The one who has the honor to bear your name."

After which the twins had been ordered to stay out of sight when he was home. But, seeing one vanish through a door once at his approach, he had plunged after her, thinking she was an intruder, and run into his wife. Since then Mary had them come in only a few hours in the morning and never took her eyes off them.

The day he was found out, Mary had caught the twins raising Daisy's nightie when it was not time to dress her or change her water. As soon as they had left the bedroom, she went in. In a little while the twins saw the lady of the house rush across the courtyard into the kitchen. On her way back she was carrying a carving knife. They were terrified and tried to follow her, but she slammed the door on them. When they peeped through the keyhole her back blocked their view, so they moved to another door. She had Daisy flat on a table, as if to operate on her, and was in a frenzy, stabbing her all over. She looked completely disheveled: a jet of water had caught her in the face. Two thin spurts rose in an arc from one of Daisy's shoulders, mixing in the air, like the water from the fountain in the garden, and her belly gushed through a rip in her nightgown. One of the twins had knelt on a cushion, with a hand over one eye, the other eye stuck, unblinking, to the keyhole. When the draft that blew through the hole made her eye run, her sister took her place. Mary also had tears in her eyes when she finally dropped the knife on Daisy and slumped into an armchair, sobbing, with her face buried in her hands. The twins lost interest in the scene and returned to the kitchen. But soon the lady called them back up to help her pack. She had decided to handle the situation with the wounded dignity of a fallen queen. Determined to punish Horace and, meantime, to adopt the appropriate attitude in case he showed up, she instructed the twins to say she could not receive him. She began making arrangements for a long trip and gave the twins some of her dresses. They followed her out into the garden, and when she drove off in the family car they finally realized what was happening and started to howl over the lady's misfortune. But, back in the house with their new dresses, they were gleeful. They drew open the curtains that covered the mirrors—to spare Horace the unpleasantness of seeing himself in them—and held the dresses up to their bodies for effect. One of them saw Daisy's mangled shape in a mirror and said: "What a beast!" She meant Horace, who had just appeared in a door and was wondering how to ask them to explain the dresses and the bare mirrors. But, suddenly catching sight of Daisy sprawled on the table in her torn nightie, he directed his steps toward her. The twins were trying to sneak out of the room, but he stopped them:

"Where's my wife?"

The one who had said "What a beast!" stared him full in the face and answered:

"She left on a long trip. And she gave us these dresses."

He dismissed them and the thought came to him: "The worst is over." He glanced at Daisy again: the carving knife still lay across her belly. He was not too unhappy and for a moment even imagined having her repaired. But he pictured her all stitched up and remembered a rag horse he had owned as a child, with a hole ripped in it. His mother had wanted to patch it up, but it had lost its appeal and he had preferred to throw it away.

As for Mary, he was convinced she would come back. He kept telling himself: "I have to take things calmly." He welcomed the return of the bold and callous self he had been in his prime. Looking back over the morning's events, he could easily see himself betraying Daisy as well. A few days ago Frank had shown him another doll: a gorgeous blonde with a shady past. Frank had been spreading word of a manufacturer in a northern country who made these new dolls. He had imported the designs and—after some experimenting—found them workable. Soon a little shy man had come by, with big pouchy eyes gleaming under heavy lids, to inquire about the dolls. Frank had brought out pictures of the available models, saying: "Their generic name is Daisy, but then each owner gives them whatever pet name he wants. These are the models we have designs for." After seeing only three of them the little shy man had picked one almost at random and put in an order for her, cash in hand. Frank had quoted a stiff sum, and the buyer had batted his heavy lids once or twice, but then he had signed the order, with a pen shaped like a submarine. Horace had seen the finished blonde and asked Frank to hold her for him, and Frank, who had others on the way, had agreed. At first Horace had considered setting her up in an apartment, but now he had a better idea: he would bring her home and leave her in the glass case where he kept the dolls waiting to be assigned their roles. As soon as everyone was asleep he would carry her up to the bedroom, and before anyone was up in the morning he would put her back in the glass case. He was counting on Mary not returning in the middle of the night. From the moment Frank had set the doll apart for him, he had felt himself riding a lucky streak he had not known since adolescence. Just happening to have been out until it was all over with Daisy meant a higher power was on his side. With this assurance, in addition to his new youthful vigor, he felt in command of events. Having decided to exchange one doll for another, he could not stop to shed tears over Daisy's mutilated body. Mary was certain to be back, now that he no longer cared about her, and she could dispose of the corpse.

Suddenly Horace started to edge along the wall like a thief. Sidling up to a wardrobe, he drew the curtain across the mirror. He repeated the gesture at the other wardrobe. He had had the curtains hung years ago. Mary was always careful to shield him from the mirrors: she dressed behind closed doors and made sure the curtains were in place before leaving the room. Now he was annoyed to think the twins had not only been wearing Mary's clothes but had left the mirrors uncovered. It was not that he disliked seeing things in mirrors, but his sallow face reminded him of some wax dolls he had seen in a museum one afternoon. A shopkeeper had been murdered that day, as had many of the people whose bodies the dolls represented, and the blood-stains on the wax were as unpleasant to him as if, after being stabbed to death, he had been able to see the wounds that had killed him. The only mirror in the bedroom without a curtain was the one over the dresser: a low mirror before which he bent just far enough for a quick glimpse at the knot of his tie as he went by absently each day. Because he combed and shaved by touch, from the mirror's point of view he had always been a man with no head. So now, after covering the other mirrors, he went by it as blithely as usual. But when it reflected his hand against his dark suit he had the same queasy sensation as when he caught sight of his face. He realized then that his hands were also the color of wax. At the same time, he remembered some loose arms he had seen in Frank's office that morning. They were pleasantly colored and as shapely as those of the blonde doll, and, like a child asking a carpenter for scraps, he had told Frank:

"I could use some arms and legs, if you have any left over."

"Whatever for, dear boy?"

"I'd like the men to make up some scenes with loose arms and legs. For instance, an arm hanging from a mirror, a leg sticking out from under a bed, and so on."

Frank, wiping his face, had watched him askance.

At lunch that day, Horace drank his wine and ate as calmly as if Mary were out spending the day with relatives. He kept congratulating himself over his good luck. He got up feeling elated, sat at the piano for a while, letting his fingers wander over the keys, and finally went up for his nap. On his way past the dresser he thought: "One of these days I'll get over my dread of mirrors and face them." He had always enjoyed being surprised and confused by the people and objects reflected in mirrors. With another glance at Daisy, who would simply have to wait until Mary got back, he lay down. As he stretched out under the covers, he

touched a strange object with the tip of his foot, and he
jumped out of bed. For a moment he just stood there, then
he pulled back the covers. It was a note from Mary that said:
"Horace, here's what's left of your mistress. I've stabbed
her, too. But I can admit it—not like a certain hypocrite I
know who only wanted a pretext to send her in and have
those sinful things done to her. You've sickened my life and
I'll thank you not to look for me. Mary."

He went back to bed but could not sleep and got up
again. He avoided looking at Mary's things on the dresser as
he avoided her face when they were angry at each other. He
went out to a movie. There he shook hands with an old
enemy, without realizing it. He kept thinking of Mary.

When he got back to the black house, there was still a bit
of sunlight shining in the bedroom. As he went by one of
the covered mirrors, he saw his face in it, through the wispy
curtain, lit by a glint of sun, bright as an apparition. With a
shiver, he closed the shutters and lay down. If the luck he
used to have was coming back, at his age it would not last
long, nor would it come alone but accompanied by the sorts
of strange events that had been taking place since Daisy's
arrival. She still lay there, a few feet away. At least, he
thought, her body would not rot. And then he wondered
about the spirit that had once inhabited that body like a
stranger and whether it might not have provoked Mary's
destructive fury so that Daisy's corpse, placed between him
and Mary, would keep him away from her. The ghostly
shapes of the room disturbed his sleep: they seemed to be in
touch with the noise of the machines. He got up, went
down to dinner and began to drink his wine. He had not
known until then how much he missed Mary—and there
was no after-dinner kiss before he headed for the little
parlor. Alone there with his coffee, he decided he ought to

avoid the bedroom and dinner table while Mary was gone. When he went out for a walk a bit later he remembered seeing a student hotel in a neighborhood nearby, and found his way there. It had a potted palm in the doorway and parallel mirrors all the way up the stairs, and he walked on. The sight of so many mirrors in a single day was a dangerous sign. He remembered what he had told Frank that morning, before encountering the ones in the bedroom: that he wanted to see an arm hanging from a mirror. But he also remembered the blonde doll and decided, once again, to overcome his dread. He made his way back to the hotel, brushed past the potted palm, and tried to climb the stairs without looking at himself in the mirrors. It was a long time since he had seen so many at once, wherever he turned, right and left, with their confusion of images. He even thought there might be someone hidden among the reflections. The lady who ran the place met him upstairs and showed him the vacant rooms: they all had huge mirrors. He chose the best and promised to return in an hour. In his dark house he packed a small suitcase, and on his way back to the hotel he remembered that it had once been a brothel—which explained the mirrors. There were three in the room he had chosen, the largest one next to the bed, and since the room that appeared there was prettier than the real one, he kept his eyes on the one in the mirror, which must have been tired of showing the same mock-Chinese scenery over the years, because the gaudy red wallpaper looked faded, as if sunk in the bottom of a misty lake with its yellowish bridges and cherry trees. He got into bed and put out the light, but he went on seeing the room in the glow that came in from the street. He had the feeling he had been taken into the bosom of a poor family, where all the household objects were friends and had aged together. But the windows were still young and looked out: they were twins, like Mary's maids, and dressed alike, in clinging lace curtains and velvet drapes gathered at the sides. It was all a bit as if he were living in someone else's body, borrowing well-being from it. The loud silence made his ears hum, and he realized he was missing the noise of the machines and wondered whether it might not be a good idea to move out of the black house and never hear its sounds again. If only Mary had been lying next to him now, he would have been perfectly happy. As soon as she came back he would invite her to spend a night with him in the hotel. But then he dozed off thinking of the blonde doll he had seen that morning. He dreamed of a white arm floating in a dark haze. The sound of steps in a neighboring room woke him up. He got out of bed, barefoot, and started across the rug. He saw a white spot following him and recognized his face, reflected in the mirror over the fireplace. He wished someone would invent a mirror that showed objects but not people, although he immediately realized the absurdity of the idea, not to mention the fact that a man without an image in the mirror would not be of this world. He lay down again, just as someone turned on a light in a room across the street. The light fell on the mirror by the bed, and he thought of his childhood and of other mirrors he remembered, and went to sleep.

V I

Several days had gone by. Horace now slept in the hotel and the same pattern of events repeated itself every night: windows went on across the street and the light fell on his mirrors, or else he woke up and found the windows asleep.

One night he heard screams and saw flames in his mirror. At first he watched them as if they were flickers on a movie screen, but then he realized that if they showed in the mirror they must be somewhere in reality, and, springing up and swinging around, all at once, he saw them dancing out a window across the street, like devils in a puppet show. He scrambled out of bed, threw on his robe and put his face to one of his windows. As it caught flashes in its glass, his window seemed frightened at what was happening to the one across the street. There was a crowd below—he was on the second floor—and the firetruck was coming. Just then, he saw Mary leaning out another window of the hotel. She had already noticed him and was staring as if she did not quite recognize him. He waved, shut his window and went up the hall to rap on what he figured was her door. She burst right out saying:

"You're wasting your time following me."

And she slammed the door in his face.

He stayed there quietly until he heard her sobbing inside, then he answered:

"I wasn't following you. But since we've met, why don't we go home?"

"You go on if you want," she said.

He thought he had sensed a note of longing in her voice, in spite of everything, and the next day he moved back happily into the black house. There he basked in the luxury of his surroundings, wandering like a sleepwalker among his riches. The familiar objects all seemed full of peaceful memories, the high ceilings braced against death, if it struck from above.

But when he went into the show room after dinner that evening, the piano reminded him of a big coffin, the silence

of a wake. It was a resonant silence, as if it were mourning
the death of a musician. He raised the top of the piano, and,
suddenly, terrified, let it fall with a bang. For a moment he
stood there with his arms in the air, as if someone were
pointing a gun at him, but then he rushed out into the
courtyard shouting:

"Who put Daisy in the piano?"

As his shouts echoed, he went on seeing her hair tangled
in the strings, her face flattened by the weight of the lid.
One of the twins answered his call but could not get a word
out. Finally Alex appeared:

"The lady was in this afternoon. She came to get some
clothes."

"These surprises of hers are killing me," Horace shouted,
beside himself. But suddenly he calmed down: "Take Daisy
to your room and have Frank come for her first thing in the
morning. Wait!" he shouted again. "Something else."
And—after he had made sure the twins were out of
earshot—lowering his voice to a whisper: "Tell Frank he
can bring the other doll when he comes for her."

That night he moved to another hotel. He was given a
room with a single mirror. The yellow wallpaper had red
flowers and green leaves woven in a pattern that suggested
a trellis. The bedspread was also yellow and irritated him
with its glare: it would be like sleeping outdoors.

The next morning he went home and had some large
mirrors brought into the showroom to multiply the scenes
in the glass cases. The day passed with no word from Frank.
That evening, as Alex came into the showroom with the
wine, he dropped the bottle . . .

"Anything wrong?" Horace said.

He was wearing a mask and yellow gloves.

"I thought you were a bandit," said Alex as Horace's laugh blew billows in the black silk mask.

"It's hot behind this thing, and it won't let me drink my wine. But before I remove it I want you to take down the mirrors and stand them on the floor, leaning on chairs—like this," said Horace, taking one down and showing him.

"They'd be safer if you leaned the glass on the wall," Alex objected.

"No, because I still want them to reflect things."

"You could lean their backs on the wall then."

"No, because then they'd reflect upward and I have no interest in seeing my face."

When Alex had done as he was told, Horace removed his mask and began to sip his wine, pacing up and down a carpeted aisle in the center of the room. The way the mirrors tipped forward slightly, toward him, leaning on the chairs that separated them from him, made him think of them as bowing servants watching him from under their raised eyelids. They also reflected the floor through the legs of the chairs, making it seem crooked. After a couple of drinks he was bothered by this effect and decided to go to bed.

The following morning—he had slept at home that night—the chauffeur came, on Mary's behalf, to ask for money. He gave him the money without asking where she was, but assumed it meant she would not be back any time soon. So when the blonde arrived, he had her taken straight up to the bedroom. At dinnertime he had the twins dress her in an evening gown and bring her to the table. He ate with her sitting across from him. Afterward, in front of one of the twins, he asked Alex:

"Well, what do you think of this one?"

"A beauty, sir—very much like a spy I met during the war."

"A lovely thought, Alex."

The next day he told the twins:

"From now on you're to call her Miss Eulalie."

At dinnertime he asked the twins (who no longer hid from him):

"Can you tell me who's in the dining room?"

"Miss Eulalie," both twins said at once.

But, between themselves, making fun of Alex, they kept saying:

"It's time to give the spy her hot water."

VII

Mary was waiting in the student hotel, hoping he would return there. She went out only long enough for her room to be made. She carried her head high around the neighborhood, but walked in a haze, oblivious to her surroundings, thinking, "I am a woman who has lost her man to a doll. But if he could see me now he would be drawn to me." Back in her room, she would open a book of poems bound in blue oilcloth and start to read aloud, in a rapt voice, waiting for Horace again. When he failed to show up, she would try to see into the poems, and if their meaning escaped her she abandoned herself to the thought that she was a martyr and that suffering would add to her charm. One afternoon she was able to understand a poem: it was as if someone had left a door open by chance, suddenly revealing what was inside. Then, for a moment, it seemed to her the wallpaper, the folding screen, even the washbowl with its nickel-plated taps also understood the poems, impelled by something in their nature to reach out toward the lofty rhythms and noble images. Often, in the middle of the night, she switched on her lamp and chose a poem as if she could choose a dream. Out walking again the next day in the neighborhood, she imagined her steps were poetry. And one morning she decided, "I would like Horace to know I'm walking alone among trees with a book in my hand."

Accordingly, she packed again, sent for her chauffeur and had him drive her out to a place belonging to a cousin of her mother's: it was in the outskirts and had trees. The cousin was an old maid who lived in an ancient house. When her huge bulk came heaving through the dim rooms, making the floor creak, a parrot squawked: "Hello, milk-sops!" Mary told Prairie of her troubles without shedding a tear. The fat cousin was horrified, then indignant, and finally tearful. But Mary calmly dispatched the chauffeur with instructions to get money from Horace. In case Horace asked after her, he was to say, as if on his own, that she was walking among trees with a book in her hand. If he wanted to know where she was, he should tell him. Finally, he was to report back at the same time the next day. Then she went and sat under a tree with her book, and the poems started to float out and spread through the countryside as if taking on the shapes of trees and drifting clouds.

At lunch Prairie was silent, but afterward she asked: "What are you going to do with the monster?"

"Wait for him and forgive him."

"Not at all like you, my dear. This man has turned your head and has you on a string like one of his dolls."

Mary shut her eyes in beatific peace. But later that afternoon the cleaning woman came in with the previous day's evening paper and Mary's eyes strayed over a headline that said: "Frank's Daisy Dolls." She could not help reading the item: "Springwear, out smartest department store, will be presenting a new collection on its top floor. We understand some of the models sporting the latest fashions will be Daisy Dolls. And that Frank, the manufacturer of the famous line of dolls, has just become a partner in Springwear Enterprises. One more example of the alarming rate at which this new version of Original Sin—to which we have already referred in our columns—is spreading among us. Here is an example of a propaganda leaflet found at one of our main clubs: 'Are you homely? Don't worry. Shy? Forget it. No more quarrels. No budget-breaking expenses. No more gossip. There's a Daisy Doll for you, offering her silent love.' "

Mary had awakened in fits and starts:

"The nerve! To think he could use the name of our . . . !"

Still grasping for words, her eyes wide with outrage, she took aim and pointed at the offending spot in the paper:

"Prairie, look at this!"

The fat cousin blinked and rummaged in her sewing basket, searching for her glasses.

"Have you ever heard anything like it?" Mary said, reading her the item. "I'm not only going to get a divorce but kick up the biggest row this country has ever seen."

"Good for you, at last you've come down out of your cloud!" shouted Prairie, extricating her hands, which were raw from scrubbing pans. And, at the first chance she had, while Mary strode frantically up and down, tripping over innocent plants and flowerpots, she hid the book of poems from her.

The next day the chauffeur drove up wondering how to

evade Mary's questions about Horace, but she only asked him for the money and then sent him back to the black house to fetch the twin called Mary. Mary—the twin—arrived in the afternoon and told her all about the spy they had to call Miss Eulalie. At first Mary—Horace's wife—was aghast. In a faint voice, she asked:

"Does she look like me?"

"No, Madam—she's blonde and she dresses differently."

Mary—Horace's wife—jumped up, but then dropped back into her armchair, crying at the top of her lungs. The fat cousin appeared and the twin repeated the story. Prairie's huge breasts heaved as she broke into pitiful moans, and the parrot joined the racket screeching:

"Hello, milksops!"

VIII

Walter was back from a vacation and Horace was having his nightly showings again. The first night, he had taken Eulalie into the show room with him, sat her next to him on the podium and kept his arms around her while he watched the other dolls. The boys had made up scenes with more important characters than usual. There were five in the second glass case, representing the board of a society for the protection of unwed mothers. One of them had just been elected president of the board; another, her beaten rival, was moping over her defeat. He liked the beaten rival best and left Eulalie for a moment to go and plant a kiss on her cool forehead. When he got back to the podium he listened for the buzz of the machines through the gaps in the music and recalled what Alex had told him about Eulalie's resemblance to a war spy. Nevertheless, he feasted his eyes greedily on the varied spectacle of the dolls that night. But the next day he woke up exhausted and toward evening he had dark thoughts of death. He dreaded not knowing when he would die, or what part of his body would go first. Every day it was harder for him to be alone. The dolls were no company but seemed to say, "Don't count on us—we're just dolls." Sometimes he whistled a tune, but only to hang from the thread of sound as if it were a thin rope that snapped the moment his attention wandered. Other times, he talked to himself aloud, stupidly commenting on what he was doing, "Now I'm in my study. I've come to get my inkpot." Or he described his actions as if he were watching someone else: "Look at him, poor idiot—there he is, opening a drawer, unstopping the inkpot. Let's see how long he has left." When his fear caught up with him, he went out.

Then, one day, he received a box from Frank. He had it pried open: it was full of arms and legs. He remembered asking Frank for discards and hoped the box did not include any loose heads, which would have unsettled him. He had it carried in to the glass cases where he kept the dolls waiting to be assigned their roles, and called the boys on the phone to explain how he wanted the arms and legs incorporated into the scenes. But the first trial angered him: it was a disaster. The moment he drew the curtain, he saw a doll dressed in mourning, seated at the foot of what looked like the steps of a church. She was staring straight ahead, with an incredible number of legs—at least ten or twelve—sticking out from under her skirt. On each step above her lay an arm with the palm of the hand turned up. "The clumsy fools," he said to himself. "They didn't have to use all the arms and legs at once." Without trying to figure out the meaning of the scene, he opened the drawer with the captions and read, "This is a poor widow who has nothing to eat. She spends her day begging and has laid out hands like traps to catch alms." "What a dumb idea," he went on mumbling to himself. "And what an undecipherable mess they've made of it." He went to bed in a bad mood. On the point of falling asleep, he saw the widow walking with all her legs, like a spider.

After this setback Horace felt very disappointed in the boys, the dolls, and even Eulalie. But a few days later Frank took him out for a drive. Suddenly, on the highway, Frank said:

"See that small two-story house by the river? That's where that little shy man—you remember, the one who bought your blonde's sister—lives with your—uh—sister-in-law." He slapped Horace on the leg and they both laughed. "He only comes at night. Afraid his mother will find out."

The next morning, toward noon, Horace returned to the spot alone. A dirt road led down to the shy man's house by the river. At the entrance to the road stood a closed gate, and next to it a gatehouse probably belonging to the forest ranger. He clapped, and an unshaven man in a torn hat came out chewing on a mouthful of something:

"Yeah—what is it?"

"I've been told the owner of that house over there has a doll . . ."

The man, now leaning back on a tree, cut him short:

"The owner's out."

Horace drew several bills from his wallet, and the man, eyeing the money, began to chew more slowly. Horace stood there thoughtfully rippling the bills as if they were a hand of cards. The man swallowed his mouthful and watched. After giving him time to imagine what he could do with the money, Horace said:

"I might just want to have a quick look at that doll . . ."

"The boss'll be back at seven."

"Is the house open?"

"No, but here's the key," said the man, reaching for the loot and pocketing it. "Remember, if anyone finds out, I ain't seen you . . . Give the key two turns . . . The doll's upstairs . . . And, mind you, don't leave nothing out of place."

Horace strode with brisk steps down the road, once again full of youthful excitement. The small front door was as dirty as a slovenly old hag, and the key seemed to squirm in the lock. He went into a dingy room with fishing poles leaning against a wall. He picked his way through the litter and up a recently varnished staircase. The bedroom was comfortable—but there was no doll in sight. He looked everywhere, even under the bed, until he found her in a wardrobe. At first it was like running into one of Mary's surprises. The doll was in a black evening gown dotted with tiny rhinestones like drops of glass. If she had been in one of his showcases he would have thought of her as a widow sprinkled with tears. Suddenly he heard a blast, like a gunshot. He ran to look over the edge of the staircase and saw a fishing pole lying on the floor below, in a small cloud of dust. Then he decided to wrap the doll in a blanket and carry her down to the river. She was light and cold, and while he looked for a hidden spot under the trees, he caught a scent that did not seem to come from the forest and traced it to her. He found a soft patch of grass, spread out the blanket, holding her by the legs, slung over his shoulder, and laid her down as gently as if she had fainted in his arms. In spite of the seclusion, he was uneasy. A frog jumped and landed nearby. As it sat there for a long moment, panting, he wondered which way it was going to leap next and finally threw a stone at it. But, to his disappointment, he still could not devote his full attention to this new Daisy Doll. He dared not look her in the face for fear of her lifeless scorn. Instead, he heard a strange murmur mixed with the sound of water. It came from the river, where he saw a boy in a boat, rowing toward him with horrible grimaces. He had a big head, gripped the oars with tiny hands, and seemed to move only his mouth, which was like a piece of gut hideously twisted in its strange murmur. Horace grabbed the doll and ran back to the shy man's house.

On his way home, after this adventure with a Daisy belonging to someone else, he thought of moving to some other country and never looking at another doll. He hurried into the black house and up to the bedroom, grimly determined to get rid of Eulalie—and found Mary sprawled face down on the bed, crying. He went up and stroked her hair, but realized Eulalie was on the bed with them. So he called in one of the twins and ordered her to remove the doll and to have Frank come for her. He stretched out next to Mary and they both lay there in silence waiting for night to fall. And then, taking her hand and searching painfully for words, as if struggling with a foreign language, he confessed how disappointed he was in the dolls and how miserable his life had been without her.

IX

Mary thought Horace's disappointment in the dolls was final, and for a while they both acted as if happier times were back. The first few days, the memories of Daisy were bearable. But then they began to fall into unexpected silences—and each knew who the other was thinking of. One morning, strolling in the garden, Mary stopped by the tree where she had put Daisy to surprise Horace. There, remembering the story made up by the neighbors and the fact that she had actually killed Daisy, she burst into tears. When Horace came out to ask her what was wrong, she met him with a bleak silence, refusing to explain. He realized she had lost much of her appeal, standing there with folded arms, without Daisy. Then, one evening, he was seated in the little parlor, blaming himself for Daisy's death, brooding over his guilt, when suddenly he noticed a black cat in the room. He got up, annoyed, intending to rebuke Alex for letting it in, when Mary appeared saying she had brought it. She was in such a gay mood, hugging him as she told him about it, that he did not want to upset her by throwing it out, but he hated it for the way it had taken advantage of his guilty feelings to sneak up on him. And soon it became a source of further discord as she trained it to sleep on the bed. He would wait for her to fall asleep, then start an earthquake under the covers until he dislodged it. One night she woke up in the middle of the earthquake:

"Was that you kicking the cat, Horace?"

"I don't know."

She kept coming to the defense of the cat, scolding him when he was mean to it. One night, after dinner, he went into the show room to play the piano. For some days now he had called off the scenes in the glass cases and, against his habit, left the dolls in the dark, alone with only the drone of the machines. He lit a footlamp by the piano, and there, on the lid, indistinguishable from the piano except for its eyes, was the cat. Startled, he brushed it off roughly and chased it into the little parlor. There, jumping and clawing to get out, it ripped a curtain off the door to the courtyard. Mary was watching from the dining room. She saw the curtain come down and rushed in with strong words. The last he heard was:

"You made me stab Daisy and now I suppose you want me to kill the cat."

He put on his hat and went out for a walk. He was thinking that, if she had forgiven him—at one point, when they were making up, she had even said, "I love you because you're a bit mad"—Mary had no right now to blame him for Daisy's death. In any case, seeing her lose her attraction without Daisy was punishment enough. The cat, instead of adding to her appeal, cheapened her. She had been crying when he left and he had thought, "Well, it's her cat—so it's her guilt." At the same time, he had the uneasy feeling that her guilt was nothing compared to his, and that, while it was true that she no longer inspired him, it was also true that he was falling back into his old habit of letting her wash his sins away. And so it would always be, even on his deathbed. He imagined her at his side still, on his predictably cowardly last days or minutes, sharing his unholy dread. Perhaps, worse still—he hadn't made up his mind on that point—he would not know she was there.

At the corner he stopped to gather his wits so he could cross without being run over. For a long time he wandered in the dark streets, lost in thought. Suddenly he found himself in Acacia Park. He sat on a bench, still thinking about his life, resting his eyes on a spot under the trees. Then he followed the long shadows of the trees down to a lake, where he stopped to wonder vaguely about his soul, which was like a gloomy silence over the dark water: a silence with a memory of its own, in which he recognized the noise of the machines, as if it were another form of silence. Perhaps the noise had been a steamboat sailing by, and the silence was the memories of dolls left in the wreck as it sank in the night. Suddenly coming back to reality, he saw a young couple get up out of the shadows. As they approached, he remembered kissing Mary for the first time in a fig tree, nearly falling out of the tree, after picking the first figs. The couple walked by a few feet away, crossed a narrow street and went into a small house. He noticed a row of similar houses, some with "for rent" signs. When he got home, he made up again with Mary. But, later that night, alone for a moment in the show room, he thought of renting one of the small houses on the park with a Daisy Doll.

The next day at breakfast something about the cat caught his attention: it had green bows in its ears. Mary explained that all newborn kittens had the tips of their ears pierced by the druggist with one of those machines used for punching holes in file paper. He found this amusing and decided it was a good sign. From a street phone he called Frank to ask him how he could distinguish the Daisy Dolls from the others in the Springwear collection. Frank said that at the moment there was only one, near the cash register, wearing a single long earring. The fact that there was only one left seemed providential to Horace: she was meant for him. And he began to relish the idea of returning to his vice as to a voluptuous fate. He could have taken a trolley, but he did not want to break his mood, so he walked, thinking about how he was going to tell his doll apart in the throng of other dolls. Now he was also part of a throng, pleasantly lost—it was the day before Carnival—in the holiday crowd. The store was farther away than he had anticipated. He began to feel tired—and anxious to meet the doll. A child aimed a horn at him and let out an awful blast in his face. He started to have horrible misgivings and wondered whether he should not put things off until afternoon. But when he reached the store and saw costumed dolls in the show windows he decided to go in. The Daisy Doll was wearing a wine-colored Renaissance costume. A tiny mask added to her proud bearing and he felt like humbling her. But a salesgirl he knew came up with a crooked smile and he withdrew.

In a matter of days he had installed the doll in one of the small houses by the park. Twice a week, at nine in the evening, Frank sent a girl from his shop over with a cleaning woman. At ten o'clock the girl filled the doll with hot water and left. Horace had kept the doll's mask on. He was delighted with her and called her Hermione. One night when they were sitting in front of a picture he saw her eyes reflected in the glass: they shone through the black mask and looked thoughtful. From then on he always sat in the same place, cheek to cheek with her, and whenever he thought the eyes in the glass—it was a picture of a waterfall—took on an expression of humbled pride he kissed her passionately. Some nights he crossed the park with her—he seemed to be walking a ghost—and they sat on a bench near a fountain. But suddenly he would realize her water was getting cold and hurry her back into the house.

Not long after that there was a big fashion show in the Springwear store. A huge glass case filled the whole of the top floor: it was in the center of the room, leaving just enough space on all four sides for the spectators to move around it. Because people came not only for the fashions but also to pick out the Daisy Dolls, the show was a tremendous success. The showcase was divided into two sections by a mirror that extended to the ceiling. In the section facing the entrance, the scene—arranged and interpreted by Horace's boys—represented an old folk tale, "The Woman of the Lake." A young woman lived in the depths of a forest, near a lake. Every morning she left her tent and went down to the lake to comb her hair. She had a mirror which some said she held up behind her, facing the water, in order to see the back of her head. One morning, after a late party, some high-society ladies decided to pay the lonely woman a visit. They were to arrive at dawn, ask her why she lived alone, and offer their help. When they came up on her, the woman of the lake was combing. She saw their elegant gowns through her hair, and curtsied humbly before them. But at their first question she straightened up and set out along the edge of the lake. The ladies, thinking she was going to answer the question or show them some secret, followed her. But the lonely woman only went round and round the lake, trailed by the ladies, without saying or showing them anything. So the ladies left in disgust, and from then on she was known as "the madwoman of the lake." Which is why, in that part of the country, a person lost in silent thought is said to be "going round the lake."

In the showcase, the woman of the lake appeared seated at a dressing table on the edge of the water. She wore a frilly white robe embroidered with yellow leaves. On the dresser stood a number of vials of perfume and other objects. It was the moment in the story when the ladies arrived in their evening gowns. All sorts of faces enthralled by the scene went by outside the glass, looking the dolls up and down, and not only for their fashions. There were glinting eyes that jumped suspiciously from a skirt to a neckline, from one doll to the next, distrusting even the virtuous ones like the woman of the lake. Other wary eyes seemed to tiptoe over the dresses as if afraid of slipping and landing on bare flesh. A young girl bowed her head in Cinderella-like awe at the worldly splendors that she imagined went with the beautiful gowns. A man knit his brows and averted his eyes from his wife, hiding his urge to own a Daisy Doll. The dolls, in general, did not seem to care whether they were being dressed or undressed. They were like mad dreamers oblivious to everything but their poses.

The other section of the showcase was subdivided into two parts—a beach and a forest. The dolls on the beach wore bathing suits. Horace had stopped to observe two in a "conversational" pose: one with concentric circles drawn on her belly, like a shooting target (the circles were red), the other with fish painted on her shoulderblades. Carrying his small head stiffly, like another doll head, among the spectators, Horace moved on to the forest. The dolls in that scene were natives and half-naked. Instead of hair, some grew plants with small leaves from their heads, like vines that trailed down their backs; they had flowers or stripes on their dark skins, like cannibals. Others were painted all over with very bright human eyes. He took an immediately liking to a negress, who looked normal except for a cute little black face with red button lips painted on each breast. He went on circling the showcase until he located Frank and asked him:

"Which of the dolls in the forest are Daisies?"

"Why, dear boy, in that section they're all Daisies."

"I want the negress sent to the house by the park."

"I'm sold out right now. It'll take at least a week."

In fact, no less than twenty days went by before Horace and the negress could meet in the house by the park. She was in bed, with the covers drawn up to her chin.

He found her less interesting than expected, and when he pulled back the covers she let out a fiendish cackle in his face. It was Mary, who proceeded to vent her spite on him with bitter words. She explained how she had learned of his latest escapade: it turned out his cleaning woman also worked for her cousin Prairie. Noticing his strange calm—he seemed distraught—she stopped short. But then, trying to hide her amazement, she asked:

"So now what do you have to say for yourself?"

He went on staring blankly, like a man sunk into a stupor after an exhaustion of years. Then he started to turn himself around with a funny little shuffle. Mary said, "Wait for me," and got up to wash off the black paint in the bathroom. She was frightened and had started to cry and sneeze at the same time. When she got back he had vanished. But she found him at home, locked in a guest room, refusing to talk to anyone.

X

Mary kept asking Horace to forgive her for her latest surprise. But he remained as silent and unyielding as a wooden statue that neither represented a saint nor was able to grant anything. Most of the time he was shuttered in the guest room, almost motionless (they knew he was alive only because he kept emptying bottles of wine from France). Sometimes he went out for a while in the evening. When he returned he had a bite to eat and then lay flat on the bed again, with open eyes. Often Mary went in to look at him, late at night, and found him rigid as a doll, always with the same glassy stare. One night she was stunned to see the cat curled up next to him. She decided to call the doctor, who began giving him injections. He was terrified of the injections but seemed to take more of an interest in life. So, with the help of the boys who worked on the glass cases, she convinced him to let them set up a new show for him.

That night they had dinner in the dining room. He asked for the mustard and drank a considerable amount of wine from France. He took his coffee in the little parlor, then went straight into the show room. The first scene had no caption: among plants and soft lights, in a large rippling pool, he made out a number of loose arms and legs. He saw the sole of a foot stick out through some branches, like a face, followed by the entire leg, which reminded him of a beast in search of prey. As it glanced off the glass wall, it hesitated before veering in the opposite direction. Then came another leg, followed by a hand with its arm, slowly winding and unwinding around each other like bored animals in a cage. He stood there for a while, dreamily watching their different combinations, until there was a meeting of toes and fingers. Suddenly the leg began to straighten out in the commonplace gesture of standing on its foot. He was dismayed and flashed his light at Walter, as he moved the podium to the next scene. There he saw a doll on a bed, wearing a queen's crown. Curled up next to her was Mary's cat. This distressed him and he was angry at the boys for letting it in. At the foot of the bed were three nuns kneeling on prayer stools. The caption read, "The queen died giving alms. She had no time to confess, but her whole country is praying for her." When he looked again, the cat was gone. But he had the uneasy feeling it would turn up again somewhere. He decided to enter the scene— gingerly, watching for the unpleasant surprise the cat was about to spring on him. Bending to peer into the queen's face, he rested a hand on the foot of the bed. Almost at once, a hand belonging to one of the nuns settled on his. He must not have heard Mary's voice pleading with him, because the minute he felt her hand he straightened up, stiff as death, stretching his neck and gasping like a captive bird trying to flap its wings and caw. Mary took hold of his arm, but he pulled away in terror and began turning himself around with a little shuffle, as he had done the day she had painted her face black and laughed in his face. She was rattled and frightened again and let out a scream. He tripped on a nun, knocking her over. Then, on his way out of the case, he missed the small door and walked into the glass wall. There he stood pounding on the glass with his hands, which were like birds beating against a closed window. Mary did not dare take hold of his arm again. She ran to call Alex, who was nowhere to be found. Finally he appeared, and, thinking she was a nun, asked politely what he could do for her. Crying, she said that Horace was mad. They went into the show room but could not find him. They were still looking for him when they heard his steps in the gravel of the garden. They saw him cut straight through the flowerbeds. And when they caught up with him, he was going toward the noise of the machines.

The Flooded House

The first thing I always remember from those days is rowing a boat round and round a small island of plants. The plants were changed frequently: they didn't get along there. Miss Margaret sat facing the stern, with her huge back to me. If she gazed long and hard at the island she might let something out, although it was never what she had promised: she spoke only of the plants, as if hiding her other thoughts between them. I kept losing hope, tired of raising and dipping the oars like hands bored with counting always the same drops of water. But I knew my weariness was a bit of deceit mixed—as I would rediscover the next time around, and the one after that—with a little happiness. So I was resigned to waiting for the few words that would reach me from that massive world gliding backward with me, drawn by the effort of my aching arms.

One evening, just before dark, I had the sudden feeling Miss Margaret's husband might be buried on the island: that would have explained why she made me circle it endlessly and then got me up in the middle of the night—on moonlit nights—to circle it a few more times. Yet her husband couldn't be on the island: according to Hector, her niece's boyfriend, she had lost him over a cliff in Switzerland. I also recalled what the boatman had told me the night I arrived in the flooded house, while rowing me slowly up "the water avenue," which was as wide as a street and bordered by plane trees with hanging seed balls. One of the things I had learned from him was that he and a handyman had filled in the courtyard fountain to turn it into an island. It also seemed to me that the motions of Miss Margaret's head—on the afternoons when her eyes went from her book to the island and back to the book again—bore no relation to a dead man hidden under the plants. On the other hand, once when she had looked me full in the face, I'd had the impression that her thick lenses taught her eyes to dissemble, and that the great glass dome over the courtyard containing the small island was meant to enclose the silence of the dead.

Then I remembered the glass walls and dome had been built before her time—and it was good to know that the house, like a human being, had performed different functions through the years. First it had been a country house, then an observatory, until the telescope that had been ordered from the United States was sunk to the bottom of the sea by the Germans, after which the courtyard had been made into a winter garden, and finally Miss Margaret had bought the house in order to flood it.

Now, while our boat circled the island, I enveloped her in suspicions that never seemed to fit her. But the enormity of her body in its naked surroundings tempted me to imagine a dark past for it. At night, wrapped in silence, it seemed even more immense, like a sleeping elephant, and sometimes she made a strange sound in her throat, like a hoarse sigh.

I had started to grow fond of her because, since being

abruptly transplanted by her generosity from penury to my current opulence, I had been enjoying a lazy well-being, and because she lent herself—as a white elephant might lend its back to a traveler—to absurd imaginings. She also had a way—although she never questioned me about my life—of raising her brows when we met as if they were about to fly off, and then her eyes, behind their thick lenses, would seem to be asking, "What is it, my boy?"

So, gradually, my feelings for her had become illusions—and if I let my memory roam free now, it's this first Miss Margaret who comes to mind, because the second one, the real one I got to know when she told me her story toward the end of the season, managed to remain strangely inaccessible to me.

But now I must force myself to begin the story at the real beginning and not linger too long over the preferences of memory.

I was very weak one day in Buenos Aires when I ran into Hector. He invited me to a wedding and stuffed me with food. During the ceremony he thought of a job for me: choking with laughter, he told me about a "dotty dowager" who could help me. She was a generous soul, he said, adding that she'd had a house flooded by means of a system devised by a Seville architect, who had previously flooded a house for a rich Arab determined to make up for the desert. Shortly afterward, Hector visited Miss Margaret with his girlfriend, told her about my books, and recommended me as a "fellow sleepwalker." She immediately contributed some money and offered to invite me to the flooded house the next summer, if I knew how to row. For some reason Hector postponed taking me to meet her, then she fell ill. She was still recovering when Hector and his girl joined her that summer. For the first few days the house was dry, but when the water had been let in they sent for me. I took a train out to a small town, from which I reached the house by car. The area seemed barren to me, but when night came I felt there might be trees hidden in the dark. The driver left me with my suitcases on a small pier at the entrance to the canal—the "water avenue." He rang a bell that hung from a plane tree. But the pale light of the boat had already broken away from the light of the house—I could see a bright dome and next to it a dark monster as tall as the dome: it was the water tower—and was coming toward me. By the pale light the boat was a greenish color. It brought a man in white who started talking before he had reached me and kept up his conversation all the way back to the house (he was the one who told me about the fountain having been filled in with earth). Suddenly the light of the dome went out. At that moment the boatman was saying, "She won't have any papers or junk thrown in the water. It's her floor and she wants it kept clean. There's no door to shut the dining room off from the bedroom. One morning when the lady woke up early she saw a loaf of bread that my wife had dropped come swimming toward her from the dining room. She was so angry she fired my wife on the spot. She said there was nothing uglier in the world than a piece of bread swimming by."

The front of the house was smothered in vines. We reached a wide entrance hall lit with a yellowish glow. From there I could see part of the great watery courtyard and its island. The water flowed into a room on the left, under a closed door. The boatman tied the boat to a large bronze frog mounted on the walk to the right, and we got off on that side and carried my suitcases up a concrete staircase. On the second floor was a corridor with glass windows that had steamed up in the smoke from a huge kitchen. There I was met by a dumpy woman. She wore her hair in a bun with flowers and looked Spanish. She said the lady, her mistress, would not receive me until the next day, but that she would call me on the phone later that night.

The bulky, dark furniture in my room seemed uncomfortable between the white walls assaulted by the raw light of a single clear bulb that hung naked in the middle of the room. The Spanish maid lifted a suitcase and was surprised at its weight. I said it was full of books, and she began to tell me about how it was "too many books" that had ruined her lady's health "and even made her deaf—and then she expects us not to shout at her." I must have done something to show the light was hurting my eyes and she said:

"The light bother you? It bothers her, too."

I lit a table lamp with a green shade that I thought would give out a pleasant glow. Just then a phone behind the lamp rang and the Spanish maid answered it. She kept saying "yes" over and over, the white flowers in her bun quivering each time she nodded. Then she seemed to be holding back the words that reached her lips in short breaths and syllables. Finally, with a sigh, she hung up and left in silence.

I ate well and drank good wine. The Spanish maid kept talking to me, but I was worrying about what would become of me in that house, and only nodded at her now and then, dipping my head like a piece of heavy furniture on a weak floor. With my coffee, I lit a cigarette, and when she picked up the empty cup, reaching through the smoky light, she told me again that the lady would call me on the phone. I kept staring at the receiver, expecting the ring at any moment, but it still took me by surprise. Miss Margaret asked me about my trip and whether it had been very tiring.

She spoke in a faint but pleasant voice. I made my answer loud and clear, pronouncing each word distinctly.

"You can speak naturally," she said. "I'll explain later why I've told Mary I'm deaf. I'd like you to feel at home here—you're my guest. All I'll ask of you is to row my boat and endure something I have to tell you. In exchange I'll be happy to contribute monthly to your savings, and I'll try to be useful to you. I've read your stories as you published them. I didn't want to discuss them with Hector so as not to get into an argument—I'm very impressionable. But we'll have a chance to talk soon . . ."

I was totally seduced: I even asked her to call me at six the next morning. That first night in the flooded house, I was so intrigued over what Miss Margaret might have to tell me that a strange restlessness kept me awake for hours. I don't know at what time I finally sank into sleep. At six in the morning a short ring like an insect bite made me jump out of bed. I waited in suspense for the sound to repeat itself. When it did I grabbed the receiver.

"Are you awake?"

"I am."

We agreed on a time to meet, and she said I could go down in my pajamas and she would be waiting for me at the foot of the stairs. At that moment I felt like a bellboy granted a short break.

The night before I had imagined the darkness almost entirely made up of trees; but they seemed to have dispersed at dawn, because now, when I opened the window, there was nothing but a vast empty plain under a clear sky: the only trees were the ones along the canal. A soft breeze rippled their leaves as they stretched across the "water avenue" from either side, stealthily touching overhead. Perhaps I would find a new life of quiet contentment among those trees. I shut the window carefully, as if to put away the view so I could return to it later on.

Up the corridor the door to the kitchen was open, and I went in to ask for some hot water to shave. Just then, Mary was pouring out a cup of coffee for a young man who wished me a respectful "good morning": he was the man in charge of the waterworks, and I heard him say something about the motors. With a smile the Spanish cook turned me around by the arm, saying she would bring everything to my room. On my way back down the corridor I saw Miss Margaret's tall, bent figure looming at the foot of the stairs, in her boat. She was very stout and overflowed the small boat like a plump foot in a low-cut shoe. Her head was bent because she was reading some papers. She had wound her hair up in a braid that looked like a gold crown. I took all this in at a glance, afraid she would catch me staring at her. From that moment until we came together I was nervous. The minute I put my foot on the stairs she began to watch me closely, with undisguised curiosity. I felt like a thick liquid squeezing down a narrow funnel. She stuck her hand out long before I reached the bottom and said:

"You're not at all like I imagined you . . . It happens to me every time. I don't see how I'm going to get your stories to agree with your face."

I tried to smile but could only nod like a horse fretting at the bit. I managed to say:

"I've been dying to meet you and to know what's going to happen."

Finally my hand found hers. She did not let go until I had climbed into the seat with the oars, facing the stern. With labored movements, she settled into her armchair, which had its back to me, breathing fitfully. She said she was studying budget estimates for a home for unwed mothers and would not be able to talk to me just then. I began to row, she controlled the rudder, and we kept our eyes on the wake we were cutting in the water. For a moment I thought it was all a big mistake: I was no boatman to handle such a monstrous weight. She had her mind entirely on the home for unwed mothers, with no regard for the immensity of her body and the smallness of my hands. In my anguished effort to pull at the oars I leaned so far forward that my eyes came flat against her backrest, and the dark varnish and wickerwork full of little holes, like a honeycomb, reminded me of a barbershop my grandfather used to take me to when I was six years old, except that these holes were stuffed with the folds of white bathrobe containing Miss Margaret's bloated shape. She was saying:

"There's no need to hurry. It'll only tire you."

I immediately relaxed the oars, fell into a sort of happy void, and, for the first time, felt myself gliding with her over the silent water. But then I became aware of having started to row again. I was as tired as if I had been at it for ages—maybe that was what had awakened me. A bit later she waved at me as if to say goodbye, but she was steering me toward the nearest frog. There were bronze frogs for mooring the boat anchored all along the walk that went around the lake. With a painful heave and words too faint to reach me, she extracted her body from the armchair and stood it on the walk. Suddenly we were motionless, and that was when she first made that strange sound in her throat which began as if she were dredging up something she had almost swallowed and ended in a hoarse sigh. I had my eyes on the frog to which we had tied the boat, but I could also see her feet, planted on the walk as steadily as any of the frogs. Everything seemed to suggest she was about to speak—or she might first make that strange noise in her throat again. If she did, or if she spoke, I would release the breath I was holding in my lungs, so as not to miss her first words. She kept me waiting for a long time and I began to let my breath out slowly, as if opening a door into a room where someone was sleeping. I didn't know if the wait meant I should look at her, but I decided to remain motionless as long as I had to. The frog and the feet caught my attention again, and I watched them out of the corner of my eye. The part of the foot crammed into each shoe was small, but a great white throat burst over the brim to become a plump leg as tender as innocent baby flesh, and the mountainous weight supported on those feet was like the fantastic figure a child might see in a dream. I had waited so long for the sound in her throat that my mind had wandered by the time I heard her first words, which made me think of water silently collected in a huge urn and now spilling over the top, a drop at a time.

"I promised to tell you . . . but I can't today . . . I have a world of things on my mind . . ."

When she said, "world," I could imagine her well-rounded shape without looking at her.

"Besides," she went on, "though it's not your fault . . . It bothers me that you're so different."

Her eyes crinkled and her face broke into an unexpected smile. Her upper lip gathered at the edges like some theater curtains to display a row of big sparkling teeth in perfect alignment.

"Whereas I'm delighted that you're just the way you are."

I must have said this with a roguish smile because I felt like an old-time charmer with a feather in his cap. Emboldened, I searched for her green eyes behind their lenses. But in the depths of those two small crystal lakes without a

-239-

ripple, her eyelids had shut and swollen in shame. Her lips began to wrap over her teeth again and gradually her whole face flushed a reddish color I had seen on Chinese lanterns. There was the sort of silence produced by a misunderstanding, and she stubbed her foot on a frog trying to clamber back into the boat. I would have given anything to turn back the clock and erase what had just happened. My careless words had revealed base thoughts that I regretted bitterly. The distance between the island and the surrounding glass walls had become a hostile space where things exchanged offended looks, as if agreeing to reject me— which was a pity, because I had started to grow fond of them. But then suddenly Miss Margaret said:

"Stop by the stairs and go to your room. I think later I'll feel very much like talking to you."

I was watching some reflections in the lake and they seemed favorable. The plants were out of sight but I felt their approval. So I ran happily up the bare bones of the concrete staircase, like a child climbing the spine of a prehistoric animal.

I had just begun to arrange my books properly in the wardrobe, enjoying the smell of fresh wood, when the phone rang:

"Please come down again for a while. We'll go around a few times in silence and when I give you the sign you'll stop at the foot of the stairs and return to your room, and I won't bother you again for two days."

Everything happened as she had foreseen, although once when we circled close to the island she gazed at the plants and seemed about to speak.

Then began an indefinite waiting period: a vague stretch of lazy days, boring moonlit nights, and all sorts of hunches and suspicions involving the husband who might or might not be buried under the plants. I knew I had great difficulty understanding others and I tried to imagine Miss Margaret a bit as if I were seeing her through Hector's eyes, then through Mary's eyes, but I was too lazy to keep that up for long and soon fell back on my selfish ways: listening placidly while I rowed, hoping that if I just sat there and waited with careless but genuinely affectionate goodwill for her to say whatever she pleased, in the end she would settle comfortably in my understanding. Or it might happen that by simply living next to her, letting myself fall under her spell, that understanding would gradually form in me on its own and reach out to envelop her. Afterward, in my room with my books, I would return to my view of the plain, forgetting Miss Margaret. And that was the view I would steal—harmlessly—and take with me when I left at the end of the summer.

But other things were happening.

One morning the man in charge of the waterworks had a blueprint spread on a table. His eyes and fingers were following the curves representing the pipes that wormed their way through the walls and under the floors. He had not noticed me, although his tangled hair seemed to bristle watchfully in every direction. Finally he lifted his eyes. It took him a minute to adjust to the idea that he was looking at me instead of the blueprint. Then he started to explain how the machines sucked in and vomited out the water of the house through the pipes to produce an artificial storm. I had not yet witnessed one of his storms—but I had seen the blurs of holes with metal flaps under the water. He said they were spouts that alternately opened and closed, some swallowing water, others spitting it out. I was having a hard time understanding the system of valves, and he had begun to explain it all over again when Mary came in:

"You know she wants those twisted pipes kept out of sight. She says they're like guts showing . . . and what if she comes by, like last year? . . . And you, sir, if you please." She had turned to me. "You've heard what I said, so keep your mouth shut. Did she tell you we're having a 'wake' tonight? . . . That's right, she puts candles in pudding bowls, sets the bowls to float all around the bed, and makes believe it's her own wake. Then she has running water sent in to sweep the bowls away."

At nightfall I heard Mary's footsteps, the gong that announced the rush of water, and the sound of the motors. But by then I was bored again and refused to let anything surprise me.

Another night, after too much food and drink, while rowing Miss Margaret around endlessly, I had the feeling I was in a crazy dream, hidden behind a mountain that glided along in the silence I associated with heavenly bodies. And yet it gave me a secret satisfaction to know the "mountain" moved only because my force was driving the boat. At one point she asked me to pull alongside the island and wait there quietly for a while. They had put shady plants with long stalks on the island that day, tipped forward like parasols that now blocked the moonlight shining in through the glass dome. I was perspiring in the heat and the plants hovered over us menacingly. I thought of slipping into the water, but Miss Margaret would have felt the weight of the boat shift and I gave up the idea. My mind had wandered off on thoughts of its own: "Her name is like her body—two big fat syllables carrying the main load and the third for her head and tiny features . . . It's unbelievable: such a beautiful night, with such a wide open sky, and here we are, two grownup persons sitting so close together and each off on his own stupid thoughts. It must be two in the morning and we're still awake . . . for what? . . . Suffocating under these branches . . . and look at her: wrapped in her solitary self, impenetrable . . ."

Suddenly, without warning, there was a roar in my ear. I was badly shaken. It took me a minute to realize she had coughed to clear her throat and was saying:

"Please, no questions . . ."

She broke off. I was choking back words I seemed to remember hearing late one night from the bandoneonist of a tango orchestra I used to play with: "So, no questions, all right? Why don't you just go to sleep . . ."

She completed her sentence:

". . . until I've told you everything."

Finally I was going to hear the promised words—when I least expected them. The silence crowded us together under the branches, but I dared not move the boat to another spot. I had time to hear myself thinking about Miss Margaret in a smothered voice, as if there were a pillow over my head: "Poor thing—so lonely, so in need of talking to someone . . . And such a huge body to manage, full of so much sadness . . ."

When she began, it seemed her words also sounded inside me, as if I were speaking them—which may be why now I can't distinguish what she said from what I was thinking. Besides, it won't be easy to put together all the words she spoke at different times and I may have to mix in quite a few of my own.

"Four years ago, when I left Switzerland, I couldn't stand the noise of the train, so I got off at a small town in Italy . . ."

It seemed she was about to tell with whom she had gotten off, but she stopped. A long while went by and I thought she would say nothing more that night. Her voice had dragged unevenly, like the trail left by a wounded animal. In the stifling silence full of tangled branches, I decided to go over what I had just heard. It crossed my mind that I had no right to do what I was doing: relieving her of her painful memories so I could fondle them later on when I was alone. But then, as if someone were forcing me to let go of that idea, others sneaked in. The someone must have been *him*: they had once been in that small town in Italy together. She had left Switzerland—after losing him there—perhaps without realizing she had not yet given up all hope (Hector had told me the remains were never found), until the noise of the train carrying her away began to drive her mad. So she had decided to stay in the area and had gotten off at the small town in Italy. But there, no doubt, everything had brought back memories that made her even more desperate. "She can't tell me all this right now, it's too private. Or maybe she thinks Hector has already told me the whole story. But he didn't say she was this way because of the loss of her husband, he just said: 'Maggie's always been a bit batty'; and, according to Mary, what's addled her brain is 'too many books.' Maybe they can't see the real problem because she hasn't confessed her sorrow to them. I wouldn't have understood a thing myself if Hector hadn't let something out, because Miss Margaret has never mentioned her husband to me."

I went on turning these ideas over in my mind and, when her words started up again, it was the night of her arrival in the small town in Italy. She was installed in a room on the second floor of a hotel. She had been in bed for a while when she heard the sound of water. She got up and looked out the window of a gallery leading into the courtyard. There were some gleams of moonlight and other lights. Then, suddenly, she saw a fountain—and it was as if she had met a face that had been watching for her. At first she could not be sure the water was not playing tricks on her, showing her only the dark face of the stone fountain, but it looked innocent enough, and she went back to bed carrying it in her eyes, careful not to spill it. The following night there was no sound, but she got up all the same. This time the water was a murky trickle, but back in bed she felt it watching her again, as it had done the night before, only now it was through leaves caught in the sluggish flow. She went on seeing it inside her own eyes, then it seemed she and the water were both contemplating the same object—so that she could not tell whether a premonition she had a moment later had come to her from depths in the water or in her soul. She had almost fallen asleep when she felt someone trying to communicate with her, sending her a message through the water, and understood why it insisted on looking at her and being seen by her. She got up in a daze and wandered barefoot around her room and up and down the gallery. But now the light and everything else had changed, as if someone had breathed a different air and another sense of things into the space surrounding her. This time she dared not look out at the water, and when she got back in bed she felt real tears, at long last, falling on her nightgown.

The next morning, surrounded by shrill women whose loud talk seemed to have caught its interest, the fountain ignored her and she decided the silence of the night had been playing tricks on her: the water could never have transmitted a message or put her in touch with anyone. Listening carefully to what the women were saying, she heard only empty chitchat. But then she realized the water was not to blame for the silly words dropping into it like wastepaper: she must not allow the light of day to play tricks on her now. To get away, she went for a stroll—and came on a poor old man with a watering can. When the old man tipped the can it let out a skirt of spray, which rustled as if a pair of legs were walking in it. She was moved and thought: "No, I can't leave the water. It must have something to say if it's so insistent—like a little girl struggling to make herself understood." That night she avoided the fountain because she had a violent headache. She decided to take a painkiller. But the minute she saw the water in the glass, suspended in the dim light, she imagined it was the same water somehow reaching out to put a secret on her lips, and she said to herself: "No, this is serious. Whoever it is knows the time to bring water for the soul is at night."

Early in the morning, before anyone was up, she went out to the fountain to study her connection with the water more closely. As soon as she rested her eyes on the water she felt them drop a thought into it. (The way Miss Margaret phrased it was: "a thought I don't care to discuss right now," and, after elaborately clearing her throat: "a shapeless thought, limp as a rag that has been wrung out too many times. Slowly, it started to sink, and I let it settle on the bottom. And there it broke into reflections that I drew back into my eyes and soul. I realized, then, for the first time, that water is the place to grow memories, because it transforms everything reflected in it and it's receptive to thought. In moments of despair you shouldn't cast your body into the water but rather your thoughts, which will come back renewed and change your whole outlook on life.") Those, more or less, were her words.

Then she got dressed and took a walk. Some distance ahead, she saw a stream. At first it meant nothing to her, until she remembered streams carried water, and that water was the one thing in the world only she could communicate with. But when she sat by the edge of the stream, letting her eyes follow the current, she had the sudden notion that this water was not addressing her and might even carry her memories off to some faraway place, wearing them down. Her eyes made her concentrate on a leaf that had just fallen into the water from a tree. It drifted for a minute, and, just as it went under, she heard a heavy tread like a dull throb. She felt the pounding of vague fears and premonitions and her mind went dark. The tread turned out to be a horse approaching from the other side of the stream. It had a jaunty gait and looked tame and a bit bored as it sank its muzzle in the water to drink. The water enlarged its teeth, as if she were seeing them through a pane of wavy glass. It raised its head dripping water from every hair but without losing its dignity, and she thought of the horses of her own country and of how different the water they drank must be.

That evening, in the hotel dining room, she recognized one of the women who had been chattering by the fountain and kept an eye on her. The woman was with her husband, whose adoring look she met with an ironic smile, and when she raised a glass to her lips Miss Margaret thought: "The water doesn't care what mouth it's in." She was so upset she went straight back to her room and had a fit of tears. Then she fell into a heavy sleep. At two in the morning she woke up tossing in bed, her soul filled to the brim with the memory of the stream. Now her thoughts argued in its favor: "Stream water is like blind hope flowing through you, beyond your control. If it's a weak stream it can easily be swallowed up in a hole and trapped there. Then it will become sad and stagnant, full of muddy silence, like a madam's head. But I must let my hopes run on and carry me along, blindly, if possible, not worrying too much about where they will lead, like water simply following its instinct, until my thoughts and memories become an irresistible current . . ." On this quickly rising tide of thoughts, she got up, packed her bags and started to walk up and down her room and the gallery, not daring to face the water of the fountain. She was thinking: "Water is the same all over the world. I can watch my memories grow in any water anywhere in the world." She was in an agony of anticipation until she had settled into her seat in the train. But then the clatter of the wheels depressed her, and she felt sorry for the water she had left behind in the hotel fountain. She remembered the night it had been murky and clogged with leaves, like a little beggar girl offering her something, innocently but with a touch of natural malice in her innocence, as if to warn her that the hope or promise she held out would remain unfulfilled. She buried her face in a towel and cried and felt better. But she could not take her mind off the quiet fountain water "standing still in the night," she was thinking, "as I prefer it, slowly sinking into silence and sleep, full of tangled plants: that's what the water inside me is really like." And, closing her eyes, she imagined herself as "a blind woman reaching out to the surface of the water, vaguely remembering a pond with plants she saw as a child, when her eyes still had some sight left in them."

At this point in her story, Miss Margaret stopped for a while, until I became aware of having returned to the night in which I was listening to her under the branches. I wasn't sure whether her last thoughts had come to her in the train or crossed her mind now, while she spoke. She was already motioning me to take her back to the foot of the stairs.

That night I didn't turn on my lamp, and, feeling my way around the room, I was reminded of another night when I had gotten a bit high on a drink I was tasting for the first time. It took me a while to get undressed. Later, in bed, with my eyes on the mosquito net, the words shed by Miss Margaret's body came back to me.

Even before she opened her mouth I had realized not only that she belonged to her husband but that I had been thinking about her too much, and sometimes in a guilty way—and for a moment I'd had the feeling I was the one hiding thoughts among the plants. But as soon as she started to speak, I had felt my body sag miserably under her weight, as if she were sinking into the water and dragging me with her. My guilty thoughts had still managed to surface once or twice, but too fleetingly to seem worth bothering with, and as her story unfolded I had begun to see the water as the spirit of a religion that revealed unexpected aspects of us in which sins had another meaning and mattered less. The sense of sharing in a religion born of the water had grown stronger every minute. Although Miss Margaret and I were the only flesh-and-blood members of that religion, the memories of my own life stirring in the water, in the pauses between the incidents of her story, had seemed to join the flock, one by one, slowly coming to life, as if traveling toward me from some distant time, after some great sin.

Suddenly I had realized a new soul was being born in me from my old one, and that I would follow Miss Margaret not only into the water but into the memory of her husband. And after she had interrupted her story, when I was on my way up the concrete staircase, I had imagined water raining from the sky and the faithful meeting under it.

But now in bed, under the mosquito net, I circled Miss Margaret's story in a different way and, to my surprise, felt myself gradually being drawn down into my old self, tormented by my own ghosts, as if the net that hold my wide-open eyes hung over a swamp where another flock, the one of my own faithful, rose and called out to me. I remembered my guilty thoughts—loaded with the intentions I knew all too well—in some detail. They had begun on one of the first afternoons, when I had suspected Miss Margaret would sweep me up like a great wave, and that I would be too lazy or weak to resist. My reaction had been to try to leave the house, but the impulse had lasted only a moment, as if I had woken up briefly and made what I thought was a move to get out of bed when all I had really done was roll over to go on sleeping. Another afternoon, I had tried to imagine—this had already happened to me with other women—what I would look like married to Miss Margaret. After thinking it over I had decided, losing heart, that if I pitied her loneliness enough to marry her, my friends would say it had been for her money and my old girlfriends would laugh at the picture of me on a narrow walk, trailing after an enormous woman who turned out to be my wife. (I had already had to follow her along the ledge that encircled the lake, on the nights when she felt like walking.)

Now I didn't care what my friends would say or how hard my old girlfriends would laugh at me: I was like a planet orbiting Miss Margaret, attracted to her by the same force with which she held me at a distance, at once remote and strangely sublime. But my flock kept asking me for the first Miss Margaret, the uncomplicated one, without a husband, before I had gotten to know her, when I could still imagine anything I wanted about her. I can't say what other thoughts were caught in the mosquito net, which vanished when I fell asleep.

The next morning Miss Margaret rang me on the phone to tell me, "Please go back to Buenos Aires for a few days. I'm having the house cleaned and I don't want you to see me without my water." She named the hotel she had reserved for me. She would let me know when I could return.

The invitation to leave set off a jealous reflex in me—first panic, then sadness. The sadness was like a heavy package that I took with me, knowing that as soon as I calmed down I would feel the stupid urge to unwrap it and examine it more closely. By the time I caught the train, I had as little hope that Miss Margaret would love me as she probably had that her husband might still be alive when she took the train to Italy. It was another time and another train, but my longing to have something in common with her made me think: "We've both suffered on the noisy wheels of trains." But the coincidence was as tenuous as if I had guessed only one of the digits of a winning lottery number. I lacked Miss Margaret's gift for finding miraculous waters, nor would I seek comfort in religion. Just the night before, I had been untrue to my own faithful, because even while they were trying to lead me back to the first Miss Margaret I had been summoning up out of the depths of the swamp other faithful that gaped at her spellbound, like bugs drunk on moonlight. The fact was that my sadness took a poet's pride in itself and in the sense of easy well-being it got from feeling unloved and misunderstood. I was the temporary meeting place where my ancestors flowed lazily into my descendants. My two sets of grandparents had been very different, and avowed enemies, but they had sworn off fighting while they passed through my life, which they had chosen to spend in more restful ways, wandering idly without ever meeting, like sleepwalkers in different dreams, and I tried not to provoke them, although if they had met and quarreled I would have preferred the fight to be short and deadly.

In Buenos Aires I had a hard time finding quiet spots where Hector could not reach me. (He would have loved to have some juicy details to add to his spiteful portrait of Miss Margaret.) I was also in a quandary trying to sort out my two Miss Margarets, hesitating between them, as if unable to decide which of two sisters to prefer and which to betray, or how to fuse them so I could love them both at the same time. What bothered me above all was being allowed only the most innocent thoughts with regard to the later Miss Margaret. My idea was to indulge all her fantasies from now on so she would confuse me with her memories of her husband and I could end up supplanting him.

I received the order to return on a windy day and set out at breakneck speed. But the wind that day seemed secretly determined to blow against time, making humans, trains, and everything else move with agonizing slowness. I was the only one to realize this as the trip dragged out endlessly. When I reached the flooded house it was Mary who was waiting for me at the pier. She would not let me row and said that on the very day I had left, before the water was let out, there had been two accidents. First the boatman's wife, Dotty, had turned up, asking Miss Margaret to take her back. She had been fired not only for dumping bread in the water but because she had been caught trying to seduce Hector one of the times he had visited the house early in the summer. Without a word, Miss Margaret had pushed her away and she had fallen into the water. Crying and dripping wet, she had left for good, taking her husband with her. Later that same evening, pulling on the cord with which she drew the dresser up to her bed (the furniture in her bedroom floated on inner tubes like the ones children swim in at the beach), Miss Margaret had spilled a bottle of liquor on a heater she used for warming some cosmetics and the dresser had caught fire. She had called over the phone for water, "as if there weren't enough of it in the room or it weren't the same water as in the rest of the house," Mary said.

The morning after my return was bright and clear, and fresh plants had been brought in. But I was jealous of the changes: they meant Miss Margaret and I would not find our words and thoughts as we had left them under the branches.

After a few days she returned to her story. That night, as on other occasions, a plank had been laid across the water of the entrance hall. When I reached the foot of the stairs Miss Margaret signaled me to stop—and then to follow her. We went all the way around the lake on the narrow walk. Meantime, she was telling me that she had left the town in Italy thinking that water was the same everywhere in the world, but that it had not turned out that way, and more than once she had been forced to shut her eyes and plug her ears with her fingers in order to be with her own water. After a stop in Spain, where an architect had sold her the plans for a flooded house—she gave me no details—she had taken a ship home. The ship was overcrowded, and as soon as she lost sight of land she had realized the water of the ocean was not her water, there were too many unknown beings lurking in its depths. She went on to say there were people on board who spoke of shipwrecks and seemed to dread the water when they gazed into its immensity— which did not prevent them from drawing small amounts of it to fill a bathtub and delivering their naked bodies to it. They also enjoyed going down into the boiler room, where torturing flames made the trapped water writhe furiously. On days of rough seas Miss Margaret lay in her cabin with newspapers and magazines, following rows of letters with her eyes as if they were ant trails or watching a bit of water swish in a jug with a narrow neck. Here she interrupted her story and I noticed she was rocking like a boat. Several times we had been out of step, our bodies swaying in different directions, and I'd had to strain to catch her words, which seemed to blow past in uneven gusts. When we got back to the entrance hall she stopped at the plank, as if afraid of crossing over it, and asked me to fetch the boat. I had to row her around for quite a while before she let out her hoarse sigh and spoke again. Finally she told me she'd had a moment with her soul on the high seas. It happened when she was leaning over the rail, gazing into the quiet deep, which was like an endless skin only faintly disturbed by rippling muscles: she began to have crazy ideas, the kind that come to you in dreams. She imagined that she could walk on the water but was afraid a porpoise would surface, and that she would trip on it and really sink this time. Suddenly she became aware of the drops of sweet water that had been falling on the salty ocean from the sky for the past few seconds. Many of the drops were bunching together and landing on deck in a heavy downpour, battering the ship as if it were under attack. In a moment the whole deck was awash. Miss Margaret looked out at the ocean again: it was taking in the rain and swallowing it as naturally as an animal swallowing another animal. She had only a vague sense of what was happening, when suddenly she shook with laughter. It racked her body before it reached her face, spreading like an earthquake with no known cause. As if to justify it in some way, she said to herself: "It must be some little girl making a mistake—instead of raining on land, she's raining on water." For a moment she sensed how sweet it must be for the ocean to receive the rain, but on her way back down to her cabin, balancing her huge body, she remembered her vision of water swallowing water and felt certain the girl was going toward her death. Then the sweetness became a heavy sadness and she went straight to bed for a long nap. At this point Miss Margaret ended her story for the night and ordered me back to my room.

The voice with which she summoned me over the phone the next morning sounded otherworldly. She said she was inviting me to a ceremony in honor of the water: it would take place that evening. Just before dark I heard the sound of pudding bowls and the quick patter of Mary's steps and my fears were confirmed: I would have to attend Miss Margaret's "wake." She was waiting for me at the foot of the stairs. As the strokes of my oars backed us into the first room, I realized I had been hearing a murmur of water that now grew more intense. There was a sideboard in that room. The ripples spread by the boat made it bob up and down on its inner tubes, clinking glasses and rattling the chains that attached it to the wall. Across the room from it floated a sort of raft. It was rounded and held a table with chairs pulled up to it, inside a rail, like a gathering of deaf-mutes nodding slightly as the boat lapped by. My oars struck a doorframe on either side and we were in the bedroom. And there I saw it: water raining on water. All around the walls, except where there was furniture—the outsized wardrobe, the bed and the dresser—hung gushing showerheads of every shape and color, fed by thin rubber hoses that extended in garlands from a large glass container resembling a Turkish pipe suspended like a lamp from the ceiling. Through the grottolike atmosphere we pulled up to the bed, which stood fairly high out of the water on long glass legs. Miss Margaret took off her shoes and told me to do the same. She clambered up on the huge bed, facing the wall in back of it, where there was an equally huge picture of a bearded white goat standing on its hind legs. She grasped the picture, which swung open like a door, revealing a bathroom. Stepping on the mound of pillows, she hoisted herself through the opening, and returned a moment later carrying two round pudding bowls with candles stuck in them. She ordered me to set the bowls in the water and said there were more coming. As I got up on the bed next to her, I fell on my face. Although I straightened up at once, I had already smelled her perfume in the bedclothes. I was setting the bowls down over the edge of the bed as she handed them to me when suddenly she said: "Not like that, please—it reminds me of a wake" (and I realized Mary had been wrong). There were twenty-eight of them. She knelt on the bed, reached for the phone, which was on one of the night tables, and gave the order for the water to be cut off. In the tomblike silence that followed we began to light the candles, hanging over the foot of the bed, and I was careful not to get in her way. When we were nearly done she dropped the matchbox, which landed in one of the bowls. Leaving me where I was, she rolled over to strike the gong on the other night table. There was also a lamp on that table—the only source of light in the room. She had picked up the stick for sounding the gong when she changed her mind, left the stick by the lamp and half rose to shut the door that was a picture of a goat. Settling back down at the head of the bed, she began to rearrange the pillows, motioning me to strike the gong. Her legs took up so much space that I had to crawl on all fours around the edge of the bed to get to it, which wasn't easy. I don't know why, but I was afraid of falling into the water, although it was only two feet deep. I struck the gong once, and she indicated that this was enough. As I backed up along the bed—there was no room to turn around—I saw Miss

Margaret lying face up under the picture of the goat, her eyes wide open, waiting. The pudding bowls also lay still in the water, like small boats resting at harbor before a storm. Almost as soon as the motors came on, the water started to roll and churn, and then Miss Margaret heaved herself off her pillows and plopped down on the foot of the bed next to me again. The current lashed by us, knocking the bowls together, rebounded off the far wall and came raging back at full speed to sweep the bowls away. One after another they overturned, the candles smoking a bit as they went out. I looked questioningly at Miss Margaret, but she was expecting my look and shielded her eyes from me with one hand. The bowls were sinking fast in the waves, swirling across the entrance hall and into the courtyard. As the candles fizzled out there were fewer reflections, and the spectacle lost its glow. When it seemed to be over, Miss Margaret, leaning on the elbow of the same arm that had provided the hand to shield her eyes, stuck out her other hand to release a last bowl caught under the bed. She watched it ride a swell for a second, but then it also went down. Slowly, she propped herself halfway up on her hands, as if to kneel or sit on her heels. With hanging head, her double chin sunk in the folds of her throat, she stared at the water like a little girl who has lost a doll. The motors were still running and she seemed more haggard and desolate every minute. Without waiting for instructions, I pulled in the boat, which was tied to a foot of the bed. I had barely climbed in and freed the rope when the current washed me away, a lot faster than I had anticipated. As it spun me around in the door to the entrance hall I looked back and saw Miss Margaret's eyes riveted on me, as if I were one more pudding bowl still holding out the promise of some secret revelation. Now I was in the courtyard, going round and round the island. I sat in Miss Margaret's armchair, letting the current take me where it pleased. I remembered the many times we had circled the island in the early days when Miss Margaret had seemed a different person to me, and fast as the current was, my thoughts began to drag me down into a bleak review of my life. I was fated to know only one side of people, and that only for a short time, like some absent-minded traveler passing through, with no idea of what he was seeing or where he was going. This time I had not even been able to figure out why I had been summoned by Miss Margaret to listen to her story without ever saying a word: all I knew for sure was that I would never really see into her. I went on circling the island with these thoughts spinning in my mind until the motors were turned off and Mary asked me for the boat so she could rescue the pudding bowls, which were going around in circles with me. I explained to her that there was no wake, that Miss Margaret simply liked to watch the bowls go down in flames . . . and I didn't know what else to say.

Later than usual, that same night, Miss Margaret summoned me again. She was nervous, and, without first clearing her throat, she took up her story at the point where she had bought the house and prepared it for flooding. Perhaps it had been cruel to displace the water in the fountain with all that dark earth. For a while, when the first plants were put in, the fountain had seemed to go on dreaming serenely of the water it used to hold. But since then the plants had kept growing into a tangle, like garbled messages, and she had to keep having them changed. She wanted the water to recall the silence of untroubled sleep or the murmuring voices of happy families (which was why she had told Mary she was deaf and could be reached only on the phone). She also wanted to drift over the water, slow as a cloud, holding books in her hands like harmless birds.

But what she wanted most of all was to understand the water. "It may be," she was telling me, "that it just wants to go its merry way, ignoring the suggestions it leaves behind. But, to my dying day, I'll believe it's harboring things it picked up in another place and somehow trying to bring me thoughts that aren't mine but are meant for me. In any case, I'm happy near it, I try to understand it, and no one can stop me from preserving my memories in it."

That night, contrary to habit, she gave me her hand as we parted. The next morning, when I went into the kitchen, the man in charge of the waterworks handed me a letter. Out of politeness—although all I could think of was getting away so I could read the letter—I asked him about his machines, and he said:

"You see how fast we installed the showers?"

"Yes—and they've been working well?"

"Sure . . . as long as the machines are kept up there's no problem. At night I pull a switch, the showers come on and the lady falls asleep with the murmur. At five in the morning I flip the switch, the showers stop and the silence wakens her. A few minutes later I pull another switch to stir the water and the lady gets up."

By then I had excused myself and was out the door. The letter said:

"My dear friend: the day I first saw you at the top of the stairs, you were looking down, as if watching your step. I thought it was shyness—but you stepped forward boldly, not afraid to expose the soles of your shoes. I took an immediate liking to you, and that's why I've kept you at my side all this time: otherwise I would have told you my story right away and you would have had to leave for Buenos Aires the next day. Which is what you'll do tomorrow.

"Thank you for your company. As to your finances, we shall be in touch through Hector. Good-bye and much happiness to you—I think you need it.

Margaret.

"P.S. In case you ever feel like writing down the things I've told you, you have my permission. All I ask is that at the end you put the following words: 'This is the story Margaret dedicates to Joseph. Whether he is dead or alive.'"